CYRUS DARIAN
and the Ghastly Horde

CYRUS DARIAN
and the Ghastly Horde

The Misadventures of Cyrus Darian Book 2

First published in September, 2012 by Prosochi.

This Edition, 2018 by Telos Publishing Ltd
United Kingdom

Telos Publishing values feedback if you have any comments about this book please email feedback@telos.co.uk

Cyrus Darian and the Ghastly Horde © 2012, 2018 Raven Dane

ISBN: 978-1-84583-966-6

Cover Art: 2017 © Martin Baines

The moral right of the author has been asserted.

British Library Cataloguing in Publication Data. A catalogue record for this book is available from the British Library.

This book is sold subject to the condition that it shall not by way of trade or otherwise, be lent, resold, hired out or otherwise circulated without the publisher's prior written consent in any form of binding or cover other than that in which it is published and without a similar condition including this condition being imposed on the subsequent purchaser.

*To my son (a new convert to steampunk) for his patience and support.
It is not easy having a possessed scribbler for a mother.*

Siam, 1875

Outside his bedroom the night jungle was alive with movement: snapping tree limbs; ferocious roars and terrified screeches of killers and their prey; the endless drone of insects and the rattle of frogs. The air was heavy with clashing scents, dank, over-ripe earth, heady night-scented blooms and fresh spilt blood – a thick pungency that left an unwelcome lingering taste.

White gauze nets across the open window kept biting insects at bay while a wide bamboo fan wafted humid air backward and forward in a vain attempt to cool the room. Darian had no idea how it was powered and he did not question it. Acceptance of the mysterious was an integral part of time spent with his paramour, the Lady. A time now coming to an end. He'd had enough of Siam, the fetid heat, the languor, the veiled contempt in the eyes of the locals for a decadent foreigner and his mistress. For all its own unpleasantness, Darian was homesick for London.

Once more he wore attire suitable for a man about town – though not exactly that of a gentleman. The alchemist favoured a more bohemian appearance in keeping with his status as a despised foreigner, a maverick – a bottle green frock coat, matching silk cravat and a splendid waistcoat made for him in gold and green hues in local silk brocade. A carefully wrought design with alchemistic and occult symbols woven into the fabric completed the apparel. He wore no hat out of vanity and carried a black ebony swordstick cane topped with a crystal orb.

Travel in sunny climes had heightened the dark good looks from his Persian inheritance. His lean frame suited the well-tailored cut of his new clothes. The sun had also added a few gold glints to his dark brown hair. He looked well, rested and pleasured to satiation. There was no hint from his appearance that he had recently experienced a near death adventure when he had been forced to battle a powerful, diabolical entity who strove to control every human soul in existence. An ambition Darian had thwarted – with some help.

Now he was ready to take on the world again. He checked his spectacles were in his pocket, travel with the Lady had given him the freedom to uncover his eldritch eyes but now their curious swirl of lilac and silver must remain hidden behind dark lenses.

Time to go home.

1

Mayfair, London, 1875

Cyrus sighed. It could only happen to him – Cyrus Darian, hedonist, philanderer, alchemist, necromancer, compulsive liar and for one brief period lasting only fifty seconds, master of every human soul that had ever existed. And the day had started off so well …

Darian had feigned a reluctant farewell and taken leave of his paramour, the Lady. Her insanely itinerant Emporium of Magickal Curios had taken them on a whirlwind tour of fascinating and romantic places. The in-lust couple had danced at the carnival along the crowded streets of Rio de Janerro, ridden an elephant around the ruins of ancient Siamese temples and made love in the moonlight in the shadow of the Taj Mahal.

Reconciled with the Lady, in body at least, Darian had returned to his familiar haunt, the London he loved and loathed with equal passion. Stepping out of the Emporium a half hour before five in the morning, the warmth and taste of his lover's parting kiss on his lips evaporated in the sharp air and was soon forgotten in his vexation. Why had the wayward shop of curios unceremoniously dumped him so far from his Mayfair home?

Darian glanced around through the obscuring fug of the London Particular, the endless toxic smog that cloaked the city in a permanent gloom. *Damnation, no sign of a Hansom cab – steam or horse-drawn.* Even at this early hour, London's streets were rife with peril, both human and supernatural in origin. Gritting his teeth, the alchemist kept a close grip on his swordstick cane and began an unenthusiastic walk home.

Inevitably, greedy feral eyes in the shadows would be tracking his progress along the dank, cobbled streets. Human opportunists he could usually handle alone, minor supernatural nuisances even more so, protected as he was by his amulet. Darian's hands strayed to his neck for reassurance and found no comforting platinum chain holding the Talisman of Greel. This was bad, very bad. He never took it from his neck, the Lady must have removed it as he slumbered beside her. *But why?*

There was no time to ponder this mystery, not with his every footstep attracting the attention of breeth. Released when some meddling fool opened a portal to a lower rung of Hell, breeth were too lowly to be considered demons, more accurately they were spectral vermin but they were dangerous. At first they had been fragile spirit forms possessing human bodies to sample the living world through vicarious pleasures. Possession usually ended in death from exhaustion and once the host expired the parasite simply moved on.

But proximity to polluting gases from the all-dominating Ephesysium Gas Works had made the breeth corporeal. Their favourite pastime was now killing and devouring humans after first hunting them down.

Until now, Darian had relied on the protection of the amulet. He had not felt this vulnerable for many years. *Why had the Lady put him in this perilous situation?*

The overhead steam tram network was silent for the night. London had switched off for a brief rest as parsons, prostitutes and pickpockets alike slumbered in their beds, not all their own. A few feral dogs sniffed through the night's debris and Darian heard the scuffle of rats fighting over a pigeon carcass.

Movement and a sinuous ugly green glow alerted him. A single breeth was emerging nearby, rising from the cobbles with a sly susurrate of hunger. Breeth rarely hunted alone, indeed their vicious fighting over prey had saved many human lives. Sure enough, more serpentine slivers of malevolence appeared behind the first arrival to its obvious anger.

Without his amulet, and knowing these creatures were immune to his swordstick, Darian had no choice but to run for his life. Sensing an easy victory, the breeth forgot their altercation and surged toward him hissing with the pleasure of the chase. A blast from his Asgard ring would not kill but might delay his pursuers. His heart skipped a beat as he realised that too had been taken from his finger. Cursing the complacency he'd indulged in while in the company of the Lady he sprinted faster, desperate for a solution.

It came to him in the form of a Hansom cab halted a few yards ahead. Snoring from the cab alerted him to the whereabouts of the driver. Breeth nearly touching his heels, the alchemist ran and hauled the very inebriated driver from his slumber, throwing him to the ground. The eager breeth began to squabble over this prize, giving Darian time to leap into the driver's seat, slap the reins onto a startled horse's rump and drive off in a clatter of iron hooves which raised sparks from the cobbles.

'Sorry, old chap,' he called back, as the man lay in an oblivious stupor, 'it's survival of the least inebriated tonight.'

If Darian gave the driver and his horrible fate any further thought, it was fleeting as he was more concerned with the welfare of the cab horse. *Surely the wretched man could have thrown a warm blanket over the animal before giving into his own drunken and exhausted state?*

Knowing how fast the breeth could move while hunting, he had no choice but to push the horse into a flat out gallop. The cab swayed precariously as they rounded tight bends on a tight angle, hard pounding hooves slipped alarmingly as the now panicked horse scrabbled for purchase. The Hansom was ridiculous in design and difficult to drive, he was perched so high above the cab and so far away from the horse, but Darian had no choice but to hang on and persevere. Pausing to cut the horse free of its harness and ride it away would undoubtedly make his eventual flight easier and quicker but the delay would, alas, allow the breeth to catch up.

As dawn lit the hidden horizon, Darian was finally able to relax and ease up on the hard-pressed valiant cab horse. All supernatural vermin including breeth had now slunk back to their lairs seeking the safety of darkness before the first glint of daylight breached the crowded skyline. He reined in the sweat-drenched animal, dismounted from the cab to caress its neck and murmured a thank you in his native Farsi. The streets were still empty, so after a short rest he climbed back into the driver's seat and continued his drive towards his Mayfair home.

As the daylight strengthened, some light brisk showers and a rare sharp easterly breeze straight off the continent did its best to clear the air of noxious gases. However, with households soon awakening, fires lit and the city's heavy industry churning into life, the weather's efforts would be lost, back into the foul miasma that did its best to suffocate London every day. But for now, it was almost pleasant. To his surprise, he began to enjoy his drive, treating it as a celebration of freedom of his victory over the breeth and the prospect of new adventures.

The tantalising aroma of good coffee and fresh baked bread halted his homeward journey. There was no rush and the rain had now turned heavier and more irksome. Darian stopped the stolen cab and finding a thick woollen horse blanket in the trunk underneath the passenger's seat – as well as a clump of hay – he placed it solicitously over the horse before entering the coffee house. There he took his time at breakfast, catching up with events during his absence from a pile of newspapers and chatting to the friendly Armenian owners.

Mixed race was a rare advantage here and enabled him to get on well with other distrusted 'outsiders' on the fringes of English society. His fluency in many languages, including Armenian also helped and after a few hours animated conversation, he was up to date with much of the capital's gossip, though he sensed the men were holding something back. They occasionally glanced out of the front window and kissed religious medals around their necks. *Curious ...* No doubt all would be revealed once he reached home, nothing got past Belial, his demonic companion in adventures.

With so many people emerging onto the streets, he considered it prudent to abandon the Hansom cab outside the café. Anyone dressed as a wealthy man about town driving a cab for hire would attract unwanted attention especially from the stalwart members of Her Majesty's Constabulary. As a valuable commodity, it would not take long for some opportunist to claim the Hansom cab and horse. He hoped it would be appropriated by a caring new owner; the brave animal that had helped save his life deserved such a reward.

Strolling at last towards his home with the city now fully awake, the clouds parted and a brief burst of April sunshine warmed Darian's lean, handsome face. As ever, many heads turned as he passed by.

As he neared his destination, a steady stream of people walking in the same direction made him pause. He could sense their unease, no, more than that, their fear, increasing with every step towards Mayfair. *How odd.* As was the balking and refusal of any ridden or carriage horse to move forward beyond a certain point. A number of abandoned vehicles lined the side of the road along with grateful local street urchins, hired for a handful of pennies to watch over the carriages and hold the horses. Cyrus noted a doleful, pining dog sat on the pavement with its lead firmly tied to garden iron railings. All of which was highly unusual. The only transport still moving towards Mayfair consisted of the huffing steam coaches favoured by the very rich. Yet even they appeared to be moving far slower than those departing the area.

What was so fascinating about Mayfair this morning? It was no more than a gracious enclave of London's wealthiest inhabitants. Whatever had generated this interest had to be more than a high profile murder or salacious scandal, why else would the horses and dogs refuse to carry on? With a sinking heart, he realised it had to be something of supernatural origin ... which meant probably he was involved despite his month's absence from the city.

His home was an elegant Georgian townhouse in a quiet square, normally of no interest to the hoi polloi of London and its address was only known to some of his many enemies and to the constabulary in the service of Her Majesty's. It was not known by this mass of silent and milling strangers from all walks of life.

As he finally approached Pleasance Square, he saw it was barricaded and a number of nervous constables were keeping the large crowd of near silent gawpers at bay. *What in Hades is going on?*

Last time the Constabulary had barricaded the Square had been six years before when a rampaging Hydra summoned to kill him had created a brief spell of gore-drenched mayhem. Then it had been easily dispatched with a few buckets of xechlotris acid. Darian had never identified the sender of the monstrous many-headed snake, perhaps this new disruption was due to another attempted attack with a creature created by dark magicke from Greek mythology? As he approached the barrier, he listened out for the angry bellow of a Minotaur or rustle of a Harpy's wings but there was only a near silence broken only by uneasy and frightened murmurs.

His next thought was Belial, the Prince of Hell who lived with him and had taken care of his home and dragoncat pet during the alchemist's dalliance with the Lady. Though in human form and therefore without all his full demonic powers, Belial could still cause havoc if provoked, had he flash fried some unfortunate denizens of the capital for annoying him? This had happened many times before, the worst one an unfortunate rampage through Vatican City. Darian wisely avoided Rome now for the faithful had proved remarkably ungrateful to him and the demon for sending so many to meet their maker. Surely their faith could never have too many martyrs? Belial's temper had added Rome to an ever growing list of places to avoid for Darian; he could not abide fooling about with disguises. He was far too vain to don false moustaches and wigs.

He hoped the demon prince hadn't been the cause of any unpleasantness this time ... unlike humans, ironically Belial, known also as the Prince of Lies, was the only being he could fully trust and the only one who could keep up with the hectic pace of Darian's eccentric and often dangerous life.

As the alchemist neared the well-constructed barrier, he felt a spectral wall of the most extreme and unsettling intensity. An eerie otherworldly cold he'd previously experienced in the company of earthbound souls but now magnified to an extraordinary degree. It was as if hundreds, maybe thousands of ghosts packed the square. Darian turned on his heel to walk away. Someone else could deal with this. He was wealthy enough now to buy another fine home in London, he'd taken this one from Bruxa, the succubus whose venom infected his bloodstream, so far with mainly beneficial results.

He was due a substantial sum of money from the recent sale of his country estate Wildewish Hall in the Cotswolds. His precious and beloved Akhal Teke stallion was stabled in luxury near Windsor with a cousin of the Queen. With his golden horse safe, there was no reason for him to hang around Mayfair if he didn't want to. He could always return in a year or two ...

'Darian.'

He pretended not to hear the querulous voice approaching through the crowd.

'Cyrus Darian ... the alchemist.'

A group of grim-faced constables barred his progress.

'Why, Inspector Brooks. It has been such a long time since I had the displeasure of your company.'

'Not long enough,' growled the stooping middle aged man, 'I take this ... this ... inconvenience has something to do with you?'

The Inspector took out a large none too clean kerchief from his Ulster and wiped his face, 'As if the city hasn't had enough problems with the turbine collapse disaster ... now this ... I have no knowledge of this situation but I am certain it is nothing the stout constables under your stalwart guidance cannot handle,' Darian replied, sidestepping the man and attempting to walk away. Several burly upholders of the Queen's peace surrounded and restrained him. He sighed. As visions of a much desired rest while Belial spoiled him, dissipated like the brief warmth of the sun. Full bellied pewter coloured clouds filled the sky with a distant rumble of thunder; Mother Nature did seem to enjoy adding her own touch of melodrama at times.

'I firmly suggest you take a look for yourself, Darian. Then tell me this has nothing to do with you.'

The constables cleared a way through the eerily silent crowds until they reached the barricade. For once Darian was speechless. Every inch of the square contained spectral forms. Hundreds of earth bound ghosts appeared in various manner of manifestation. From little more than audible sighs or indistinct, vaguely human shades, to detailed luminous recreations of their last known appearance before death. All stood stock still. All were fixated on one spot ... Darian's townhouse. He swore a violent oath in Farsi. This ghastly horde was waiting for him.

Darian shrank back, eager to get away and escape into the fearful but fascinated crowd. But it was too late. As one the phantoms turned and stared at him through sightless voids instead of eyes. Darian felt the full force of their seething fury and resentment as whispering voices from unmoving mouths addressed him as one ...

'Master ...'

Aware that his beloved friend had returned, the demon prince raced from the house and onto the abandoned street, scattering spectres with a warning growl. The damned things were vermin, debris from spent human lives that should have moved on after their deaths. The ghosts had been gathering in increasing numbers after Cyrus's destruction of the Technomicron and had refused to move. Belial had tried railing at them with threats of sending them Hell bound to suffer eternal torture – but unfortunately a brief flash of power from the dying book had been enough to bind them to the alchemist. Nothing could move them. *What a bore.* The thought of setting off on another adventure with this lot in tow would be amusing if not so vexing. He ran over to Darian and ignoring the scandalised watching humans, whirled him around in a tight, welcoming embrace and kissed him on the mouth.

'It was that accursed book, wasn't it?' Darian sighed, forcing his gaze away from the unwilling army of the dead awaiting his command. 'I didn't destroy the damn thing quickly enough. The Technomicron held just enough power to capture earthbound souls and bind them to me. Bugger.'

'Let's go home, my friend,' urged Belial. 'All the curtains are drawn and the circles of protection are in place. Maybe they will get bored and return to their haunts.'

Inspector Brooks stepped closer. 'Not so fast *gentlemen,*' he sneered signalling to his men to block Darian and his flamboyant young companion. 'You cannot ignore this horrible aberration. I will not have a London thoroughfare blocked by ... by ... these spooks. It's not natural.'

'That's why it is called the supernatural, Brooks.'

'That will be Inspector Brooks to you, Darian.' The man replied through clenched teeth. The insolence and arrogance of this foreigner was an old wound reopened. 'They are here because of you. Get rid of them.'

'Sorry old man,' Darian returned, allowing the unnerving aura of the demon with the golden beauty of an angel but the cold, old eyes of something infinitely evil to clear a route through the constables, 'that is a matter for your churchmen ... send them in armed with plenty of holy water and bibles. Waft some incense about ... whatever it is that they do.'

As Darian attempted to walk away from the square, a piercing scream from a female gawper confirmed his worse conviction: the ghosts were following him, floating past the barriers and into the crowds triggering pandemonium. The alchemist could do without the bother of having people trampled to death in a headlong panic added to his already long list of crimes. So, reluctantly, he turned around and vaulted back over the barrier into the square. As expected the phantoms also turned as one and followed him back.

Seething, Brooks watched in impotent fury as Darian and Belial strode through the wall of phantoms. Too afraid to follow them over the barrier, he shouted, 'Don't you think we haven't tried that, Darian. We have had archbishops, cardinals and the church's official exorcists. Even a handful of bloody Catholics and Hebrews. Nothing will shift these infernal ghosts.'

He bellowed in fury to the young men's indifferent backs, 'Do you hear me, Darian? It's down to you!'

2

In his study, Darian collapsed onto an old leather chair and allowed Belial to pour him an over generous measure of fine cognac. Instead of savouring the warming amber liquid, he downed it in one and held the glass balloon up for another. And another. Only then did he speak, his voice barely audible above the hearty roar of a log blazing in the hearth and the background droning of the phantoms ... one word over and over again ... *Master*.

'How long have those wretched things been here?'

Belial sat down opposite him. After first pouring himself a cognac and raising his glass in a toast to his friend's return, he related the tale of the apparitions' appearance in Mayfair.

'The first ones must have arrived just after you destroyed the Technomicron and disappeared with the Emporium and the Lady. They were here when I returned to the house. But there were only a handful of apparitions to begin with.'

He took a sip of his drink then continued, 'No one beyond me and Misha could see them at first. And the animals of course ... the refusal of people's horses to enter the square and their pets disappearing were the locals' first clues that something weird was amiss.'

Darian glanced around, missing the scrabble of small talons against the parquet flooring, 'Talking of pets, where is my dragoncat?'

Belial shrugged, his indifference fuelled by his desire not to share Darian's affection with anything – including devoted pets.

'She was here this morning, tucked into her breakfast and hasn't been seen since. She enjoyed chasing the ghosts at first but got bored. Nothing solid and bloody to sink her fangs into.'

Darian decided not to be too concerned, the strange creature whose origin, species and true gender was still a mystery, was free to roam where she wanted and often disappeared for a long time on some mysterious mission of her own.

'Anyway,' Belial took up the narrative again, 'as more and more arrived, the combined spectral energy caused the stronger ones to glow at night. Can you imagine the furore that caused? It was hilarious. Then as the numbers of spooks kept increasing, they could all be seen by day and night. That is when the residents bolted and the square was cordoned off.'

'An understandable reaction,' Darian replied. 'Even I as a necromancer and well accustomed to the sight of ghosts, balk at so many. I suspect the toxic fog from the gasworks is enhancing their coherence ... it does with the breath.'

Darian glanced up at the windows, unused to seeing them hidden in the morning. What dismal light there was to filter through the London Particular had to be welcomed and enjoyed.

'Er, Belial, old chap. Why are all the curtains still drawn?'

All the rooms were lit by candle sconces but late morning was a brief time when there could be some natural light. Unlike most of modern London, Darian refused to have gas lighting and heating from the all powerful Ephesysium Gas Works Company, who's cheap and readily available but often dubious products poisoned people and the air alike. It was highly corrosive and a menace to those who treasured their antiques and delicate furnishings like Darian.

'Believe me, my friend,' Belial answered, 'you won't want them open ... but see for yourself.'

Darian rose from the chair and pulled back the burgundy velvet drape to be confronted by dozens of spectral faces pressed hard against the glass, all murmuring their monotone, one word chant.

'Every window is like that,' the demon continued, 'right up to the top floor and the skylights. Dashed inconvenient. And it is getting worse with each new unwelcome arrival.'

Pulling back the drapes with a shudder, Darian nodded agreement. It was more than inconvenient, it was downright creepy. The heavy, velvet curtains would remain pulled resolutely shut.

'I don't suppose you have heard from Miles? I could do with one of his ingenious inventions right now. A Phantom Disintegrator or something of that nature.'

Belial laughed without humour.

'Do you honestly think his *charming* wife will ever let him talk to you again? No doubt she is Lady Hardwick by now. She had poor, smitten Miles in her American eagle talons from the first moment you introduced them. You were an idiot to ruin her honour, Darian,' the demon continued. 'Sir Miles Hardwick is a far more useful friend and ally than some ghastly ex-heiress from Wyoming or wherever.'

'What can I say?' Darian replied with a shameless grin. 'I am a rogue and a cad and cannot resist a challenge. Especially one in the formidable form of Miss Athena Dedman.'

Belial nodded in agreement; he wouldn't be here if it wasn't for the alchemist's inability to give into temptation and risk taking.

'So, what have you brought back from your stay with your paramour?'

Somehow the demon managed to bite back any too obvious contempt for the shapeshifter who had won Darian's body if not his heart; a contempt born of sheer jealousy and genuine concern for Darian's wellbeing. He watched with bemused interest as the alchemist emptied out his pockets.

'I bought this from the Emporium,' he announced, holding up a stone knife, the handle in the form of an ugly Mayan idol carved from human bone. Its skeletal form and blade still had brown stains from long-past human sacrifices. 'One of their wretched death gods, I believe.'

'Ah ... *Yum Cimil*,' Belial laughed as he took the gruesome weapon from his companion and held it up to the candlelight for greater scrutiny. 'He is far uglier in real life and has the worse foul breath in Hell. And no sense of humour. Like all of the other South Amerindian deities. They make most tedious company to say the least.'

Darian showed him another object purchased from the Lady, a large orb of rainbow quartz, beautiful and with a curious flaw deep within its depths. 'Look closely, old chap. What can you see?'

Belial peered into the orb, at once entranced by spectrum of rainbow colours gleaming in its depths, until he saw what appeared to be a crouching black imp created by a flaw from the crystal's fiery creation. What passed for a face was frozen in a grimace of pure hatred.

'It wouldn't be a real imp,' Darian ventured, 'captured and contained by the crystal?'

The demon examined the orb once more and shook his head, 'A trick of the light, no more. A humorous trinket. I hope she didn't charge you too much for it.'

Darian's knowing grin spoke volumes, not all items from the Lady's shop were purchased by gold. Or purchased at all, he reached again into the depths of his burgundy frock coat to reveal what appeared to be an oriental thumb trap, an item small enough to be secreted and not missed straight away.

Belial sighed. His beloved companion's light fingered ways were as compulsive as his lying and philandering.

'One of these days, she will succeed in killing you. At least make it for something worthwhile and not a valueless trinket.'

Darian gave a slight, indifferent wave of a hand, it was not the first time the demon had scolded him over his wrongdoings. What right did a fallen angel from Hell have to lecture him? It was an amusing situation.

'I think she has already taken her revenge, my friend,' Darian mused. 'Not only did my beloved dump me on the wrong side of town and at a hideously inconvenient time, I found myself bereft of the Talisman of Greel and my Asgard ring.'

Belial's eyes darkened with anger and concern. What was that fickle bitch playing at, leaving Darian so exposed to danger?

'Think nothing of it, Belial,' soothed Darian with a reassuring smile. 'I am here, safe, am I not? It will take more than a few hell-born sewer rats to stop me from getting home.'

'Home ... to you,' Darian added, shamelessly exploiting the demon in human form's only weakness – his accursed, unbreakable devotion to the alchemist.

Over a light, simple supper of cold meats, cheese and bread washed down with an excellent old Merlot, Darian had a brain wave.

'Belial, old chap, I suspect we are both over-thinking this situation with the spooks. I am their master after all. I will simply command them to go away.'

3

Shoreditch

Count Nicolai Bartrev, dispossessed Russian nobleman and world-weary soldier of fortune knocked back another disgusting shot of raw gin. How could these heathen English drink such a foul brew? He raised the glass, ready to dash it against a flagstone hearth but paused. The natives were unused to this custom and could create a violent protest.

'*Mne pohui*, let them,' he swore under his breath and watched as the cheap glass shattered into a hundred fiery diamond shards: a brief flash of beauty before landing in the ash and filth of the hearth. He readied himself for a brawl but apart from a few bleary eyed glances, no one objected, not even the rotund landlady of the dilapidated gin house. She'd well overcharged him for the alcohol and could bear the loss of one glass ... or even three.

He had nowhere else to go. Virtually penniless, the last of his money spent on passage to London, Bartrev faced a future with no direction, no goal beyond surviving. His family lands now belonged to the Tsar, Alexander III and his thousand erstwhile loyal servants had probably hired gypsies to curse him to perdition for abandoning them to the Romanovs. He had fought his mercenary way around Europe – there was no shortage of wars – and like a piece of flotsam, finally washed up on the rain-sodden shores of England. Catching a locomotive at Dover, within hours he had traded the clear skies and salted air over the Channel for the stench, grime and claustrophobia of the nation's capital.

A mixture of awe and dismay coloured his arrival into the East End of London. It was undeniably the richest city in the western world, fortunes could be made – and as easily lost here.

CYRUS DARIAN AND THE GHASTLY HORDE

Nowhere in Mother Russia had such gleaming modern technology, not even Saint Petersburg and certainly not his stolen ancestral lands where nothing had changed since the Middle Ages. Everything around him appeared to be in constant frantic motion. The chug and huff of steam driven vehicles, the marvel of the overhead steam trams whose network of tracks crossed the skyline like the work of an insane spider. Day and night, the constant beam of street and home gaslight did its best to illuminate the all-pervading gloom. All were near incomprehensible marvels to Bartrev. Less welcome was the perpetual poisoned air that permeated every street and alley, a foul smelling miasma so thick at street level it was possible to walk without seeing your own feet.

Amid all this modernity, humans, hardworking horses, lurking dogs and scruffy pigeons bustled through the overcrowded streets, living components of the vast machine that was London. In Shoreditch, buildings crammed hard against their neighbours, many leaning as if fighting for their space on the narrow, cobbled streets, some so tall with wide overhangs, they shut out daylight adding to the overall gloom. Bartrev had never seen so many people crammed into every space in teeming slums, beneath which open sewers ran down the narrow, winding and chaotically arranged streets.

Bartrev drank alone now, though he had been pestered at first on his arrival at the dockside inn. A tall, broodingly handsome man, with the robust build of a peasant, with the refined features and bearing of an aristocrat, he attracted the attention of the inn doxies, eager for a new face – and body – to reward their company with guineas ... or more likely shillings. A couple of the older strumpets would have enthusiastically done it for farthings or a shot of gin.

He dismissed them with an authoritative growl, and reaching into his great coat, dug out a battered, dog-eared book. He had spent his last coins on a cheap bottle of gin, the only white spirit on sale, indeed it was easier to obtain and cheaper than drinkable water. He hoped the liquor would be similar to vodka – to his displeasure it wasn't but after the initial odd taste and raw burn to the back of his throat, the gin spread welcome warmth through his body. He could understand its pernicious power to numb the senses of the poor and wretched, as did the cheap and often deadly vodka that was a scourge of the working classes back in Russia.

He forced aside such dreary thoughts, he was indeed down on his luck, a hunted exile in a strange land but he would not give in to gin-sodden despair. He was young, strong and intelligent, a man of honour and courage despite his circumstances. This seething, filthy city was also a place of opportunity and enterprise. Tomorrow, his adventure would begin again. Tonight was a time to rest, to recover his strength, so doing his best to relax, Bartrev settled down to read by the merry blaze in the hearth.

Though still early afternoon, Bartrev intended to spend the night by the hearth in the inn, there was nowhere else to go. Though used to the privations of sleeping rough on military campaigns, this was a bewildering pandemonium of a foreign city. The last thing he expected was to be addressed in Russian. No doubt recognising the Cyrillic script of Bartrev's book, a young Jewish man, an immigrant to England, cautiously introduced himself.

'I apologise for this impolite interruption but I see you are reading *A Nest of Nobles*.'

'Indeed,' Bartrev replied still pleasantly surprised at hearing his mother tongue. 'This is the first work of Ivan Turgenev I have attempted.'

'How are you finding it?' the man inquired.

'I am grateful for the presence of Helen ... a noble and resolute woman.' Bartrev smiled as he answered and beckoned for the young man to join him by the hearth, grateful for the company of someone sharing his language and knowledge of literature.

'Turgenev does seem to create weak and vacillating male characters but the beautiful Helen is indeed a delight.' His new companion answered. 'I find it also a pleasure to see an aristocrat from our home land reading a work in our native tongue, most nobility favour French literature and customs these days.'

The man held out his hand, 'My name is Mikhail Levin ... though I have now adopted the name Michael Lewis. England is my home now. By your accent and bearing, you are an aristocrat therefore if you are here, sir, in this lowly place, can I take it you are no friend of Emperor Alexander?'

Bartrev shook Lewis's hand but did not answer this query. There was every chance the Tsar had sent out spies to track him down. He could not trust anyone now, but in this man's favour the Tsar was an aggressive anti-Semite. Within the hour, he and the former Mikhail Levin had become friends, something that would have enraged the reigning Romanov ... which gave Bartrev some small satisfaction. He agreed to accept the man's offer of hospitality and walked the short distance to a seething, overcrowded tenement.

Inside the cramped confines of Levin's home, his pretty, heavily pregnant wife Hannah had done her best to keep the place clean and orderly. The addition of another mouth to feed did not concern her and she made Bartrev as welcome as her husband had. These were good people; the Count was determined to earn enough money to repay their kindness but how? As Bartrev settled for a comfortable night on a makeshift bed of blankets on the floor before the hearth, he began to ponder on the many changes of fortunes over the last two years. From respected young aristocrat with a vast rural estate to hunted fugitive and then on to bloodstained mercenary. Now he was penniless, grateful for the hospitality and generosity of a family who would be despised and persecuted back home in Russia. Their blameless lives in danger from other aristocrats like himself.

He was a disposed, hunted exile – all because of the recent discovery of an ancient and valuable secret, a family treasure that he refused to hand over to the Romanov Emperor. The cost of such defiance was high but there were powers in the universe that should remain hidden from mankind.

4

'Well, that worked well.'

Darian stepped back into his home, grateful for the occult barriers woven and carved into the fabric of the structure which kept the phantoms from pouring inside through the walls and windows. In a burst of optimism, he had stridden out of the house and in a loud voice, commanded the ghosts to return to their haunts. The only response was an increased wave of their roiling resentment towards him and the now tedious loud drone of 'Master.' They crowded towards him, a wall of spectral debris, animated by residual willpower and insanity. Darian steeled himself from bolting back into the sanctuary of his home, desperate to find a way of dispersing the phantoms.

He had tried to single out a well-formed ghost, recently deceased by its modern apparel. He'd found one of a tall felon, the shadowlike form of a hangman's noose still draped around its crooked, stretched neck. Any attempt at reasoning with the phantom was futile. It stared at Darian with its sightless orbs blazing with fury, hating being bound to this living human as much as Darian hated its bondage to him.

'I say, old chap,' Darian said in reasonable tone, 'you don't want to be here and I certainly don't want you either ... so why not be a good spectre and sod off ...'

If Darian's words were heard and understood by the apparition, there was no sign, no spark of awareness. It continued to waft closer to him, the only sound emanating from the ghost was that single, unwilling word ...'Master.'

He resisted the wild urge fuelled by exasperation, to grab the ghost by the shoulders and give it a good shake, make it listen to him but he would have only connected to freezing air. Darian and Belial had returned to the house, defeated by the powerful spell of the Technomicron, a baleful influence living on after its destruction.

'I feel like a prisoner,' muttered Darian, 'I am quite certain if I tried to go anywhere, I would not be alone. The damned things are determined to follow me about to the ends of the earth. Maybe even beyond that.'

'I'm afraid that seems to be the case, Cyrus,' answered the demon, as unhappy about the situation as his friend. 'Time to get researching through that extensive library of yours. Even without his lordship about to help creating an anti-ghost device, I suspect any answer will be occult in nature.'

Darian sighed, 'No disrespect, but I find it difficult to believe a demon prince even one in human form cannot send this lot scurrying back to their graves in immortal terror.'

Giving a nonchalant nod of agreement, Belial settled down in an armchair in the study, the only windowless living room in the townhouse.

'The Technomicron's hold over them seems unbreakable, Cyrus. And what could I threaten them with? Fiery bolts of hellfire would just go straight through them, incinerate some harmless tree. I cannot curse them to eternal damnation … hardly an incentive to move on from their earthly bonds. At the moment, you are stuck with your spooks.'

The demon intended to keep his friend company during the night as Darian would not sleep in a room where throngs of angry spectres pressed up against every windowpane. Though the heavy curtains were drawn, just knowing they were there was most disconcerting to the highly strung alchemist. But Darian had no plan to sleep, he held out his hand to Belial.

'Come on old chap, you can read in every human language ever spoken. Help me search through the grimoires.'

Belial rose to his feet with a low growl and grabbed an unopened bottle of cognac; it was going to be a long night.

By the next morning Darian was already claustrophobic and pacing the floor like a caged tiger. Nothing had changed, his phantom followers had not moved or ceased their chanting. Over breakfast he questioned Belial, 'How can you stand it, old chap? You've put up with this nuisance for weeks.'

'Must admit it hasn't been much fun taking care of the house with that tedious crowd of wafting ectoplasm outside.' The demon answered with a yawn of boredom, 'But remember, I can stroll past them and take my pleasures in the city beyond.'

Darian did not question what those pleasures entailed. Ignorance was the best stance when it came to sharing your home with a Prince of Hell. But if Belial could walk out past them, so would he and damn the consequences.

'By Hades and all that dwell there! I am going out. If that crowd of spectres follow me, so be it.'

He strode out of the kitchen seeking a light coat and his crystal orb-topped ebony cane with Belial following close at his heel doing his best to dissuade him.

'I understand your frustration, my friend ... better than any living being ... but this is insane. The ghosts will follow you wherever you go, triggering mass hysteria. Riots, panic, chaos. Who knows what mayhem, fear-crazed people will cause? The pandemonium you will create marks you as a legitimate target for the police and the militia. You know how fearful the establishment is of any form of anarchy.'

'What are the authorities going to do? Arrest me for possession of spooks?' Darian's determination had not wavered. 'Wherever they take me, the ghosts will follow. I am already in jail so what have I got to lose? Out of my way, Belial, I am going for a walk.'

Belial stood in front of him, barring his way. 'If they kill you, the ghosts will most likely go. Don't think the authorities haven't thought of that. I am certain the square is ringed with official assassins. It will only take one accurate bullet to end this.'

He spun Darian around and forcibly removed his coat. 'Get back to the library. We have yet more serious research to do today.'

Reluctantly, the alchemist agreed, though his intuition told him this would continue to be a futile occupation. So far nothing had turned up. His well stocked library of mysterious tomes, grimoires and ancient treatises were all written at a time when the concept of the enormous power available now would be inconceivable. The Technomicron was a product of this age of mechanical wonders. There would be nothing written in the past to deal with the continuing fallout from its destruction.

There were other ways to seek information, all of which held no pleasure for Darian. One was to reverse the spell of Summoning and send Belial back to Hell to seek guidance from those on a celestial plane of existence, such as the Old Gods and Goddesses. But there was no guarantee that the prince would be allowed to return back to him in human form again. It was not worth the risk of distressing and angering such a powerful being just to find out a method of spectral pest control.

The other was to utilise Darian's skills at necromancy, a dangerous occult pursuit that nearly cost him his life last time he succeeded in reaching a soul. Not the easy task of contacting an earthbound spirit but risking all to reach beyond the *Veil* between the living and the dead and deep into the realms of the afterlife. *The Beyond*. Only a matter of earth shattering urgency would induce him to try something like that again. Whatever solution existed for ridding him of these damn nuisances, Darian had to find it for himself.

5

Bartrev awoke just before dawn, stiff from an evening sleeping on the floor but thoroughly refreshed after the most secure sleep since his flight from Russia. He tidied away the blankets, lit the range and boiled some water for tea and a wash in the sink. Already the city outside was awake, if it ever slept and he took in the view from the small window. Here most people were hurrying to their daily chores on foot and there was the occasional clatter and rumble of horse and donkey drawn carts. Above, criss-crossing the dirty fog cloaked skyline, were the steam trams. Noisy wonders of modern transportation, their trails of blackened smoke added to the fug.

Battling their way through this complex network, steam driven dirigibles bobbed across the city like a flotilla of dirty clouds. Bartrev had seen airships in many cities in Europe but never in such number. Some were huge to provide public transportation, others were fleet, sleek private vessels of the very rich.

'Quite a sight aren't they ...' Lewis had joined him by the window to gaze at the dirigibles. 'Nothing like that in the old country ... yet.'

He threw Bartrev's coat at him and gestured towards the door, 'This may come as an unwelcome shock to a fine gentleman like yourself, but this morning you are going to earn your keep. And learn some more English.'

As they battled through the crowded, narrow streets, Bartrev could see why so many people fled to London, nobody noticed him; it was easy to be lost in a city of strangers. Lewis led him to a shop in Pitfield Street, where East End deprivation rubbed shoulders with the city's wealthy. It was a place full of skilled artisans. Silk-weavers and piano-makers jostled for space with inns and slaughterhouses. The stench of carrion and the woeful call of doomed beasts added to the organised chaos.

His new friend was a skilled craftsman, a clockmaker and repairer. As they stepped inside, the heartbeats of many clocks from the grandest grandfather to elegant small carriage clocks greeted them, beautiful pieces of polished rich woods, gleaming brass, silver, gold and mother of pearl inlays.

'This is how I earn my living,' he announced, throwing back a curtain to reveal another room, 'and here is where I give my mind free rein to create, 'But don't mention this to Hannah ... she doesn't approve of me wasting time on frivolities.'

Bartrev stepped into a world of wonders, gleaming clockwork gadgets of all manner of purpose and many whose usage was unknown filled every space on the floor and packed the shelves.

Complex animated wood and metal figures showed Lewis's playful side. Moving tableaus of juggling clowns, dancing circus dogs or haunted houses with fleeting ghosts and skeletons popping out, were extraordinary in their beauty and exquisite craftsmanship.

'You are a genius, sir,' an entranced Bartrev said in awe. 'These delightful playthings alone could make you very rich.'

'I wish my wife shared your faith,' Lewis replied with a rueful grin, 'but I hope you are right.'

He returned to the main shop and handed Bartrev a broom, 'But until that time, my new friend, we must work.'

So a privileged aristocrat who had once ruled an estate as large as a minor European principality, with over a thousand servants at his every whim, found himself in command of a broom ... and to Bartrev's astonishment, enjoying it. The quiet rhythm of Michael Lewis's shop, the whirr and tick of the clocks and the to and fro swish of the broom were curiously relaxing. To the outside world he was no more than a humble shop worker and for the first time in a year, Bartrev relaxed his constant vigil from the threat of assassins.

Lewis was a man in great demand for his skills, fine horse-drawn and steam carriages pulled up outside the shop all day with a steady stream of commissions and repair work. Bartrev could easily imagine that his new friend's diligence and skill would soon see him propelled out of the slums of Shoreditch and into a pleasant, outlying village like Finchley. The man deserved it. The day passed pleasantly enough but Bartrev became aware of a distinct agitation in the clockmaker's manner as the afternoon stretched on and an early twilight darkened the streets as the sun became lost behind the high buildings and obscured by the day's outpouring of industrial smog.

'Come, my friend,' Lewis murmured, his eyes fearful and darting towards any lengthening shadows. 'Help me close up the shop.'

Unfortunately for his peace of mind, the valet of a well-heeled customer arrived just as Lewis prepared to bolt the door. His hand shaking, the clockmaker stepped back and did his best to welcome him into the shop. Much to his credit, Lewis hid his agitation well and did not try to rush the customer's manservant, whose master's requirements for a new long case clock were demanding and precise. It was only when the man finally left two hours later that Lewis gave into his fearful state.

'We must hurry home, London's streets are no place for a sane man to dwell in after dark.'

'But you have me at your side now,' reassured Bartrev. 'No lurking gutter snipe or scoundrel is a match for a seasoned soldier as myself.'

Lewis smiled sadly and patted the count on his shoulder, 'In any other city, I would be pleased to agree with you. But this is London and there are worse things to fear than dippers and busters to contend with.'

'Since 1840,' he explained, hastening his steps, 'we have been plagued by monstrous foes of an occult nature. An arrogant and inept sorcerer named Thelonius Budd inadvertently broke through a portal into a minor rung of Hell and inflicted the curse of a plague of primitive demonic forms on the nation's capital.'

Bartrev shook his head in wonder, 'I have heard such rumours of course, but dismissed it as envious gossip. No city in the world has such wealth as London.'

'Oh it is true, all right,' continued the clockmaker with a deep sigh. 'The most numerous fiends Budd released are blaggers and breeth. Blaggers are like rats, feeding off carcases but will take vulnerable lives when they can ... they are particularly fond of human infants. Breeth are perhaps more problematical. They seek to possess human bodies in order to enjoy our senses, ousting the poor victim's soul in the process. An irreversible process'

'So how do we fight these monstrosities?' The warrior soul in Bartrev demanded.

'We don't. We avoid.' Lewis replied, steering the big man out of the shop and locking it with many heavy bolts, 'That is why we must make haste, every minute of nightfall increases their number.'

The man's anxiety to get home was all too apparent. He bustled along, nearly at a running pace, keeping his head down and walking close to the centre of the road despite the thronging traffic and milling crowds.

'Always keep clear of dark alleyways,' he advised the Russian. 'That is where the monsters wait until the last rays of sunlight are gone.'

Ahead of them, a horse-drawn Hansom cab stopped abruptly as the tired old beast baulked, striking sparks off its ironclad hooves. The reason became clear as a marching footfall neared, powerful and metallic in manner, sending pedestrians scattering off the streets. The clockmaker grabbed Bartrev's arm and hauled him into the nearest shop doorway. Astonished, Bartrev witnessed a squadron of huge men, clad in red painted metal armour, marching down the centre of the street, forcing the traffic from their path by the arrogance of their conduct. Their armour whirred and hissed with steam and clockwork powered enhancements to make the wearer stronger and faster and they carried large intimidating weapons.

'Mechmen,' Lewis whispered, not disguising his contempt. 'They were once the private army of some aristocratic megalomaniac but when he was financially ruined by the Great Turbine Disaster, Her Majesty's Government took them over.'

Bartrev shook his head in wonder, 'How could anyone fail with an army of such Titans under their control?'

Lewis laughed openly, the Mechmen were now out of earshot, 'One man bested them. The notorious alchemist Cyrus Darian who lives in London. Created a potion that turned their armour into dust.'

'He sounds a fascinating man, one well versed more in science than the dark arts by the sound of that concoction,' Bartrev replied, 'I would love to meet him.'

Lewis carried on his journey home, hurrying more after the delay caused by the passage of the Mechman squadron. Darian had been a past customer – the clockmaker had repaired an exquisite orrery in the man's strange and otherworldly home. Lewis had been generously rewarded for the task and working on the beautiful, complex device had been a great pleasure but there was no reward on Earth that would make him go near Mayfair now ... not with wild rumours of frightful apparitions surrounding Darian's home.

'A man to avoid at all costs, my friend,' Lewis warned. 'Death and danger follow him around like a faithful dog.'

6

Downing Street, London

The mysterious disappearance of Britain's Prime Minister after the Great Turbine Disaster had resulted in a sudden power vacuum. A country reeling with the aftermath of so much destruction needed strong leadership. One Sir Enoch Bowring was only too happy to give.

Wild speculation surrounded the whereabouts of the last PM. The reality was more bizarre than any theory brought forward in the disaster's aftermath. Only a handful of people knew his predecessor Sir Edgar Quibbe had been a hell-spawned minor demon or that he had tried and failed to control every human soul in existence by literally emptying Heaven and Hell using a book of dark spells called the Technomicron. To achieve that aim he had combined the ancient occult power of that notorious grimoire with energy boosted by two massive steam powered turbines,

Again, unknown to all but those closely involved, Cyrus Darian and his team of adventurers had thwarted this dastardly scheme. To everyone else Quibbe was an ill-advised and ambitious politician who had championed a plan to build two vast turbines to blow London's crippling, poisonous pollution out into the North Sea. He was one of many financially ruined when the towers blew up, destroying a large area of North London.

Sir Enoch was not one of the people in the know. He accepted the most likely theory that having forced through the ill-fated project and committing huge resources and finance from the state coffers, Quibbe could not live with the enormity of the scheme's destructive failure and loss of innocent life.

The newly elected Prime Minister did not dwell on the fate of his predecessor, not with the country needing firm guidance and restoration of their faith in the establishment. Like him, ignorant of its true purpose, the Queen herself gave her blessing to that damned overblown project. But right now, when he wanted to be supervising the rebuilding of the Hampstead Heath area where many homes and businesses had been demolished in the catastrophe, the wretched Mayfair ghosts affair consumed his time.

A gruff man, built like a prize fighter, bullish with pride about his humble origins and strict religious faith, Sir Enoch sat heavily at the head of a conference table and gestured that the participants be seated. He had surrounded himself with successful and determined men of action. There would be no fawning around the inbred idiot younger sons of the aristocracy in Bowring's government. He threw down a report onto the table with an unfortunate porcine grunt of impatience.

'So, now we have our dubious Persian trouble maker back in London ... why hasn't this problem been resolved?'

Head of Scotland Yard, Herbert Grimley spoke first. 'Mr Prime Minister, sir ... Cyrus Darian has indeed returned to his Mayfair dwelling and is clearly the focus of these apparitions. Inspector Brooks and his men witnessed him commanding the ghosts to return to their graves. They all ignored him.'

'If this foreign necromancer Cyrus Darian is powerless to remove the problem he no doubt created in his vile meddling with demonic occult forces, then his usefulness to the situation no longer exists.' Sir Enoch decided. 'We must utilise the more permanent solution.'

'Sir, with all due respect,' a senior civil servant piped up in alarm. 'The last government thought this man most useful to the country and gave him full protection.'

Sir Enoch growled his disapproval and glared at the speaker, a leading figure from the Department of Inventions and Technological Advancement. 'Despite considerable latitude and plentiful time, Darian has not given us the promised new fuel source he claimed to have invented. Therefore that protection is cancelled. Starting from now.'

The Prime Minister stood up abruptly. 'We have focused too long on the problems caused by technology. That ill-thought up extravaganza to clear London's air has led to death and destruction and loss of faith in those who must shoulder the burden of Great Britain's leadership. Now is the time for a new crusade ... against the forces of evil and the supernatural that plague our society.'

He slammed his fist down on the table with violent force, sending documents flying and spilling glasses of water.

'I am going to transform this country's decadent society and bring it back to God. No more breeth and blagger infested streets. No more alchemists and necromancers. No more magic. No more terror inducing apparitions weakening the country's morale. Commencing with no more dissolute foreign mavericks like Cyrus Darian!'

To the Prime Minister's delight, no one in the meeting opposed him, instead they rose as one to their feet and applauded his impassioned speech with enthusiastic cheers. It was obvious even to a blind fool that the country needed strength of purpose and he, Sir Enoch Obadiah Bowring, self-made millionaire and God fearing man was the right one to give it.

'In some ways, these ghosts have done us a favour,' Bowring continued, puffed up with delight at the enthusiastic show of support. 'The clergy report record numbers of people swelling their congregations, new churchgoers eager to save their souls now proof of the afterlife is undeniable. We must build on this fear.'

He leant forward, rotund face flushed with fervour, 'This is the first day of a glorious future for Britain and the Empire. I will instruct the police, militia and the covert operations squads. They must use skill and discretion but I must have Darian permanently eliminated ... from life itself. An act that will free London from the phantom scourge and send out a chilling message to all those who dabble in ungodly acts that they will be next.'

Short-sighted, puritanical fool, thought one participant in particular. *It doesn't matter that Cyrus Darian still hasn't come up with a new fuel source for Britain and its growing Empire. Darian needs continued protection not persecution from the government especially when he commands an army of the dead. The military potential of this situation are clearly lost on that jumped up ironmonger of a Prime Minister. An army of obedient phantoms that cannot be harmed but could spread terror and panic through any opposing forces? This is a prospective resource far too valuable to lose to an assassin's bullet.* Major Earnest Greville Stroude, head of Military Intelligence had the power to undermine Bowring's orders and he fully intended to do it.

The Prime Minister surrounded himself with able men, equally as zealous as their leader but they were too concerned with the nation's moral fibre, on spiritual matters and rebuilding trust in figures of authority. Stroude was more concerned with security for the Queen and her many and growing domains. Envious eyes around the world coveted the success and wealth of the British Empire. He knew they would love to weaken and undermine it in order to grab what they could in the resulting disorder like slavering, ruthless hyenas around a fresh kill.

This must not happen. The morning's meeting with the new Prime Minister left Stroude angry and with a sour taste in his mouth at the wasted opportunity if some idiot with an itchy trigger finger assassinated Cyrus Darian. There was no time to lose, if he was to secure the safety and co-operation of the alchemist, to ensure the development of the prospective new fuel source and the possible use of this army of ghosts for the greater good of the Empire. He decided to meet the man straight away … alone.

Stroude was no coward, a gleaming line of hard-earned medals on his dress uniform spoke volumes about his bravery. He proudly and stoically bore the scars of battle, from many wounds including a sword slash that had taken his right eye. But even he hesitated as his hired steam coach chuffed and hissed to a halt close to Pleasance Square. The crowds of frightened but fascinated onlookers had not diminished, nor had the presence of the clergy leading well-attended groups in loud prayer and rousing hymns. The indisputable existence of the ghosts had helped recruit many converts to the established church and probably too many others.

The road leading up to the barrier resembled a sombre carnival, street merchants sold hot chestnuts, ale and mulled wine. Some had fashioned crude cloth spectres on sticks to sell as toys. Clearly the Prime Minister had not considered the possibility of allowing this to turn into an attraction. Come to London to see the sights, The Tower of London, The Monument and The Ghosts of Mayfair. But then Bowring was a humourless puritan and a short-sighted fool

'Sorry, sir,' muttered his driver, 'but this is as close as I can get you without endangering the crowds.'

'Take it right up to the barrier, driver, they'll get out of the way soon enough.'

As the cumbersome steam coach edged through the throng, Stroude ignored the howls of protest and angry hammering against its brass sides. These people were nothing for a man of his mettle to fear; the Major had fought fearsome Xhosa hordes in Africa and survived battles in the Crimea with honour. The gawping hoi polloi of London had an easy choice ... move out of his way or be crushed under the iron wheels of his coach. The hired driver was not so ruthless.

'Sorry, m'lud. I don' wanna 'urt anyone nor catch a glimpse of them there h'apparitions. Sling me in the nick if you want, but I ain't moving a h'inch closer.'

'I'll double your hire,' Stroude insisted, unused to being thwarted by the working class. 'There is nothing to fear. Whatever these things are, and I suspect it is no more than a monstrous hoax, a magician's illusion using smoke and mirrors, they cannot harm you.'

'Not fer all the tea in China,' grumbled the driver, putting on the brakes with a show of defiance. Unwilling to waste any more time, Stroude alighted but refused to pay.

'I will give you double the fee if you wait for me here. My appointment will not take long.'

Ignoring the driver's colourful oaths ringing across the crowds, the major strode forward, his commanding presence alone helping to clear the way. He observed a group of people gathering at some railings. Someone had fixed a large chalkboard with a list of names of any apparition identified by members of the crowd. He gave the inventory a cursory glance ... recognised many well known executed felons, no doubt this was adding to the tremors of fear that had spread from this once unremarkable London square and out across the civilised world. Good. Fear was the weapon Stroude desired to control.

To one side were mismatched bands of anxious people huddled around religious types reading loudly from their various holy books, close up to the barrier were others hopeful for a sight of their loved ones, many were pleading with the ghosts to reveal if their departed were amongst them. Stroude shuddered at this maudlin spectacle, a carnival of death.

Bracing himself, the major looked across the barriers into the deserted square ... empty of the living but thronged with the spectral essences of the dead. Eerie human shapes drifted close and through each other, often many merging before restoring their fragile individuality. Some were stronger, their shapes clearly defined ... almost recognisably human but for baleful voids where their eyes should be. Others were faint fragments and wisps of fading memory. He shuddered but was undeterred, sharpened steel and well aimed projectiles were all he feared. What could these things do to him?

He marched through, there were enough gaps to be able to sidestep the apparitions but it was not enough to avoid the cold sense of dread emanating from their ethereal forms. Each day and night more arrived, Stroude was aware that in the near future, making his passage through on foot would become impossible, there would be far too many of the things to negotiate a path through them. Today, bravery and quick reflexes got him through the spectres but the effort still left him shaking, his mind assaulted by the sheer aberration of their existence in this plane and hardening his resolve to have them forced under official control. If they could rattle a man of his resolve, what could they do to a rabble of enemy soldiers?

7

Despite his extensive collection of occult books, not one offered even the smallest hope of a solution. Darian slammed the last ancient vellum tome shut with a sigh of defeat. Even his Chaldean Book of the Dead copied from cuneiform clay tablets, bound in dragon skin and written with basilisk blood had failed to yield any clue to a solution! And if that hadn't contained an answer, what would? He sat in his well secured library, a long room packed to the ceiling with mahogany bookshelves crammed with ancient, esoteric tomes, any one of which would have condemned Darian to a fiery agonising death at the stake in less enlightened times.

In pride of place in the centre of the room was a large orrery, a magnificent 17th century clockwork masterpiece. On slender brass limbs, the planets encircling a highly polished pure gold sun were polished orbs of semi-precious stones. Once the device was in motion, delicate music as from movement of the celestial spheres played to augment the orrery's beauty. Darian treasured the machine but it could do nothing to help him with this dilemma. Nor could the other devices of scientific calculation, astrology and sorcery packing the room. Collectors' pieces and curiosities to the hostile and suspicious, useful working tools to Darian. Usually.

Without Sir Miles Hardwick about, he could not seek a technological solution. Where in Hades was the inventor? Perhaps he had succumbed to the voracious passion of his amazonian beloved, the formidable Athena Dedman? Darian needed his friend back now ... damn the love-struck fool.

The continued imprisonment in his home was unbearable, Darian considered escape into an opiate induced dream world but nothing would change on his recovery ... the damned ghosts would still be there. But without a better solution, he left his library and sought out sanctuary. Belial would not approve, as a demon, he cared nothing for the fate of humans – none – except Darian. The demon prince's obsessive love and devotion to Darian was a cruel curse, a twisted punishment on a Fallen Angel who was once a being created out of cosmic love for all creation. But it was a curse Belial gladly accepted even though it condemned him to life on Earth in weakened human form. He was in no hurry to go back to Hell.

Darian shamelessly exploited this situation to keep the demon in his life, not for any emotional reasons ... what better protection could a man have than his own personal demon on hand? Even one who fussed around him like an old nursemaid at times! At ease with each other's company and willing partners in adventure and decadent pursuits, the concern over his welfare was an easy price to pay for Belial's company.

It was no good. Darian needed to take some stolen time away from his dilemma and accept the demon's disapproval a small price to pay. He cautiously made his way to his laboratory, doing his best not to alert Belial. He was not in the mood for a lecture on morals from a creature who boiled human heads alive for fun.

No one human entered this most esoteric of Darian's rooms, he alone knew the spell that unleashed the intricately wrought magickal lock of silver and star stones. Once inside, he was surrounded by the tools of his main trade, alchemy ... the potent and much derided blend of science with ancient magickes.

As he lit the central candle sconce, the warm flickering light shone on shelves packed with multicoloured glass jars of potions, catalysts and chemicals. On the floor lay many chests of lead or stone to store the more volatile and dangerous substances including a whole black mandrake root and a jar of glowing pitchblende. Curious wooden boxes from far flung corners of the globe held mysterious, rare ingredients such as voodoo grave dust, dragon scales and powdered moon diamonds. From hooks dangled bunches of dried Tannis leaves, Celestial Orchid and other rare plants. Decorative glass and precious stone phials held precious drops of Styx river water, mermaid tears and unicorn blood. Hidden behind these delicate and irreplaceable treasures was a plain, scuffed wooden box, where he stored the gateway to his dreams.

He lit a fire and settled in a well-worn, comfortable red velvet armchair and opening the box, took out all he needed to chase the dragon to wherever it would lead him.

Brutal heat hit Darian like a blow, as if he was thrown into a furnace in a desert setting. His heart plunged to despair as he recognised his location, last time he'd been here, the wind from the Nile was gentle, benign. Moonlight had bathed what had once been his home, caressing the colourful tiled walls with silver. Hope and love still existed within the palace walls. The night air was perfumed with sandalwood smoke, enlivened by the music of many fountains and laughter from within the candlelit chambers.

When he was stolen from this place by a force he could not control, Darian had left his heart behind and all that was good in his forever damaged soul. Returning only in opiate dreams, the visions had tantalised and tormented him, always taking him to the exterior of his home but never within. Yet still he had welcomed them for he recognised the laughter, knowing it was her. His beloved young wife.

This time, the visitation was terrible beyond words, a vision of desolation, ruin and despair. Nothing remained of the gracious compound beyond one short course of broken wall bricks, the only clue to what once was a small palace beside the Nile. There was nothing left of a large grove of palm trees that once gave shade to the building and provided such sweet fruit it seemed grown for the goddesses of Egypt. But Bast, Sekhmet and Maat had turned their haughty faces away from this place, abandoning it to the desert wind and conquering sand.

Darian fell to his knees and sobbed. What was this dream telling him? A dream that had the raw touch of reality, how could he deny his skin was seared by the midday sun, his throat painful, raw from the heated air? His hand reached down and felt the burning sand that had stolen his home.

Was this a sign it was all too late? That the years spent trying to return to a past adventure in time, back to his soul mate, his one true love were futile? Was all that remained of that charmed time in ancient Egypt including his wife no more than wind-blown dust?

He stumbled back to his feet and wandered the site without knowing why, perhaps seeking some artefact, some clue to what had gone. But there was nothing, even the tiling had been scoured off the remaining section of mud brick wall by the raking desert winds. He felt the wall crumble at his touch. Soon that too would be lost to the sand.

Darian turned to the Nile, at least the mighty river and giver of life still continued its majestic, enigmatic passage through Africa. It was wide here, slow and meandering as if exhausted from its long journey from its remote source. He walked, the distance longer than he remembered, to its banks and watched the snow white egrets swoop low over the deep waters. A dangerous place to stand, crocodiles would never lose their appetites whatever the era but he was beyond caring …

To his astonishment the river rose to engulf him … a river that was a wakeup call from an insistent demon with the shock of a jug full of ice cold water thrown in his face. Curse that Belial! He hated the opiate induced dream but it showed him a mystery, one he wanted to know more about. What era had he returned to? What had happened to the palace?

'Sorry my friend,' Belial murmured unconvincingly, 'but against all the odds, we have a visitor. A Major Stroude.'

Pulling out a silk kerchief and wiping his face, Darian replied with ill grace, 'Evidently, a madman or a fool. I will be down as soon as I have changed. Another fool has doused me in water.'

Belial began to stride away then turned, growling with a long running bitterness,

'I am the fool? And this from someone deliberately poisoning their mind, a weak coward unable to face reality.'

Anger cleared Darian's head and he leapt to his feet ... just as the demon planned.

'Come on, Cyrus. Don't keep our guest waiting. I am intrigued to know what he wants.'

8

Stroude was surprised to be ushered into the alchemist's home by a well-dressed manservant, assuming Darian's staff would have fled at the first appearance by the ghosts. His conjecture turned to bafflement when the young man joined him in a reception room, brazenly offering him a drink from a well-stocked cabinet. No servant would dare to be so impudent.

Accepting a tumbler of excellent single malt whiskey, the major took stock of his surroundings. The Georgian townhouse had not been altered to be in line with contemporary sensibilities but was furnished and decorated in the light, bright fashion of the Regency period. There was no tell-tale rank odour of gaslight, instead there were glistening, large crystal chandeliers and silver candle sconces to light the rooms. Stroude had forgotten the attractive warm dance of candlelight, he was another caught up in the rush for progress and to modernise his dwelling with gas lit lights and heating.

The décor in the high ceilinged rooms had polished floorboards covered with richly coloured silk Oriental rugs in jewel colours. The walls were painted duck egg blue and were hung with delicate Chinese silk coverings in shades of jade and gold. The furniture was delicate, expensive and exquisite with several examples of genuine Chippendale items. So much in contrast to the dark colours and heavy furnishing so popular in modern homes.

The mantelpiece and shelves were not crowded and stuffy with too many ornaments but what was there was carefully chosen for its elegance of design and occult overtones, imitating a shudder from the major, reminding him that he was alone in the lair of a potentially dangerous man and his eerie partner.

Fortified by the whiskey, the major contemplated the young man, now brazenly sitting opposite him. Stroude's conclusions were not good. The silken, golden good looks and manner were unsettling, as were his coldly intelligent and malign eyes ... the beautiful but deadly gaze of a predator in the body of an angelic youth. Rumours about Darian's decadent lifestyle abounded, the presence of this gilded boy and his high status in this household confirmed Stroude's judgement.

Before he could dwell further on this depraved matter, the master of the house entered the room. A tall man, younger in appearance than his alleged years, darkly handsome, elegant and highly-strung in manner. He wore the louche, luxurious clothing of the city's artistic community which added to his air of nonconformity. He had all the attributes of an outsider by his lack of title or breeding and openly defiant behaviour. One who had no interest in fitting in with English society, perhaps holding it in contempt. A man, the major surmised, who had no loyalties except to himself and who made enemies easily. Stroude was convinced his earlier assessment had been right and this was indeed a dangerous man.

'We have become unused to casual visitors,' Darian said, taking a seat opposite the major. 'A vexing infestation of ghosts is most inconvenient and off-putting to potential guests.'

After introducing himself, Stroude replied, 'Then I take it, this *inconvenience* is not of your making?'

The alchemist gave a humourless smile, 'Only a madman seeking total seclusion would dream of putting up such a defence around their home, I am neither insane or a recluse.'

'Yet they appear to serve you.'

Darian held up his hand and was immediately given a balloon-glass of cognac by his eerie companion without a word passing between them. Stroude shuddered at the intimacy such an action represented. Darian's long fingers curled around the glass stem and he took a swig of cognac before answering.

'To my exasperation, Major Stroude, they do not serve me well enough. Any attempt to send them away leads to abject failure. I must assume this makes me a marked man. No doubt Her Majesty and her government want this situation concluded swiftly.'

Did nothing get past this strange, enigmatic man?

'Indeed,' Stroude agreed, 'but it will be difficult to persuade anyone that you had nothing to do with this *inconvenience*. The spectres chose you, a man rumoured to practice the dark arts and necromancy and not some unfortunate innocent.'

'Yet the truth is, Major, I had nothing to do with this summoning of the earthbound dead,' Darian lied easily. 'Whether anyone is prepared to believe that or not makes no difference.'

Stroude sighed. He was used to dealing with straightforward military men of action, this foreigner steeped in mystery and intrigue left him wrong-footed and unsure. A matter not helped by the sinister dark spectacles that hid Darian's eyes veiling the windows of his soul. And what a complex, dark soul! Stroude's own eyes scanned the reception room again; its discreet opulence and elegance as befitting a man of affluence and taste and who revelled in defying conformity. But closer scrutiny revealed a preference for the outlandish. A nightmarish oil painting by Fuseli glowered from above the mantelpiece, depicting a man trapped in his bed by a terrifying female monster, a succubus. The major shuddered as a primal fear of the unknown crept unwanted into his veins.

'You are correct, Darian, with our new Prime Minister holding the reins of power; a forthright Christian zealot, he wants all trace of the supernatural eliminated from the Queen's realm ... that includes all sorcerers, alchemists and creatures escaping from Hellish regions.'

Darian's companion laughed, a deep melodious sound undermined by a chilling undertone. 'A fool's errand. Pandora's Box has been flung wide open and cannot be so easily closed.'

'Could you be the man to do it?' Stroude quizzed, all the while doing his best to ignore the intense and hostile scrutiny of the alchemist's demonic companion. 'It would remove the sword of Damocles over your head and secure your future in this country and the Empire ...'

'I never do anything that gives me a disadvantage,' Darian replied. 'And nothing would ever make me accepted here as an

Englishman. Thank Hades.'

Arrogant too, thought the Major, beginning to doubt his decision to protect this man to gain the army of the dead.

'Pity,' replied Stroude through gritted teeth. The atmosphere of this house, this triumphant shrine to all that was occult and unseemly, had become claustrophobic despite its bright and spacious dimensions. An unpleasant feeling made much worse by the presence of constant mocking scrutiny of Belial and the knowledge that a ghastly horde of spectres surrounded this building.

'Darian, let me make it clear. Your position is untenable. Bowring wants you dead in an attempt to rid the city of these ghosts. You are a prisoner in your home. I can offer you the only solution to this dilemma.'

The alchemist lay back in his chair and gave an extravagant yawn and stretch, 'I wish I could say I was intrigued but I am not. Any dealings with this government, and its military, has been a grave disappointment to me in the past.'

Stroude gestured to the curtained window, 'And you have so many other choices? Hear me out, Darian. I can get you away from London, somewhere safe. All I ask in return is your co-operation.'

'Go on …'

The major leant forward, 'Use this army of the dead for the good of Great Britain and the Empire. Can you imagine what a weapon of terror you have at your disposal? *Our disposal.*'

Darian searched for glimpses of insanity in the major's flint grey eyes but found none. 'My dear man, I want rid of these wretched encumbrances not traipse around the world's battlefields like some ghoulish Pied Piper.'

'From what I have heard about this new prime minister,' Belial interjected for the first time, 'he would never allow this to happen. Not exactly the Christian way of warfare.'

Stroude shrugged, 'I will have that shot of whiskey after all … if the offer is still forthcoming.' He waited until Belial handed him a crystal cut tumbler of single malt before continuing. 'Obviously such a force must be employed with great circumspection.'

Darian laughed, full-throated and genuinely amused. 'And news of an army of earthbound dead terrifying enemy troops into a panicked retreat will somehow never reach Bowring's ears?'

'I believe with skill and discretion … yes. All attributes I believe you have, Darian.'

'Major Stroude, do I look like someone prepared to lead any battle for queen and country? I am the antithesis of everything you stand for … I have no class, faith, status or nationality. My only loyalty is to myself. I prefer the company of sinners to saints, harlots to that of ladies.'

The major knocked back the whisky then stood up and walked towards the door, 'Then you are a dead man. I offer the only solution and protection to your predicament. Here is my card, should you come to your senses. Send your …' Stroude's words tailed off as he hesitated, what was the golden haired youth? Not human, that was now certain. He left the card on a nearby table and stormed out and head down, repeated his stoic march through the hard-pressed throng of spectres.

'A brave man,' noted Darian, 'if one on a fool's errand. And one who will attract the unfavourable attention of this new Prime Minister before long.'

He turned to Belial, 'I have to get out of here, old chap. I am trapped by these spooks and at the mercy of my still living enemies. Can you get Miles back? Much as I hate admitting this, I need him.'

9

Florence

Sir Miles Hardwick approached the entrance to yet another mausoleum of an art gallery and stifled a sigh of trepidation. His feet ached and his stomach churned with the after effects of luncheon, a suspect, overly pricey seafood pasta. The prospect of following his bride around more echoing corridors lined with great works did not cause him to feel any enthusiasm. The new Lady Hardwick had turned out to have a voracious appetite for culture and he looked back at the early days and nights of their extended honeymoon with a pang of nostalgia for languid afternoons spent resting in their hotel in Venice and long nights of passionate lovemaking.

Now with the heady days of early marriage over, mundane issues began to crowd Hardwick's mind. They were nearly broke. Darian had given them a generous wedding gift of gold sovereigns but Athena who had been brought up as a wealthy heiress before her father's financial ruin and subsequent demise left her penniless, had become used to a lavish lifestyle. Their stay in Paris had been a nightmare, with Athena ordering exquisite and exclusive gowns from the feted genius and fashionable couturier Worth. The newlyweds had left France without settling his bill although for the time being Hardwick had managed to keep the unsavoury truth from his bride.

Hardwick had no savings and no capital he could access. Money made from his ingenious inventions slipped easily through his hands from a deeply ingrained gambling addiction. To his shame, he had relied too long on that wretched alchemist to subsidise him. As a married man, it was time to take responsibility for the first time in his life. The trouble was he hadn't a clue how to do this ... .not without Cyrus Darian. The man he had solemnly sworn to Athena he would forever shun.

Within an hour, the combined effects of the bad seafood and fatigue overwhelmed him. Fortunately, a chattering gaggle of middle-class English ladies were only too happy to take Lady Hardwick under their wing and include her on their tour, enabling her to continue exploring the gallery. Hardwick felt better after the welcome discovery of a public lavatory. He then sought the shade of a nearby café where he partook of a glass of brandy to settle his stomach.

Within minutes he became aware of a ruddy-faced, stocky man, hot and stiffly uncomfortable in an expensive, fashionable outfit.

'Beg your pardon, sir,' the man said hesitantly, 'such an intrusion would be unpardonable back home but we are both Englishmen alone in a foreign clime and our wives are already acquainted.'

Hardwick had lost most of his inhibitions regarding mixing with social inferiors, a side effect of his long liaison with Darian and as a consequence welcomed the man to join him.

'Josiah Emery Pringle,' this new companion announced with an awkward smile. 'Maker of the finest steel in Her Majesty's Empire.

'Hardwick,' the inventor replied, 'and as for the steel I can avouch for that. I only ever utilise Pringle Steel in my workshops.'

The delighted industrialist pumped Hardwick's hand with a firm, calloused grip, 'Then this is a happy circumstance, your Lordship. While our womenfolk gawp at a load of old daubs, we can discuss the more important affairs that concern us men.'

'Indeed,' grinned Hardwick, it was time to be honest with himself that the weeks of travel had now paled and he longed for news of home. No, more than that, he longed to be home. He missed his workshop and the thrill of creating. He missed the smell of steam and oil and metal and the satisfying sound of a device once just an idea, purring into precision action. Most of all, he missed pushing the boundaries of his imagination and technology to make something extraordinary and new. All activities the new Lady Hardwick deemed unsuitable for an aristocrat and a gentleman.

Athena's enjoyment of the cultural highlights of old Europe had not waned, only this morning she spoke avidly of her desire to travel to Greece. This was bad news, for Hardwick was unsure if he had enough funds to pay for a passage home ... at least in the style Athena would expect.

'Rum business that, in London,' Pringle began as he sat down at Hardwick's table. 'The missus was all for moving down there but I've put my foot down. There's nowt in that filthy city that is good for man nor beast.'

Hardwick gave a slight bow of his head in agreement, unwilling to discuss the Great Turbine Disaster with anyone, not when he had missed being incinerated by seconds, rescued by the twin amazons of Athena and the Lady ... his attention sharpened up as Pringle continued, this clearly was another problem besetting the capital.

'Aye, there are no ghastly apparitions haunting our Sheffield streets, unless you count the ladies of the Temperance Society. Once planted, our dear departed stay dead and buried.'

Hardwick's natural suspicions rose, trouble, ghosts and London all added to one possible cause ... his erstwhile partner in adventure and inventions, Cyrus Darian. 'Tell me more, Mr Pringle, I have been out of touch with events back home ... this being our honeymoon.'

Pringle gave a knowing wink and proceeded to relate the tale of the bizarre haunting of Pleasance Square, Mayfair. His voice appeared to fade, the words lost as a cold shadow of trepidation made time stand still for Hardwick. It had to be Darian and some lingering consequence of saving the world from the evil Technomicron. There could be no other logical conclusion. Hardwick wanted to be there, for all his treachery, lies and arrogance, Cyrus Darian was the closest to a friend, maybe even to a brother that the inventor had ever known. Life around Darian was never dull, usually downright dangerous but always thrilling. Hardwick loved his new wife but a life of domesticity and debt had never been in his plans. But how could he go home, back to an alliance with the notorious alchemist and keep Athena's love?

An hour passed, then another, the time blurring as Pringle's hospitality and rough-hewn congeniality took over. Hardwick knew he was getting drunk, inhibitions loosening as they sat together in the heady Italian spring sunshine, a companionable euphoria developing between them even the sewage stench from the nearby river Arno could not dampen. By the time the swish of fine fabrics and the light waft of flowery fragrance announced the return of their spouses, Hardwick had worked himself into a determined resolve. He was master of his fate … and of Athena's. They would return forthwith to London, accepting the generous offer of a passage home on Pringle's steam yacht. Hardwick would brook no argument.

Hardwick's plan to assert his marital authority seemed a good idea at the brandy-fuelled time. Athena had listened to his slurred and over-loud public announcement with remarkable poise and forbearance. She had taken gracious leave of the Pringles on behalf of them both and frogmarched her husband to the nearest carriage for hire to take a silent, seething journey back to their hotel.

Unfortunately, once the servants were out of earshot, her tirade against Hardwick's appalling behaviour in front of his social inferiors, had fallen on deaf ears. He had fallen into a deep sleep, sprawled across the bed and was oblivious to her torrent of ire. Athena retired to the balcony, her hands gripping the marble balustrade, grateful for the strength of the cold stone. It reflected the mood of her heart. The honeymoon was over. Below her the city's ancient beauty was a cruel reminder of what she would lose once back to London, that roiling, infested cesspit with Cyrus Darian at its dark heart. How could she ever expect to keep Miles away from his malevolent influence once back in England?

Darian and his reckless misadventures were a dangerous, foolish addiction to her husband, one she fully intended to break forever. But her plan could only succeed by a prolonged absence from the alchemist's corrupting influence. To return home now would be a disaster, to their marriage and to Miles Hardwick's very soul.

10

Darian faced the prospect of another day and night sealed up in his house with an uncharacteristic display of ill grace, shoving a pile of old tomes off the table and giving them a desultorily kick across the floor for good measure. No wonder his dragoncat kept away. Wise creature. Even Belial had given him a wide berth that morning. The alchemist was in such a foul mood that even Stroude's insane offer began to have more appeal. Darian had never experienced a problem without an apparent solution before, the curse of the Technomicron had the upper hand and this was unacceptable.

Grabbing his swordstick, he marched to the front door, flinging it open.

'Go away! I don't want your servitude and you don't want my command over you ... .so just bugger off!'

The spectres remained, a ghostly wall of forms packed close together as yet more had gathered overnight, glaring with their sightless hatred, unable to stop their dreary murmuring of submission, *'Master, Master ...'*

'I mean it ... bugger off!'

Darian felt hot, strong hands on his shoulders as his demon companion yanked him back into the house.

'You can be an idiot some times, my friend,' Belial growled, 'but never a suicidal idiot. It would take just one well aimed shot from a sniper and London's ghost problem could be over.'

Belial glanced around the surrounding rooftops before slamming the door shut. 'They will be there, if not now, later today. How many times do you need reminding? This government wants you dead.'

'Nothing new then,' Darian mumbled, struggling to recover his composure. 'Name me a government in the world who doesn't.' He had to accept there was no known way of dispersing the spectres and the answer lay elsewhere. He returned to his study, at least spending time pondering this would distract him from the crushing claustrophobia for a few hours.

The long day drew on marked only by the rhythmic ticking of the house's many fine old clocks, something he did not normally notice but now the sound was driving him to insanity. He needed to escape, if not to the outside world then to the inner world of his dreams. Darian decided to indulge in some more chemical assistance to gain a few hours oblivion from the endless claustrophobia and lack of progress. With Belial out seeking news of the globetrotting inventor, Darian chose to chase the dragon again as his opiate of choice. He knew that he risked returning to that desolate place and the sad ruins of his past home in ancient Egypt but opium dreams were unpredictable, he could just as easily find himself somewhere pleasure-filled and delightfully decadent.

Darian decided it was worth the gamble, his nights before the arrival of the wretched ghosts were always wild and hedonistic adventures. He loved the theatre both risqué and respectable, the company of ladies of ill-repute whether high-class courtesans or the exotic, cheap girls of certain preferred bawdy houses. He was equally at home at eminent scientific lectures or East End music halls, elegant soirees of the titled or seedy gambling dens. Of course, the more high class the event, the less welcome he'd receive from other participants. This amused him greatly. His wealth opened doors that one of his reputation and breeding would normally find barred shut.

Within minutes, all his expectations of an escape into dreams were dashed, his opium and laudanum supplies were missing, even the stuff he'd secreted away from the demon's knowledge. Damn that Belial. Since when did a High Prince of Hell become so sanctimonious? A bloody infernal nursemaid. Seething, he returned to his library, the floor strewn with discarded books from his last outburst of frustration. Those accursed spooks were getting to him, robbing him of his usual insouciant poise and self-control.

At least the demon had left a half full brandy bottle

untouched on the floor, Darian grabbed it and took a big swig straight from the bottle in case his companion returned and wrested it off him. He slumped at his desk, his normally mercurial mind for once stumped for a solution.

Distracted by loud buzzing, Darian watched an early emerging bumblebee bustle and blunder around the room. How the hell did that get past his defences from the outside world? Or survive the caustic air that was anathema to all insects in London beyond fleas, lice and cockroaches. Now fascinated by the unlikely intruder, he gazed at the creature's attempt to navigate what must have been an alien and confusing environment, no flowers, no open spaces. It eventually hovered, buzzing loudly, above one shelf of eclectic artefacts, choosing one in particular to land on; a brass, gold and copper-inlaid thumb trap. At first sight simply a geegaw to amuse at dinner parties but Darian knew it was a far more complex and dangerous object of oriental design. This was an example of potent magickal equipment of ancient and unknown origin. One he hadn't explored fully yet.

The bee crawled into one end … and disappeared. Darian examined the thumb trap carefully, even held it to his ear to discern any buzzing from within but the insect had vanished. Extraordinary. There was so much more to learn about this device he'd stolen from a Tibetan temple. He placed it back on the table, curiosity aroused. Damn his own soul to Hades! What a fool he had been. This was a sign, a wakeup call from someone or something. The bee was possibly a natural thing but not this device. He could not control or banish the ghosts but perhaps he could trap them.

Excited by this revelation, his mind spun with possibilities. Of course it would need that blend of the occult and clever practical engineering. It would need Hardwick, wherever that henpecked fool was. Patience was never a virtue Darian embraced among his many vices. There had to be someone else who could help him. His gaze caught the candlelight gleaming from the brass and semi-precious stones of his orrery. Of course. Hardwick was not the only genius in town. That clever, nimble-fingered clockmaker, Michael Lewis had designed and crafted beautiful instruments and clever devices of greater complexity and sophistication. In this case, more useful than Hardwick's big machines and weapons. Would he work for Darian? Of course the clockmaker would, nobody refused a gold-laden purse.

11

The creature shuffled into its lair, throwing down the bodies of its three brace of scrawny city pigeons, their feathers coated with rank pollution and fresh blood.

The charnel house it had made out of an empty marble sarcophagus was now a permanent home for the creature. It reeked of death. Bones of its prey, gnawed free of every last trace of flesh and marrow lay strewn in piles, encroaching on the patch of dank earth used for sleeping through the long hours of daylight. It had lived in this makeshift lair for many months. Once a peaceful, abandoned corner of an old cemetery, even birds no longer alighted on the branches of surrounding trees, such was the fear it created throughout those of the natural world.

The animals that had happily dwelled among the overgrown graves and monuments to long forgotten human dead, had long since fled, or had fallen victim to the monstrous thing. It had fed on rats, rabbits, foxes and cats and pigeon. It was hungry, very hungry but the main source of its need was not sustenance but revenge. Eating human flesh would be the final step towards its eternal damnation but it could not be any hapless passer-by or lost, wandering mourner. It would have to be Cyrus Darian who would meet his long overdue end between the creature's slavering jaws.

It was time to move on ... or change appearance to something smaller.

The creature had been human once, well, almost. A demonic half-bred heritage cursed him to a life of shapeshifter. Abandoned to die on a stinking midden heap by his fear-crazed mother, the baby had been found in time and raised by a kindly elderly man, a clergyman who was also a scientist. With his help and guidance, the creature had held on tight to his humanity and his faith, obediently following the scriptures and leading a quiet, introspective life. Named Cambion, his life had been turned upside down by the old man's peaceful death. The world and all its cruelty had crowded in on a gentle and shy young man who had only wanted to live a good, simple life and to shun the reality of his being.

Rescue and purpose had come in the dubious form of Cyrus Darian. In return for a high wage and a comfortable home of his own, Cambion had agreed to be used for the alchemist's nefarious schemes. The shapeshifter had refused to thieve or take lives but had accepted employment as a spy, changing to many forms such as a rat, hawk – even an infestation of biting fleas to help his employer. Cambion had seethed with self-loathing, hating every use of his demonic power to assume animal forms. Each change had seemed to diminish his precious hold on humanity and tarnish his immortal soul.

Cambion had felt he should be grateful for the acceptance and friendship of the rest of Darian's entourage of adventurers, for the comfort and relative safety. But the reckless, amoral life of the alchemist and his team had rankled and clashed with Cambion's deeply held religious beliefs. How could he justify associating with a man who flouted every law and openly consorted with loose women, criminals and worse of all ... a demon? Belial was no less than a Prince of Hell in human form.

In the end, it had become unbearable and he had betrayed Darian to a group of religious fanatics in return for a promise of sanctuary and shelter in their monastery. Of course it had ended badly. He had thought they'd wanted Darian to make him see the error of his Godless ways, repent and renounce his demon companion. In reality, they'd wanted to torture and kill him. Lied to and used again, Cambion had fled, surviving Belial's furious and horrifying revenge. Guilt-ridden, confused and angry, Cambion had given into his hidden instincts and became a ravening beast, convinced he was beyond redemption, beyond forgiveness. He bowed to his fate to be a monstrous hell-spawned being, determined to end his life. But not before first ending Darian's – the architect of his downfall.

CYRUS DARIAN AND THE GHASTLY HORDE

In the form of the beast, his mind was less conflicted. A creature of pure instinct, an insane amalgam of fur, feathers, scale and claw. It had no scent but exuded an energy that chilled the blood of all that came close. Few survived its predation. The human within rarely surfaced now, becoming less in control with each day and each kill. The beast enjoyed its power, the taste of hot, fresh blood and the crunch of bone. Cambion's human soul withered into a festering core of resentment simmering within the hulk of the beast.

And now the time of waiting was over, after nights of becoming an owl and flying low over the alchemist's dwelling, watching with curiosity as spectres gathered in increasing number in the square it became clear they were awaiting the same man. One night his patience was rewarded. All the phantoms were focused on Darian's front door, all murmuring their one word incantation of *Master*. If proof was needed, the man himself appeared briefly on the front doorstep, as vain, arrogant and handsome as ever. The beast's vigil in the cemetery was at an end.

12

The gaslight's attempt to illuminate the foul gloom filling the narrow street like a solid, reeking wall was as doomed as the doxie's attempt to get some business from Belial. He enjoyed all human pleasures of the flesh but he had high standards. This scrawny, inebriated woman was of indeterminate age. Her front teeth had been knocked out by her whoremaster and she wore a new, stolen, feathered hat crammed and pinned onto her lice-ridden hair. The hat's bright colours highlighted her poverty and degradation. The demon could smell through the miasma, the stench of unwashed flesh, stale sex, cheap gin and desperation.

He had no need to push past her clumsy advances, even in her bleary-eyed state, she could sense the danger from him and she shrunk back against the dank wall of the inn with a squeal of alarm. Belial threw her a shilling, not out of kindness but to shut her up. He was on a mission and could do without the distraction of the hue and cry on discovery of her body or a violent confrontation with local ruffians, however enjoyable the prospect.

As expected, the streetwalker ran off down the street, away from her pimp to spend all her windfall on gin, leaving Belial to concentrate on self-control as he entered the inn. Much as he desired creating some bloody mayhem as a diversion, a more subtle approach and bribery would gain him more answers. A quick glance through the pipe smoke and grimy light and Belial found his prey. Three men he recognised from one of Hardwick's nearby workshops. The demon reached their table just as one looked up and spotted him, Belial held the man's shoulder in a vicious grip, pinning the engineer back down in his seat before he could flee.

CYRUS DARIAN AND THE GHASTLY HORDE

'Gentlemen, did I hear one of you offering me a drink? How kind, I accept your hospitality.'

Belial's trawl of the inns around the inventor's workshops was to no avail, even the fearful presence of an insistent demon loosened no tongues. He had to accept they genuinely did not know where Hardwick was. Which was a shame, he was in the mood to boil a few heads that morning. Maybe later.

He returned home via steam Hansom to find the defences around Pleasance Square now fortified with a battalion of Mechmen. Surly and rebellious, the crowd of gawpers were pushed back further from the boundaries, the hawkers and churchmen forcibly removed under protest. With each new spectral arrival, there were rising hopes of spotting a departed loved one, the angry crowd did not want to be refused sight of the ghosts. But it was hard to protest against the near solid wall of mechanised metal-clad titans, armed with a bristling array of lethal new technology.

This was going to be awkward.

The demon made his way through the crowd; his aura parting the way as people instinctively shunned the blond young man with the confident, feline stride. Getting past the Mechmen would be more problematical, chosen for their height and brawn not brains. The power of suggestion would go over their heads, only something physical would get through to these walking rust buckets. Though living in human form, weakened Belial and had reduced his full infernal powers, he could still muster up plenty of chaos. In fact he relished any excuse to wreak havoc, oblivious to any consequences as befitting one of his princely status in Hell.

The obvious solution would be to unleash a few bolts of hellfire, incinerate a Mechman or two and stroll past the ensuing chaos. But Darian frowned on extravagant mayhem so close to his home. Too much mess and inconvenience.

Belial needed a more subtle solution.

Darian had once defeated the Mechmen with a volatile potion which reacted with the metal in their armour causing it to rust almost instantly and then collapse into dust. Belial knew that they all still feared this substance not knowing the alchemist had great difficulty recreating the unstable formula. The demon glanced through the crowd and soon found a perfect subject for suggestion – a ruffian in ill-fitting clothes with a half-consumed gin bottle in one ragged pocket.

Belial put one slender hand on his shoulder and paused while shivers of fear and cowering submission juddered through the man's scrawny body. The victim went limp, silent, only held on his feet by Belial's strong grip.

'You are determined to get to the ghosts and you will not let those mechanical fools stand in your way.'

'They will not stand in my way,' echoed the man like an automaton.

'In your hand is the special formula created by Cyrus Darian. The liquid in your gin bottle is in fact, the formula that dissolves their armour.'

'Dissolves their armour.'

'You will run towards the Mechmen and tell them what you have in your hand … if they threaten to shoot you, throw it at the nearest one.'

'At the nearest Mechman.'

The demon let go of his victim who collapsed at first in a sprawling heap on the cobbles. 'Do it now.'

Belial sauntered past the crowd and waited as close as he could to the barrier, meeting the unnerved gaze of a nearby armoured soldier with an impudent wink. Within seconds there were shouts and commotion as his puppet met his fate, cut down by a blaze of weaponry, the resulting flames intensified by the gin. With all eyes turning to the unwitting human torch, Belial leapt the barriers and strode unnoticed through the passive spectres. In theory, he had caused mayhem but he reasoned it was only a small amount compared to past spectaculars. Like Rome.

As he approached the front door, Darian appeared and hauled him into the house. Once again the light of animation and enthusiasm flashed through his lilac and silver eyes. Belial was relieved, the old Cyrus was back.

'Forget that henpecked fool, Hardwick. I have a plan and I need the clockmaker, Michael Lewis. Bring him to me now.'

Even a being as blindly devoted as Belial baulked at this. *'Thank you, Belial, thank you for risking your existence on earth by walking those filthy human streets. Thank you for exposing yourself to the vile cesspits of human-infested inns to find Hardwick.* You know Cyrus, if I wanted to experience hell on earth, I'd create my own.'

The demon's sarcasm was not lost to Darian, aware he had pushed him too far and not for the first time. But it never took much to get Belial back on his side. Darian held the demon's slim, pale face in his hands and kissed him on the mouth, lingering long enough to weaken Belial's resolve. It worked. It always did.

13

A note? A note! Left on the bed of their hotel in Florence, Athena Hardwick held out the offending missive in her fingertips as if it were something poisonous and forced herself to read it again to make certain she had not imagined its outrageous contents.

My dearest wife, my heart, my love,

You are so clearly enjoying your tour of Europe's treasures and I am loath to be the instrument of such cruelty as to tear you away prematurely. Sir Obadiah Pringle and his lovely wife Myrtle have kindly offered to accompany you anywhere in the world your heart desires. They are commonbred but decent, trust worthy people of financial substance. I know you will be safe in their company.

I must return to London at all haste to attend to urgent matters of my business affairs.

I yearn for the day when we will be reunited.
Your devoted and loving husband,
Miles

A hoax ... it had to be. Her husband was many things but never a pathetic, snivelling coward ... except ... Who was she fooling? There was no doubting the signature and phrasing of the missive. Athena knew exactly what that 'urgent matter' entailed. There was only one thing that would make Miles Hardwick forget his duty to his wife. Cyrus Darian. Well, that conniving, immoral foreigner was not going to get away with it. At her insistence, her husband had broken all ties with Darian and she didn't care if every ruin in Europe and the Orient crumbled to dust, she was going to return to London and end this insidious hold over Sir Miles Hardwick once and for all. Permanently.

She swiftly changed out of the extravagant, bustled day dress of peach and cream silk and into a practical travelling gown of more sensible toffee brown linen then rang for the hotel staff to pack up her boxes, ready for despatch back to England. She gathered up her jewellery and some essentials into a small valise on her own, intending to travel fast and light after her errant husband.

As she rushed out of the hotel and onto the street, she took a deep breath and prepared to hail a cab, not willing to waste time waiting for one of the idle, gossiping doormen. This was not something a lady in her position should ever have to do but she did not want to waste time, with Hardwick already at sea. It was only then that Athena encountered a brutal truth about her situation. She had no money. Her purse contained only hairpins, a small comb and a glass phial of light cologne. All her life, she had depended first on her father then her husband to pay for anything she needed in life. She had no need of pin money when they had both been so generous in answering her every whim. This was a disaster. That idiot of a spouse assumed she would be happy accepting the hospitality of the wealthy Pringles, social climbers and people who would not expect a lady to pay her way. Whether he meant it or not, this dependency was a trap. One she refused to fall into.

She still had her jewellery ... that could be sold to pay her passage but she would resent the sale of every treasured gem and fully intended to make both Hardwick and Darian pay dearly for her loss. Her cheeks flushed with embarrassment, certain the cab driver thought her an abandoned mistress as she commanded him to drive her to the most reputable jeweller in Florence and not some dubious, clandestine back street fence. This was humiliation enough but she still wanted the best possible price for her gems.

It was within the tastefully luxurious rooms of Signor Fanelli, feted jeweller to the Italian aristocracy that Athena Hardwick received her second shock of the morning. In hushed, discreet tones, the manager looked up from his examination of her jewels.

'I'm sorry Senora, but these are ... fake.'

The so-called family jewels of the noble Hardwick dynasty were all carefully crafted copies of the originals. The only genuine stones were from the rings and necklaces given to her by her beloved late father. Things of the greatest sentimental value to the orphaned Athena.

Should she swallow her pride and return to be the unwilling guest of the Pringles? Or bear the loss of her most precious things to pursue that craven wretch of a husband?

Athena had never accepted the easiest path in life. She was feisty and determined, very much her father's heir.

In a flash of inspiration, she remembered a gift given to her by an obscenely wealthy Texan oil magnate. A suitor, who had sent the ring to calm her pique when he married some milksop from Boston instead of her. The ring meant nothing to her.

'What about this one?' she said.

She wrenched the ring off. It was a large, diamond and platinum set with a central fire opal, the rare, dark purple stone flashed with a bright inner fire that seemed magical. It was the least sentimental and most valuable of her gems.

Astonished by its beauty, the manager hastily gave her a generous price without quibble, unwilling to let such an astounding ring out of his grasp. He knew it would make him a handsome profit. To Athena's relief, the magnificent jewel was more than enough to pay for a one-way passage to England in considerable comfort as befitting a woman of her status.

Let the seas between Italy and London rage. Let the skies unleash deluges and thunderbolts. She had no fear of monstrous leviathans rising from the deep or marauding hordes of savage pirates. Let them fear her! Nothing was going to stop her catching up with her disappointment of a husband.

Her arrival at the Arno's main wharf was a considerable shock and gave her confidence a substantial knock. In the past, ushered from luxury vessels to the comfort of a waiting landau, Athena had never taken much notice of surrounding harbours. Now the full impact of this one's chaos was like a slap in the face. The stench, the noise, like the first morning at Babel, the hordes of disreputable looking mariners and equally suspect passengers. Athena had never felt so alone, so vulnerable without a gentleman at her side to guide her safely through the morass of humanity.

A group of ragged and heavily armed Middle Eastern sailors, in Athena's mind more likely pirates approached her, their boldness and lack of respect alarming. Worse for wear with drink, they began to heckle her with lewd suggestions and gestures that needed no translator to comprehend. Even under her heavy veil, she was certain they saw her cheeks burning with shame. Never one to give into vulnerability, Athena realised this situation was clearly too dangerous for a woman on her own however courageous. She was out of her depth and her plan to confront her husband and Cyrus Darian would have to be delayed.

Turning on her heel, Athena returned to the puzzled driver of the hired landau and demanded to be taken back to Florence. At least there was an alternative, passage home across Europe by locomotive, travelling first class of course. She would hire a local girl as a ladies maid and a male servant to stand guard outside the carriage door. That way her status and reputation could be maintained.

With a difficult and delayed sea passage, Hardwick might indeed find his wife waiting for him in London. It would be an interesting reunion.

14

Shoreditch

At the sound of a firm, insistent rap on the door, Bartrev's instincts were to search for a weapon, anything to defend himself and his friend. He cursed himself for foolishly thinking himself secure in the teeming chaos of Shoreditch and painfully aware of his vulnerability, he stood armed only with a broom among whirring clocks and precise mechanisms which were hardly adequate against ruthless and violent men like the Tsar's agents in London. But the clockmaker seemed unbothered by a visitor so early, though the shop was not due to open for another hour.

'Relax my dear friend,' urged Lewis, 'there is no need for alarm. I recognise that knock well, we have an important customer.'

Bartrev remained unconvinced as the other man went to unlock the front door. What could be so urgent? And there was no mistaking the weary reluctance in Lewis's voice. A good-looking ... no ... beautiful blond youth slipped through the half-opened door with the silent agility of a cat. Immaculately attired, the young man gave a humourless smile that did not reach his chilling blue eyes. Inhuman eyes. Bartrev shuddered, instinctively aware to the primal depths of his soul that this seemingly angelic youth was far more dangerous than a battalion of Mechmen or a team of Tsarist secret agents.

Lewis made no attempt to introduce the eerie visitor or offer hospitality, somehow Bartrev knew the thought of handing over a cup of tea to the man would be highly inappropriate, that he existed on far darker fare.

'So,' sighed Lewis, 'what does he need fixing now and with such urgency ...'

The being raised his hands to show he had not brought

anything to repair. 'Mr Darian is most unfortunately indisposed and cannot venture out. He has a new and most vital project that needs your unique skills to succeed.'

His cold smile broadened. 'And of course, you will be most handsomely rewarded ... as always.'

'I will lock up the shop.'

Bartrev was puzzled by the instant acquiesce of the clockmaker. He had often remarked during conversations that he never closed his shop even when ill or desperate to make up a backlog of repairs and orders for new devices. What compelling hold did Cyrus Darian have over him? He glanced at the youth again, chilled by his aura of restrained evil and curious but potent power. No henchman came in such a muted form, the threat of a stiletto knife hidden in a velvet glove or deadly poison in a glass of wine.

'I'll get my tools,' Lewis muttered as he turned to his companion, 'tell Hannah I may be late, even away for some time but reassure her I am in safe hands. She knows Cyrus Darian will treat me well.'

'Well I don't know that,' countered a wary Bartrev, 'I do not intend to allow you to go alone.'

In truth, as well as wanting to protect the clockmaker, Bartrev was desperate to meet Darian in person. The one man in London ... maybe in the world with the esoteric knowledge that could help him shake off the Tsar and his relentless minions.

'The more the merrier,' laughed the stranger, 'I can send an urchin around to break the good news to your pretty wife, Lewis. Tell her that after this job, she will be living with you in some peaceful, wealthy area of London far away from the cesspit of Shoreditch.'

Darian's hold over the clockmaker was now all too apparent; his wealth offered the family hope and security for the future. What better incentive was that?

Outside, a hissing, chuffing Hansom waited, partly obscured by the clouds of grey steam from its twin rear funnels, one of the new, faster models to take to London's streets. The boilers of the older ones had an unfortunate tendency to explode without warning, spewing fast-moving death in the form of shards of jagged red hot metal to endanger more than the cab's unfortunate passengers and driver. Many an unsuspecting passer-by met an untimely and unpleasant end from a steam cab accident.

Seeming oblivious to the risk, the others climbed into the cab without hesitation, clearly the dangers of modern technology was accepted as the price of living in London. Bartrev pondered that perhaps his Mother Russia was not unwise in her reluctance to embrace this brash, new world.

Once on route, the sound of the cab's churning pistons and rumble of metal tyres drowning out their conversation from the driver, the still unnamed being leant forward, 'As you seem bizarrely unaware of Mr Darian's current difficulty, I must warn you we may have to be rather ... dramatic at our final approach to his home.'

Bartrev's jaw set into a grim line, this situation was getting worse by the minute, 'Are you going to enlighten us?'

So, the story of the haunting was real after all. Lewis put a hand on the Russian's arm to restrain him, 'There is no need to concern yourself, Nicolas. Mr Belial here will make sure no harm comes to us.'

'Indeed,' Belial replied with an unconvincing grin and an unnerving flash of what seemed like fangs, 'I just hope neither of you have weak hearts or minds and are not frightened of ghosts.'

'I heard the rumours on the streets but thought it was a hoax or an exaggeration,' muttered Lewis, his face pale in the dim, smoky light of the steam Hansom.

'Ghosts?'

Bartrev instinctively crossed himself. He came from a haunted land, the unrelenting centuries of invasions, starvation, brutal winters, raging diseases and cruel pogroms had scattered the spiritual remains of so many dead from violence and despair to roam unshriven. Did any Russian not believe in ghosts? The count doubted it. The spirits of the dead should only remain on the earth for forty days before seeking eternal rest. Those left roaming never gathered in groups.

'*Da,*' replied Darian's messenger in Russian, '*prizrak, spiridon, rusalka.*'

Belial enjoyed the look of horror on both men's faces; Russians, they were a superstitious race regardless of what faith they followed, so delightfully easy to frighten.

'All true,' Belial continued with a mocking grin. 'A great and ever-growing gathering of the city's earthbound spirits. And a dashed nuisance.'

He then tapped at the roof of the cab with his silver skull-topped cane to signal the driver to stop. Out of sight of the other passengers, the demon climbed up to the driver's seat and used his influence to make the elderly driver approach Pleasance Square and its annoying barriers at full speed. Nothing, human, Mechman, police or gawpers alike were to impede the heavy vehicle's head long progress. The coach must appear to a runaway, out of control.

No doubt Lewis and his Russian would scream in genuine terror adding authenticity to the ruse. Accustomed to easy access to his friend's home, Belial returned to the cab, ridding the square of these vexing ghosts could not come soon enough.

The journey continued on uneventfully with the two human passengers unaware of what had transpired between Belial and the driver. They were too lost in their own thoughts about what they would face in Mayfair and what was their part in Darian's plans.

As the view outside the windows changed from crowded, filthy tenements to stolid middle class homes and finally to the wide, tree-lined thoroughfares and gracious Georgian townhouses of Mayfair, the pace of the vehicle stepped up. No cause for alarm at first as this was a quieter region of London with less thronging traffic but as the steam cab picked up speed and began to sway, Belial saw concern spread in his fellow passengers' eyes. Good. Let the screaming begin.

From a sharply sloping rooftop, Stroud's top marksman waited with the innate patience of his calling. Unnerved at first by the shimmering, ghastly forms crowding the square below, with considerable difficulty, the assassin had learnt to ignore the spectres ... they had no interest in him. And like him, they waited for any glimpse of their mutual target. The alchemist.

The government agent had fostered no belief in an afterlife and did not expect to see any of his many victims returning to haunt him. The sight of the ghosts had shaken him badly, bringing with them the concept of some ghastly form returning from the grave seeking vengeance. He steeled himself to concentrate on the assignment, using his inner self-discipline to stop himself from searching the faces of the dead below on the street for anyone he had dispatched to what he had erroneously thought permanent oblivion. This would be his last assignment, the cold, calculating and clinical world he once knew and understood was now shaken to its core.

Earlier that day, Darian's companion-bodyguard-manservant had left, pushing through the ghosts as no more annoying than a cloud of flies. The marksman had shuddered: there was something not right about the golden-haired young man and the unnerving sensation that he was aware of his master's nemesis on the roof. Nonsense of course – a lifetime of training had made the assassin careful at silent concealment and not once had the youth actually glanced up in his direction. Yet even the memory of that sensation sent an echo of the earlier shiver of unease. Used to eradicating enemies of the Queen and Empire with precision and skill, he had never endured such an assignment. *Come out of your fortress, you bastard and let's get this over with.*

Hours passed with no sign of Darian or the other man. Instead his usual, focused concentration was reluctantly drawn to the army of silent ghosts, the swirling mass of human shades. He began to spot individuals among the shimmering mist of spectral energy, a young woman in Georgian costume whose neck was bent at an unnatural angle ... a victim of the gallows. Another killed by hanging was from a still earlier age, no more than a child. Innocent and guilty alike, lost souls who could not pass to their eternal rest. How could he doubt the existence of life after death after seeing these phantoms for himself? Time to change his life, to repent and seek spiritual restitution for all the lives he had taken. But not until he had despatched Cyrus Darian, the man was a threat to British society and the Empire. A worthy and honourable choice of a last kill.

He did not detect the hover then swoop of great wings above him or his coming death until he was overwhelmed by long, cruel talons and sharp fangs.

Cambion had merged many beasts to become a hideous airborne fury when he spotted the lone assassin on the rooftop readying to take out Darian. An outrage, the alchemist was its prey! Its prize! So swift, the human concentrating on Darian's home was killed without emitting even a brief gasp of surprise, his clothing, flesh and bones rent into chunks of gore and devoured completely leaving only the long range rifle on the rooftop. The creature took out its ire on that too, crushing and rending the wood and metal weapon into many jagged pieces.

Cambion took over the assassin's vigil, blending into the skyline as a city crow on a rooftop. No one would notice it.

15

Bartrev gripped the sides of the wildly swaying cab as its speed became reckless, sparing no traffic in its way. He saw white-faced pedestrians running and throwing themselves from its path and the drivers of horse-drawn cabs practically pulling the teeth out of their nags in an attempt to steer them from the vehicle's path. The driver must be insane. He could not stand by and let this mayhem continue.

With difficulty, he moved towards the door, intending to clamber out and up onto the driver's seat to seize control but before he could act further, Bartrev felt a hand grasp his arm and pull him back, its touch burning his skin through his heavy wool jacket. Shocked, Bartrev spun around to be fixed by the young man's eyes, as clear and blue as glacial ice. Without knowing why, the Russian returned to his seat in unprotesting silence to the fearful astonishment of Lewis.

The screams and protests grew louder as the out of control Hansom veered towards the Pleasance Square barriers and the battalion of shocked Mechmen. With Bartrev still in a curious daze, Lewis finally understood what was happening, a deliberate ploy to crash through the blockade of the alchemist's home under the guise of a runaway cab. '*Tshchatel'nyi, drug moi* ... Hold tight, my friend!' he cried to Bartrev as the inevitable collision rocked the steel frame of the cab, sending it skittering onto its side on the teetering edge of two metal wheels.

All became the blur and crash of splintering wood and tearing metal as the world turned upside down in a blaze of sparks and the defiant roar of a dying dragon. The front section of the cab had crumpled into a blazing ruin half buried in a brick wall, its driver had been thrown from his position above and behind the carriage. He was now reduced to a shambles of torn and charred flesh. Belial was first to his feet. He leapt up with a silent, cat-like agility and once out of the stricken cab, reached down for Lewis. He did not bother rescuing the Russian, the man was not part of Darian's plan.

Dazed and confused, Bartrev snapped out of his fugue with no memory beyond trying to stop the runaway cab. Around him, the now empty seat was ruined and beginning to smoulder as fire from the stricken engine began to spread. The whole vehicle was primed to explode at any second, and with primal strength born of instinct, the big man found the speed and energy to vault up and leap clear of the wreckage. Once safe, his legs gave way from shock and he watched from the damp cobbled ground as the Hansom exploded in an intense ball of angry flame.

Nobody came to his aid. Through the haze of black, oily smoke, Bartrev made out a sea of pale, shocked faces beyond the wrecked barrier where many Mechmen lay on their backs, as helpless as upended gigantic beetles. The Russian glanced around him, where the reason for their reticence became apparent. The spectres packed every inch of the square: remnants of too many lives trapped on Earth where they no longer belonged.

They had no interest in him, this he kept repeating as a mantra as he steeled himself to rise to his feet and follow the diabolical youth crossing the square with a terrified Lewis in tow. *Shadows cannot harm the living,* the Russian insisted to himself, *they have no substance beyond their translucent appearance.* Bartrev strode, head down, doing his best to ignore the phantoms. None moved out of his way, their sightless gaze and remaining trace of free will were all focused on the alchemist's home. He had no choice but to push on, meeting the ghosts head on, receiving a shock of intense cold through his body and into his soul as he passed through them. They left an impression of their past lives on Bartrev, like a tainted taste in his mouth. A lingering memory of their sorrow, fear and fury. Their invasion of his life repulsed him but he had no choice but to barge his way through to the sanctuary of the Georgian townhouse of their master.

Bartrev followed the youth and Lewis through the front door into an elegant hallway where at last he encountered the infamous alchemist in person. Tall, at least a decade older than his companion, Cyrus Darian was clearly charismatic despite eyes hidden behind darkened glass. Though obviously a foreigner, he spoke perfect English, perhaps too perfect betraying his exotic heritage.

'Belial, old chap, I really must admire the discreet manner of your return to my home.'

The youth gave a wicked grin then turned and left the house leaving the visitors with Darian who ushered them into an imposing formal parlour, no different from that of any contemporary man of wealth but for the bizarre nature of the ornaments: an eclectic collection of statues of ancient, forgotten gods, intricate Japanese amulets and scientific instruments from the Arab world. Bartrev found them fascinating, his search for a man of arcane knowledge was finally over.

'I must apologise to you, gentlemen. I was not expecting you to be delivered to my home in such a dramatic manner. But please forgive Belial. To him chaos and mayhem are a normal part of his existence.'

Shocked at his cavalier attitude, Bartrev ignored the urbane manner of his host and muttered, 'Chaos that cost an innocent man his life, no doubt leaving a family destitute and grieving.'

The alchemist gave the slightest of shrugs, indifferent to the fate of the cab driver, further enraging Bartrev who fought back a powerful urge to punch Darian's face. He'd seen too much of this disinterest towards human life among his fellow Russian noblemen and it still rankled.

'You must allow Belial some latitude,' Darian murmured, gesturing for his visitors to sit down by a table. 'He is human in form but all pure blood demon by nature.'

Shaken to the core of his being, Bartrev glanced across to the clockmaker and realised he had known this about Belial all along. The strangeness of Bartrev's life in London deepened. Was there anywhere else in the world like England's capital? A place of astounding new wonders, flying craft that crowded the filthy skies and steam driven vehicles that shook the narrow streets like miniature earthquakes. Yet one with a deep seam of evil, human and demon alike, dwelling together in the teeming slums and fancy homes of the rich.. He had never been so homesick since his exile, Bartrev longed for the clean, sharp air above the steppes, the crisp, pungent aroma of the pine forests and the honest smiles of the people working on his vast estate.

'You really have nothing to fear from my companion, at least while you remain an ally of mine.'

Bartrev's anger was unabated, 'I take that as a threat, Darian?'

The alchemist appeared to be amused, 'By Hades no, why would I deal out something so mundane. I will leave that nonsense to petty criminals and politicians. No, treat my statement as a well-meaning desire to preserve your life. Belial has a hellish short fuse. Now, please allow me to offer you refreshments. Maybe something stronger than tea after such a shocking conclusion to your journey?'

The Russian's anger and suspicion remained, but Lewis appeared to have recovered his composure and accepted a cup of very fine Arabian coffee.

'Please, Mr Darian, don't tell me the orrery has malfunctioned again. It is indeed a masterpiece but so very old.'

'Not at all,' Darian reassured. 'Not after your extraordinary care and craftsmanship. Thanks to you, my little jewelled planets will remain safely in their orbits for many centuries to come.'

Darian reached into his pocket and produced the oriental thumb trap, if that was what it was, the alchemist now doubted that rather mundane purpose. It was far more than a cheap trick from a circus conjuror. He handed it over to Lewis.

'As you are all too aware, I have a tiresome problem with a growing army of subservient but idiotic ghosts. Nothing will induce the flimsy beggars to desist and depart. I need to commission a device that will trap and contain them.'

Lewis held the thumb trap up to the light, examining its filigree ornamentation. This was not the artistic whimsy of its creator … it was a script, perhaps an ancient spell in some unknown language.

'It is so small,' the clockmaker murmured to himself, in appreciation for the intricate craftsmanship.

'How large does it need to be?' Darian replied, 'the phantoms are weightless, so insubstantial that thousands can occupy the top of a pinhead.'

'Like angels.'

Darian glanced across to the big Russian, 'No, not like angels. You have just met one of their Fallen. Hardly a being without substance, wouldn't you agree?'

The alchemist enjoyed observing the shocked shiver from Bartrev, whose relationship to Lewis was yet to be discovered. 'Anyway, do you think that between us, we can create a small, portable device to capture and contain my spectral followers?'

Darian paused as the gifted clockmaker carefully examined the mysterious device, his furrowed brow betraying his anxiety. Lewis knew his client would not easily accept the wrong answer.

'I am sorry, truly sorry, Mr Darian. I am a humble maker of toys – mere fripperies and mender of all things clockwork. This device was created by a genius, a master mage well steeped in the occult.'

'As am I,' Darian replied with an encouraging smile. 'I can work on the occult components if you can create an ingenious contraption, a portable, miniature maze constructed of magickally charged materials. I have faith in you, Lewis. I know you can do this.'

'Why should he?'

Bartrev's interruption was brusque, 'Dabbling in such matters is wrong. It is blasphemy and disrespect to the spirits of the departed. It is also dangerous to body and soul. Mr Lewis has a wife and a baby on the way to look after.'

Lewis glanced up at the Russian, his eyes imploring him to keep silent but a determined Bartrev ignored him, 'The ghosts are your problem, Darian. Not ours.'

He turned to leave, but Lewis grabbed hold of his arm to stop him.

'Forgive my impetuous friend. He has only my family's best interests at heart. Of course I will do what I can to help you create a device.'

Darian sprung to his feet, animated by optimism, 'That is

settled. We will waste no more time and get started straight away. Bartrev, old chap, if these dealings with the restless dead offends you, the solution is simple ...' He gestured towards the door, 'you are not a prisoner ...'

A combination of loyalty to Lewis and pragmatism made the count remain. The spectres kept the world, including his enemies at bay. Of course Bartrev did not want to leave his friend alone in such weird and dangerous company. Darian lived with a demon. An unimaginable concept back in his deeply religious Mother Russia. Bartrev was outraged. Bartrev had dedicated his life to the pursuit of honour and integrity and tried to be a force of good against evil. This was why he had fled Russia with his secret, why his life was forfeit to the Tsar's ire. His troubled thoughts must have been transparent, his unease and wary looks towards the door in case Belial returned giving him away. Darian attempted to put the count at his ease.

'It may seem curious to one not accustomed to dwelling at such close proximity to the supernatural world, but my dealings with humanity have taught me what a treacherous and fickle species we are. I confess I am among the most notorious and untrustworthy of our kind. But paradoxically, Belial, High Prince of Hell is the only being I can trust with my life. And with yours.

The assassin on the roof was gone. Belial had noticed this earlier as he strode across Pleasance Square with the clockmaker and his big Russian in tow. The demon was disappointed; he had looked forward to dispatching the sniper himself. He climbed up to the roof in a series of cat-like leaps to discover nothing remained of the lurking killer beyond the taint of freshly spilt blood. Another predator had beaten him to his prize.

But who or what? Something big and fast enough to overpower the man without a single shot given off in self-defence. Something animal-like – no, something monstrous, able to devour the government agent whole, clothing, bones as well as flesh, leaving nothing beyond the smell of gore; something strong enough to reduce the assassin's rifle to a pile of debris.

A minor demon? Possible, but none was foolish enough to act without Belial's permission. High Princes of Hell, even in human form were entitled to due respect for fear of truly hellish consequences to the transgressor.

That left a lowly half-breed demon otherwise known as a shapeshifter and that made Cambion (once companion-in-adventure turned heinous traitor) the obvious suspect. Cambion would only have removed a threat to Cyrus because he wanted to kill the alchemist himself. But while Belial lived (and as an immortal, his opposition to the shapeshifter would be eternal) he would not allow that to happen. Death itself would not bring an end to Cambion's torment should he harm one hair of Cyrus's head.

Belial was bound forever to the alchemist, a bond of cursed, unrequited love that could never be fulfilled or returned without destroying Darian. A cruel curse he would not want lifted, even if such a feat could be achieved. He wanted to love Darian and bore the pain with the stoic grace of a Fallen Angel.

As he returned to the street, ignored by the ever-present spectres, he looked up to the rooftops, hoping Cambion was still there, hidden as a sparrow or rat. He smiled, made a gesture, human in origin, old as mankind itself ... symbolically drawing a knife across his throat with one finger. Let the traitor know his days were numbered.

16

Momentarily distracted by a dirigible passing too close to his window, Major Stroude shook his head at the extreme folly of its captain. A hard-pressed engine racketed with distress, leaving a following trail of sooty smoke. He became alarmed; it was approaching far too close, enough for Stroude to see sparks flashing from the controls and the shocked, blanched face of its young pilot. The floundering dirigible's envelope was starting to sag adding to the danger. Nature saved Stroude from disaster. A timely gust of west wind directed the stricken machine away from his office on the embankment with feet to spare and sent the airship dipping low over the Thames. With luck, the worst that could happen was a rough landing on the river unless of course the passengers ended up tipped into the Thames, the foul river was too toxic for a human to survive a soaking.

Ill-handled dirigibles were a growing menace above the capital, piloted by inexperienced, reckless fools with too much money and no common sense had added to the death toll from airship collisions. He, the operator and his passengers had just survived thanks to a narrow escape created by luck. Stroude did not give the young man much chance of making old bones if he continued to try to master the crowded air above London.

Shaken by the near collision, Stroude returned to his desk and forced himself to concentrate on the document on his desk, the Prime Minister's private report to him on the campaign to rid the United Kingdom of all occult influence. A meticulous, long winded report in a cramped, repressed script that spoke volumes of the writer's character. Stroude was not surprised by Enoch Bowring's short-sightedness, there were many supernatural forces and objects that could be utilised to further the interests of the Empire. Stroude had not given up his plan to harness the eerie power of Darian's army of ghosts. The major also considered deliberately infecting prisoners with the demonic parasites known as breeth, in order to create a powerful force of supernatural soldiers. But first he had to find a way to control the breeth.

What did surprise him was the subtlety the Prime Minister insisted on being deployed in the campaign's initiation. For once a wise move in a time of civil unrest and distrust of the ruling establishment. Too brutal an attack could trigger worse than unrest but outright rebellion. For example, the rural poor, unable to afford traditional doctors, were reliant on herbal remedies and midwifery from goodwives also known as witches. In cities the abundant charm shops packed full of bizarre remedies and spells were a mostly harmless distraction that placated the teeming dwellers of slum tenements. – when they weren't drunk on cheap gin.

Instead, Bowring wanted to clamp down on the occult by stealth at first. He wanted Stroude to recruit a covert force from the countries seminaries; eager young men from top families chafing at their allotted place in life and willing to do something more valiant than preaching dry sermons to a church full of bored and dozing parishioners. There would be many to choose from. Many families from the aristocracy and gentry had *spare* sons who would not inherit or follow a career in the military but were shipped off to fill their duty quota in the established church. Stroude doubted there was a genuine vocation amongst these young men, perfect raw material for the major to mould to his way of thinking.

The document went on to state any artefacts found with genuine magickal powers were to be seized and taken to a secret, sanctified site, a convent run by a closeted order of Church of England nuns. Built on the site of a much earlier Christian site, this holy place would be perfect to contain the demonic artefacts until they were destroyed. Stroude winced at the waste of so much useful power but as he reflected on the report his mood lifted to euphoria. Excellent. The Prime Minister had given him the manpower he needed to gather the artefacts and instead of following orders to destroy them, Stroude would consider it his patriotic duty to requisition them for Queen, Country and Empire.

His only opposition was a group of cloistered women? Hardly an obstacle to a man of his determination and strength of will, bolstered up by his youthful new team, he would make them his own private Holy Army. A brigade as loyal and fanatical as possible, putting the country's interest above the orders of a mere commoner of a Prime Minister. A jumped up industrialist with a knighthood only granted a year before, a short-sighted and unintelligent fool.

A greater problem Stroude faced in his long-term plan to control the supernatural was dealing with the breeth, the creatures released from a hell dimension to infest the streets of London, preying on its citizens. They were oblivious to all blandishments and exorcism by ordained ministers. Only a powerful mage with knowledge of the workings of Hell itself would have any hope of containing the occult vermin; exactly the sort of person the current leader of Her Majesty's government wanted to destroy. A dilemma and a paradox the major was committed to resolve.

17

Could any sea journey have been more tortuous and hag-ridden? A sweat-drenched Sir Miles Hardwick lay on a bed in his cabin, doubled up with the stomach-churning gripes of extreme seasickness. Despite frequent changing, the linen bed sheets were soaking and crumpled. The medicines from the on board physician untouched, Hardwick could not face the foul-tasting concoctions. His stomach had already been weak and empty from copious voiding after the bout of food poisoning in Florence. All the ostentatious comfort of Josiah Pringle's massive steam yacht did nothing to soften the horrors of the journey.

He had arrived at Livorno, the nearest seaport to Florence to find it bathed in pleasant spring sunshine. The warm, sea-scented air was still with a cloudless pale blue sky above. It augured well for a pleasant voyage home. The sudden change as Pringle's steam yacht chuffed out into the open sea was almost supernatural in its speed. Black clouds flashing with lightning boiled up over the horizon and overtook the ship in a fury-driven rage.

A series of violent storms and heavy seas battered the *Sheffield Queen* and pursued the thankfully sturdy vessel like an ancient Greek curse across the Mediterranean. No sailing ship could have survived such an onslaught: a thought that gave some scant comfort to the stricken and humiliated Hardwick. Well accustomed to the turbulent passage of dirigibles, his reaction to the sea voyage was most unexpected.

At least his beloved Athena was spared the indignities of the journey, safe in the rough-edged but generous company of the Pringles. She would be angry of course, knowing he was returning to the forbidden company of Cyrus Darian but harsh realities had to be faced. Hardwick was penniless, his once obscenely wealthy heiress wife was penniless. The alchemist was generous to those who helped him, at least financially. If Darian ever had a heart or conscience, they had long been burnt out of his damaged, bartered soul. Hardwick was no fool but a man forced to be pragmatic by circumstances.

He dozed off, mercifully carried away to many hours of pain free oblivion unsullied by troubled dreams or fever-induced delirium. A polite rap on his door from one of the vessels discreet and efficient stewards woke him to a sense of relief. The tumultuous motion from the *Queen* as she gamely battled high seas had stopped. The pain had finally eased from his stomach and limbs. Even the raging headaches that had felt as if his skull was being crushed in a vice had lifted. He was weak but on the mend.

He welcomed the cup of milky tea and dry toast proffered by the steward and the good news that the seas were calm, the sky clear and England's white cliffs within sight on the horizon.

18

Vexed, Lady Athena Hardwick paced the platform of Vienna's railway station. She was not the only aggravated passenger braving the billowing smut-laden smoke and hot steam from a station full of locomotives eager to move but stalled. Impatient as chained, monstrous leviathans, the locomotives groaned and belched out their fumes to no avail. Nothing was allowed to leave Vienna that morning.

Gradually in a wave of rumour and astonishment, the news filtered through the large throng of stranded passengers and rail crews. An attempt on the life of the heir to the Austro-Hungarian Empire had blown up the imperial train, derailing it and blocking all rail exits from the Austrian capital. To the world this was a momentous near disaster, an event that could change the course of the world's history. To Athena, it was merely yet another annoyance on her journey, postponing her confrontation with her husband. There had already been one broken down engine in Tuscany, a herd of the most stubborn goats blocking the line in the Tyrol and now this.

If she were a less worldly-wise woman, she might think it was deliberate; some sort of hex put on her by Cyrus Darian, no stranger to dabbling with the occult. But apart from the Vienna outrage, the hold ups were all too petty to be Darian's work. His vanity would demand something more spectacular than a wayward herd of goats.

With the confusion creating a melee, Athena decided to act in a positive and determined manner. She gathered together her staff of two and with their belongings piled onto a purloined trolley marched straight out of the beleaguered railway station. It was obvious nothing would move out of Vienna for some time. Refusing to let this tedious setback delay her, she would hire a coach with fresh horses and find an alternative route further up from the Austrian capital, one not affected by the disaster.

The city was at a standstill. It seemed this titled American woman was the only one who wanted to get on with everyday life instead of standing in the streets debating the near assassination with anyone who would join in. Rich and poor alike mixing as the horror and its possible consequences sunk in. Wretched people, Athena cursed, it wasn't as if their prince was harmed.

Foot tapping with her vexation, she set her man to seek a suitable vehicle for hire, something reliable and most certainly not a dirigible. The last time she had travelled in one of those infernal machines, she had become travel sick, struggling but failing to hold onto her dignity. It would not be permitted to happen again.

She glanced around the strangely motionless square, darn it; time itself appeared to be paused in contemplation of the calamity. Puzzled, her gaze caught the only movement around her, a shimmer in the middle of a parade of elegant buildings. One edifice of white stone stood apart from the others, poised as if in transit from somewhere else ... could it really be the Emporium of Magickal Curios?

Hope flared in Athena's heart, it must be! How many other buildings could change their appearance and travel anywhere they wanted? The Lady was here in Vienna. A dangerous and unpredictable individual, Athena still considered her an ally despite the shapeshifter's unseemly and torrid relationship with Cyrus Darian. Ordering her servants to grab the luggage, she strode across the square and up the steps to the Emporium's grand entrance. Of course all was deception. The insanely itinerant shop could be in one of an infinite number of guises as could its mysterious and beautiful owner.

Though Athena stood before a grand old house beloved of the Austro-Hungarian aristocracy, this was illusion. That it was really an esoteric and mysterious emporium stacked chock full of extraordinary curios and magickal objects from all over the world and maybe through time itself was hidden from any passer-by. The American woman knew the interior well, having travelled in the emporium twice before. She had learnt to steel herself from its world of strangeness, the voodoo dolls, ancient idols and bottled curses. But she saw no cluttered ephemera as she stepped through the heavy mahogany and gilded doors.

She found the Lady waiting in the foyer, a grandiose design of ornate columns, marbled floor and large ancestral paintings, all over hung by a vast golden chandelier hanging with a multitude of branches sparkling with cut crystal. The woman was now an imperious Austro-Hungarian princess, her carefully coiffed blonde hair piled high and adorned by exotic feathers, her ample cleavage highlighted by a waterfall of perfect teardrop pearls.

The Lady was magnificent and totally fake, all that Athena could see was created by glamour, by deep old magicke no human could master. The American woman could not care less. Here she would find sanctuary and company. Here she would find the swiftest route home to London.

'Pay off your servants, my dearest Athena,' the Lady murmured with a strong Austrian accent. 'You won't need them if you want to travel with me.'

For once, Athena did what she was bid without any argument, the Lady was an answer to all her anxiety, saving her a long, perilous journey across Europe and enabling her to save the last of her dwindling money. Once the servants' dues were settled, Athena followed her hostess into a copy of an elegant parlour where someone or something had set out a silver tea service and stands of mouth-watering Viennese cakes and pastries. Athena could not remember when she had last eaten and decided for once to forgo the ladylike pose of refusing sweet treats. Her Amazonian figure was as trim and athletic as ever and could bear the consumption of sachertorte without straining her tight corsetry.

Refreshed, Athena smiled at her saviour, sitting opposite her with a fine bone china cup and sauce in hand. She had never seen the Lady eat and wondered if she ever did and if so, what it was she consumed. It was probably best not to know. The shapeshifter raised her cup high in a toast, 'Our boys have been busy recently. I think they are overdue a sharp lesson in not taking their womenfolk for granted. Will you join me in taking them to task?'

Athena raised her own cup and smiled in agreement. This was perfect – transport home and a powerful ally. Her husband would rue the day he abandoned her in Italy to pursue his pathetic obsessive devotion to that loathsome foreign criminal.

19

Oblivious to any curious bystander or passing constable, a gang of burly men kicked in the door of the clock mender's shop and ransacked the premises with ruthless efficiency. They sought the Russian nobleman or clues to his whereabouts but found nothing to further their murderous mission. Frustrated, they took out their anger on the shop's contents, customers' priceless timepieces and children's clockwork toys alike fell prey to their heartless destruction in a crash of shattered wood, discordant jangle of bells and a shower of broken cogs and springs.

On leaving, they discovered an angry mob of locals had gathered outside. Lewis was a foreigner, a Jew, one of so many refugees and immigrants in the area but he was also a man they had accepted as one of their own. One who fixed the old and well-worn pocket watches and clocks of locals for free and never asked questions of their origins. A well-built young man stepped forward to challenge the intruders but backed off as one of them produced a pistol and levelled it at his face. No one doubted the raider's intention to use it.

Another of the thugs produced a leather purse and poured out a handful of gold sovereigns into his hand, speaking with a strong accent, addressed the mob.

'This is yours if you can tell me where the Russian and the Jew can be found ...'

No one answered but as the men returned to their nearby heavily armoured steam coach, a notorious and aging local doxie approached and was observed slinking away moments later, with more newly gained wealth than she could have earned in a year on her back in a cat house or pushed up against a filthy alley wall.

It appeared she had seen Lewis and his new friend leave but an hour earlier with Cyrus Darian's manservant. At last their prey was within their reach, at least that was what they believed as they headed for Mayfair. Only one of their number spoke English and he had been too preoccupied tracking down the Tsar's enemy to take much notice of current affairs in London.

They arrived at Pleasance Square to a scene of chaos. The charred remains of a steam Hansom smouldered beyond the wreckage of a wooden barrier across the entrance to the square. Its driver still remained in the wreckage, a horrific sight of burned and contorted flesh and bone, a grotesque parody of a human being. Close by, a Mechman lay on his back, alive but helpless, trapped like a stricken beetle by his malfunctioning body armour that had been damaged in the collision with the doomed Hansom. No one, not even one of the Mechman's squad did anything to help their downed comrade or attempt to douse the blazing vehicle. There was no mystery as to why, the Russian agents' minds raced with the enormity of what stood packed into every inch of the square. An army of ghosts.

It was too much for one of the agents, who sank to his knees, placed his head in his hands and whimpered in terror. Another began to pray loudly in his native tongue. Prayers that carried across the morning smog and to the attention of the nearest angel. One of the dread Fallen. The demon prince Belial. He left the others and walked out into the square, ignoring the chaos he'd created, to observe the gang of Russians. His sharp senses caught the scent of cordite from recently discharged hand guns. *Trouble.* Belial returned to the house and caught the alchemist's eye, addressing him in the alchemist's native Farsi, *'What have you done to upset the Russians this time?'*

'Haven't a clue, old chap,' Darian answered in English, looking across the room to his guests. 'But I suggest the answer could lie with Count Bartrev.'

Lewis knew something had changed, saw the tension rise between Darian and his demon. 'What is going on?'

'Russians,' Belial replied. 'A gang of heavily armed and determined Russians to be exact. Lingering nervously at the other side of the barricade. Time to let us know why they are here, Bartrev. I have many ways of making you tell the truth.'

'Which you really wouldn't want him to use,' warned an intrigued Darian. A gang of human enemies, however well armed were no real threat to him but his curiosity was aroused by the presence of a foreign nobleman with a humble clockmaker. The adventure was afoot; at least it would be if he could get control over his annoying spectral encumbrances. He waited quietly until Bartrev saw sense and told all. There was nothing like having a Prince of Hell sitting a few feet from you to loosen the tongue and speak only the truth.

With no other choice, Bartrev gave a sad smile of apology to Michael Lewis. His attempt to keep his new friend safe from his relentless pursuers had failed miserably. He also realised with some irony that there was nowhere safer than in Darian's home, surrounded by the phantasms and guarded by a powerful demon. Bartrev realised he had put poor Lewis and his wife in danger, he owed it to them to come clean.

'Four years ago, I inherited Yaregi, the vast family estate beyond Ukhta from my beloved father. He had been killed fighting for the Tsar on one of his interminable wars for more territory beyond Russia's already expansive borders. Our leader's greed knows no bounds. At first, my new life as a landowner far away from my studies in St Petersburg was uneventful. I was glad of the time to mourn my father and comfort his bereft people. Uneventful until the arrival of a group of clerics from a monastery on the furthest outpost of my lands.'

Darian smiled, mysterious monks were always a good component of a potentially lucrative mystery. Intrigued, he leant forward as the Russian continued.

'Their fear was impossible to dismiss, it seemed they guarded an ancient secret for so many centuries and so successfully, there had been no need to tell the incumbent rulers of my ancestral lands.

'Until but weeks before when a rogue monk, seduced by ambition and the wealth of the Tsar sold him the secret. I knew then my position as Count of Yaregi was doomed. What could my loyal supporters and farm hands do against the Tsar's army? The monks told me the secret and its new hiding place before fleeing for their lives. As did I.'

'Odd,' mused Darian out loud, 'if they wanted it to remain a secret, why tell you?'

'Because someone had to know.'

The Russian's enigmatic reply left Darian perplexed and desperate to discover what the monks had hidden, something the Tsar thought worth usurping the power of an important and wealthy landowner. Something he had to have for himself.

For Belial, there was no mistaking the acquisitive gleam in the alchemist's eyes, shining despite the masking of his dark glasses. Another wild and hopefully dangerous adventure beckoned at last but not without solving the problem of the wretched spectres. It would be impossible to be clandestine with thousands of spooks in tow!

'Cyrus, *azizam,*' the demon's honeyed voice soothed with a Farsi expression of affection. 'One thing at a time. Why don't you start work on the ghost trap with Mr Lewis while I deal with our unwelcome visitors?'

The demon licked his lips, eager for some bloody mayhem, 'Don't concern yourself, Count Bartrev. The Tsar will be most inconvenienced and have to send more agents.'

20

'Just in time, Hardwick,'

The inventor's heart leapt and he spun around to find a familiar but unwelcome figure. Damn it, Darian still had his demon companion in tow. He had hoped the alchemist would have reversed the Summoning spell after their last adventure and sent the evil devil back where he belonged. How Hardwick hated the evil youth's insolent smirk and hell-forged powers however muted in human form. Though he had tried many times to make him see sense, Hardwick could do nothing about Darian's cynical manipulation of the demon, his shameless exploitation of Belial's cursed emotions. It was a perilous knife-edge path that could so easily go too far with disastrous results.

On arriving back in London, Hardwick had made straight for his main workshop which was contained in the mews and coach houses of all that was left of his aristocratic but penniless family's London estate. Now owned by a rich industrialist, owner of a notoriously foul chemical factory, the mansion remained beside the mews, a silent, ever-present reproach from past ancestors of Hardwick's inadequacy with money. He had missed the familiar workshop where the ideas bubbling over in his creative mind first became drafts on paper nailed to the walls then solid reality. So many wondrous engines and devices wrought in brass, copper, wood and glass brought to throbbing, whirring life by steam, clockwork and sometimes even aided by alchemy courtesy of Darian.

As he walked through his creations, his feet echoed on cold flagstones, setting up eddies of dust, triggering a reflex action. He picked up a clean oil cloth and began to wipe months of dust from the machinery, his hands lovingly tracing the curves of the great brass wheels and gears that helped generate galvanic power.

He belonged here, a hardworking inventor and not the bored, titled master of some country estate overseeing the tenant farmers and organising fox hunts and game shoots. Hardwick certainly was more at home here rather than on some endless trawl around Europe's cultural centres. What wonder of Renaissance art could compare to the precision and near perfection of his elaborate devices, what work in stone to his of brass and steel?

He felt a twinge of deep guilt over abandoning Athena, one that disappeared as his hands caressed the shiny brass hub of a new steam vehicle he'd devised. Its sleek curves the only manufactured part of a machine which would be swifter and smaller than the existing steam driven coaches, it would cut through London's traffic like a knife through butter. If it ever got finished.

The demon's arrival spelled trouble and distraction, the downside of Hardwick's reluctant association with Cyrus Darian. 'How did you know I was here? I have only been back in London for four hours.'

Belial's beautiful face broke into an angelic smile, ruined by the dark corruption glimmering in his Fallen eyes, 'You upset many of your staff by closing up the workshop, just to be led around Europe on a leash by your harridan of a wife. And there is nothing like the promise of gold and the threat of having your head boiled to hasten news my way.'

'I take it Darian wants my help,' Hardwick sighed, ignoring the expected insult, his dreams of spending time locked in his workshop making exciting new things dissolving into nothing, like a waft of fresh air daring to intrude on London's pernicious smog.

Grabbing his arm in a hot, steely grip, Belial steered him away from the unfinished pieces of the inventor's dreams, 'Trouble is, Hardwick, Cyrus has a small problem causing us some considerable vexation. There is only one good, safe method to get to his home now; we need to travel in your dirigible. I'll explain on the way.'

Hardwick sighed, Darian's *small* problem was no doubt a

massive understatement. No one made enemies as easily as the alchemist and no one lost friends so effortlessly. And of course, there was the Pringle's wild tale of an army of ghosts occupying a Mayfair square. One he would have dismissed as nonsense if it wasn't for Darian's constant, dangerous interaction with occult forces.

'I'll need to prepare the *Dauntless* for travel and as you have frightened off my workforce, you had better help me.'

Hardwick was satisfied by the look of horror on the demon's face, Belial as Hell spawned royalty had an abhorrence of manual work. Good, a little act of revenge for all of the creature's constant stream of mocking jibes but a satisfying one all the same.

Belial's reluctant *help* was more hindrance so it took many hours of the inventor's lone, hard toil to get the canopy of the *Dauntless* inflated and its engines stoked up with sufficient steam power to fly above the capital, high enough to avoid the towering steam tram network and low enough to navigate through the filthy air. Hardwick was proud of his airship, rightly so, it was the pinnacle of contemporary technology, its smooth ride and precise handling a credit to his genius.

Somehow, through gritted teeth, he managed to get her flight worthy without a well trained crew in attendance. In Hardwick's eyes the *Dauntless* was beautiful, her now taut canopy a subtle shade of sepia, her cabin of rich mahogany, her metalwork brass polished to mirror shine. Hardwick took the wheel and ordered the demon to cast off, something surely he could do without denting his royal status. Belial complied with a fierce contemptuous growl and a reluctant glower but at last the dirigible lifted clear of its bonds and floated free.

As London lay beneath them, Hardwick realised how much he had missed this dreadful city, a seething, roiling anthill of human life and ambition crammed into its dark, dirty and overcrowded streets. He had no idea why, he had seen the luscious sunlit slopes of Tuscany's breathtakingly gorgeous countryside, Renaissance cities of heart-rending beauty. The haughty, ice-capped splendour of the Alps and the fairy tale villages nestling in their lush, green valleys. Yet it was this foul, depressing sprawl that he called home. Madness? Most likely, an infectious insanity caught from Darian who refused to live anywhere else than London.

Belial joined him on the flight deck as they approached the outskirts of Mayfair.

'There is a small matter I hadn't mentioned yet ...'

Belial began but the inventor held up his hand to interrupt, 'The ghosts. I know. News like that travels far and fast.'

The demon was visibly relieved, he had no idea how Hardwick would react to the sight of thousands of phantoms, fainting in shock or panicking while at the controls of an airship would have been unfortunate.

'Why do you think I came home early? Someone needs to get Darian out of trouble ... again.'

They arrived above the entrance of Pleasance Square as a sudden rain squall lashed at the canopy and the brisk wind fought with the dirigible for control. It took all of Hardwick's considerable skills to keep the *Dauntless* ready to moor behind Darian's home against the buffeting and lashing rain. Enough concentration to overlook the uncanny forms below, becoming shimmering and translucent from the downpour. At least the squall sent human onlookers scurrying for shelter, leaving only a miserable squadron of Mechmen to guard the barrier.

Hardwick looked down from his craft and gave a mirthless smile at their discomfort. Like most sane people, he loathed the metal-clad titans, a brute force designed purely to intimidate, threaten and kill with a soulless efficiency. That there was a man at the centre of the suits of modern armour seemed not to matter, once inside their bullet-proof cladding, all traces of humanity disappeared. But flaws in their design made them vulnerable and not just to Darian's short lived but effective rust eating potion. Heavy rain could seep through chinks in their brass and iron carapaces and disrupt their motion and weapon controls. So they did not leave their post guarding the barrier but shut down their power, leaving them immobile and ineffective as metal statues. Good. Hardwick knew he had the knowledge and technology to make the Mechmen near invincible but he never would. There was something not right, not English, damn it ... simply not cricket ... about these creations.

'No wonder it has taken so long to translate,' Darian announced with a grin of triumph and relief as he studied the thumb trap's inscription through a Galvanic Minutiae-Scope. The many hours of exhaustive study of the tiny, skilled carving into the metal had finally rewarded him as the object gave up its secrets ... well nearly. 'I believe the language used is Chaldean but the words are scrambled into a hellish code.'

'Can you decipher it?' asked an equally fatigued Lewis whose long hours working with the mercuric and unpredictable alchemist was at least bolstered by knowledge his wife Hannah was well and safe. Her letter arrived in a bizarre manner, in keeping with everything involving Darian. A curious and otherworldly creature that appeared to be Darian's pet, arrived bearing the letter in its fanged mouth. The small creature, apparently named Misha was now curled contentedly at Darian's feet, making a sound between a cat's purr and a dragon's growl.

Occasionally, Darian would reach down and caress the unnatural winged beast's red and gold fur as an aid to concentration. Lewis hoped it was a shapeshifter and had arrived at their home in the form of a human messenger. The thought of Hannah being frightened and some harm coming to their unborn baby was chilling. But her letter was reassuring, Hannah had been taken by some apparently human agent of Darian's to a lovely big house in the leafy suburb of Finsbury Park, cared for by kindly maids and she felt safe and protected. It seemed though clearly a maverick and against all accounts of his character, Darian was a man of his word.

Wiping his tired eyes with a kerchief, Lewis was pleased he had at least made progress. While Darian battled with discovering the occult secrets of the thumb trap – for want of a better description for the object, he had built a similar looking device that contained an ingenious one-way entrance. Once anything entered, it could not leave. There was much heated debate between the two men whether this version should be a permanent trap. Lewis believed it should, Darian was uncomfortable about trapping earthbound human souls forever. Not through any sense of altruism for the lost and wandering spirits of the departed but unleashing an army of ghosts was a power he was loath to lose.

Both men were agreed that any attempt to dismantle the original device was too dangerous without knowing the secrets it contained. Where was the fly? Had it died instantly or had it been transported to some weird, unknown dimension? One able to break into their own reality through a hellish portal resulting in unknown but most likely dire consequences. Darian was a risk-taker but not a fool.

'This could take an eternity to unscramble,' Darian admitted, fortifying himself with a swig of fine old brandy. 'Make me another device like that but with an unleashing mechanism only I can operate and your work with me will be over. You can go back to your pretty wife.

'The alchemist refilled his glass, 'I suggest you stay in Finsbury Park, no one but you knows I own that house. It would be dangerous to return to Shoreditch now the Tsar's agents know about you and Count Bartrev'

Lewis looked aghast as the full impact sunk in, 'But our things ... pitifully few and not much to a man of your considerable means, but they are all that is left of our lives, our families back home in Russia.'

'Already taken care of. Your possessions are safely with your Hannah.'

Lewis wiped away a tear of relief, 'How can I thank you, Mr Darian?'

Smiling, Darian raised his brandy glass in a salute to the clockmaker, 'There is no need, just make me a spirit trap ... a Ghostbinder that only I can control.'

He put down the glass and resumed studying the coded inscription on the original device, 'Oh and let me take care of Count Bartrev in future, you wouldn't want danger from more Tsarist agents following you to Finsbury Park. Not with the new baby so close to gracing this sorry world.'

Darian was right, damn him, thought Lewis bitterly, feeling like a treacherous cur. The Russian nobleman had become his friend but would always bring danger in his wake. They had found Bartrev once, they would easily find him again. Lewis nodded a reluctant assent.

'There is no need to be concerned about your noble friend, he will be safer with me and Belial,' Darian attempted to reassure the clockmaker. 'Indeed, we shall do all we can to solve his problem with the Tsar.'

He wants the monk's ancient and secret power for himself, Lewis realized but kept silent. He had fled Russia seeking a quiet, safe life for his family, something that could only be achieved by finishing his task and having nothing more to do with ghosts, demons, ancient secrets and dangerous men like Cyrus Darian.

A deep, purring vibration above them interrupted their study, Lewis leapt to his feet, alarmed but Darian steadied him with a reassuring pat on the shoulder, 'No need for concern, old chap. I'd recognise that sound anywhere, the perfectly tuned engine of Hardwick's dirigible, *The Dauntless*. We have good company.'

21

A furtive group of men huddled around a table in the smoke laden fug of a Lambeth public house, the Crooked Crown, located down a narrow winding alley well away from the main streets. They did their best to fit in, gripping pints of ale while trying to look inconspicuous in their borrowed shabby workmen's clothing and with suspiciously pale, soft hands. It did not work. Unlike the other men relaxing beneath the one spluttering, faulty gaslight that added noxious fumes to the smoky miasma, this gathering did not roar with laughter over bawdy banter or try to feel up the strumpets frequenting these establishments and who would do it in the alley outside for a measure of gin or a glass of porter.

Other aspects of the men's true identity filtered through, one wore an eerie gold and lapis lazuli ring set with what looked like a real, moving eye. Another's blue velvet waistcoat of gold embroidered moons and suns burst through his overcoat, borne ever outward on the man's expansive belly.

One with a sweaty brow pulled a red kerchief from his pocket followed by dozens of others tied together in a string of rainbow hues, another's inner coat pocket occasionally wriggled and squirmed before a sleepy white rabbit poked its head out to reveal its hiding place.

They were all small time mages, sorcerers and illusionists who had come together, putting aside their often bitter rivalry, united by one cause. Some force, some knowledgeable and probably government force was ruining their businesses. Everyone spoke of people they knew in the magic world suddenly disappearing, their occult goods taken away. It was a frightening scenario, anyone could be next. So far it had been just the seriously powerful practitioners that had gone, but it could only be a matter of time before they were all targets

'They have taken Giraldo The Astonishing,' muttered one, pulling down his cloth cap low over his face, peering beneath the brim for any nearby snoopers. 'Cleaned out his store of tricks and illusions as well. It is as if he had never existed.'

'No loss,' grumbled another. The corpulent form of Harry Sturgess, aka Mesterior, 'The only thing astonishing about Eddie Grover was how he got away with such a dreadful act for so long.'

The others gave a collective shudder at this dire news. The word on the street indicated all initial disappearances had been of major league players in the supernatural world and occultists of considerable power and reputation. If the mysterious abductors were now targeting small fry like Giraldo it meant they were all now in danger.

'Why haven't they taken Cyrus Darian? He is top of any list of dabblers in the supernatural,' whined one of the illusionists, a dapper little man named Alberto aka Bert Higgins.

'I suspect the fact his home is guarded by an army of ghosts and he has a high ranking demon for a sidekick might be an explanation.' Mesterior snapped back, he had no time for idiots, not with the fear spreading like contagion through his community. The men returned to brooding over their ale, needing the dubious and no doubt watered down fortification, this meeting was going nowhere beyond swapping horror stories.

Throughout the gathering, one man remained silent. A genuine fakir from India, Mohan Haridas rarely spoke but when he did, the others listened as if he was the font of all ancient, oriental wisdom. The elderly Indian slapped both hands onto the table, his deep, heavily accented voice brooked no dissent, 'This started not long after Darian's ghosts appeared, terrifying the populace. I do not believe this is a coincidence. Cyrus Darian is always in the centre of any problem in our community.'

The others nodded in agreement, the man was equally despised by the magicians and the British establishment, Darian lived by his own rules, not giving a damn who he trampled over to achieve his goals. There was not much honour among the occultists but he was giving even them a bad name.

'We must contact him directly, see what he knows,' Haridas continued, 'and I suggest we pick Reggie to be the one. You have had the most dealings with the man.'

Reggie Dunne, aka The Great Miraculous, failed illusionist and piss poor magician, nearly choked on his ale, coughing up a quantity of the brew over his clothes, to the amusement of men on the nearest table.

'Take yer bloody time, mate. The night has just begun.' Jeered one, unheard by Reggie. He was afraid of ghosts, now he knew they existed. It brought back his terror of discovery since he did away with a rival magician in a deadly feud over a glamorous assistant they had both coveted. A stupid feud as the lovely flame-haired Nancy loathed the pair of them with equal venom and ran away with a dashing and titled stage door Johnny. The thought of meeting the angry spirit of The Great Mystic Mage kept the murderer awake at nights. At least it did since the day ghosts turned up at a square in Mayfair.

What if the dread, drowned form of Ali Pasha aka the Great Mystic Mage was amongst them ... pointing an accusing finger at him for all to see? To be honest, it had been more of a ridiculous accident involving a cloak and a deeper than it looked puddle than an actual murder but Pasha was still dead so the details seemed irrelevant. All of this lay heavily on his mind as Reggie presided over a clandestine meeting of other men of mystery in a Lambeth public house.

'I am not going to walk through that square past all those awful ghosts just to speak to Darian,' Reggie announced knowing that was exactly what the others wanted him to do. There was no other way to get to the man's house. Reggie was indeed the only one to have had successful dealings with the notorious alchemist, necromancer and all round friend of the otherworldly. A relationship now come back to haunt him. 'I won't do it!'

'Of course you will, dear boy,' Mesterior's grey streaked ginger beard greasy from an earlier meal came into close view as he leaned into Reggie's face causing the younger man to gag. 'Either that or a pernicious rumour will be started, naming you as the possessor of great occult power and a renowned and notorious necromancer. That will soon spark their interest.'

Reggie stood up abruptly, knocking the table and sending the beer tankards flying, the men on the nearby table roared, cursing their disapproval at such wanton waste of good – well that was pushing things –wanton waste of ale.

'If I go down, I'm taking every one of you with me,' Reggie's threat sent shudders through the group of magicians.

'You wouldn't dare,' sneered Alberto, 'we should stick together in this time of peril.'

'Stick together?' Reggie's voice became high pitched, tinged with rising hysteria, 'Don't make me laugh. Where was all this brotherly solidarity when you half-inched my new floating sun and moon illusion? Eh?'

'Calm down my good man,' Haridas soothed, guiding him back into his seat with well-practised authority. 'We must indeed forgo all past enmity to protect our select little community.'

He leant forward to whisper in Reggie's ear, 'What if there was a way to get you past the ghosts, straight into Darian's home. Would you go there then to speak for us all? Remembering it is the safest place from our unknown mutual enemy?'

Reggie conceded that prospect had some appeal. He had not forged an actual friendship with the alchemist, he doubted that was possible knowing the man's reputation for double-dealing but certainly they were on speaking terms and had conducted some successful business in the past.

'If you can arrange it, I will do as you ask.'

'Excellent!' Mesterior pronounced, beckoning over a serving wench, 'Ale all round to celebrate … on you Reggie of course … you were the one who spilled our drinks.'

22

If Darian was pleased to see the inventor back, he showed no sign of it as he continued studying encryptions through the Minutiae-Scope.

'Before you get too settled, old chap,' he said without looking up from the scientific instrument, one of Hardwick's inventions, 'could you give Lewis a lift to his new home in Finsbury Park after luncheon?'

'My new home?' Lewis gasped as the alchemist reached into a pocket and threw him a set of keys.

'You wouldn't expect me to live in dreary suburbia? So bourgeois. It's all yours. Enjoy the peace and quiet and ghastly fresh air.'

Hardwick shook the clockmaker's hand, a man whose work he had long respected and admired, 'What has he dragged you into this time?'

'Creating what our mutual friend has called a Ghostbinder,' Lewis explained handing him over the prototype to examine. 'Something to trap the ghosts.'

The inventor took the device, marvelling at its carefully wrought intricacies. It was ingenious, as expected from a master craftsman like Lewis. But it would never work. Even if the spectres could be lured inside, the Ghostbinder could never hold them. It had no energy source, something of great and enduring supernatural power that would bind them forever within the trap.

'I know what you are thinking, my friend,' Lewis continued. 'It needs an addition beyond the ken of a simple artisan. It doesn't help that our mutual patron wants to be able to release and return the spectres at will.'

'Cyrus!'

'Oh come on, Miles!' Darian finally stood away from his desk.

'This is me we are talking about. Why in Hades should I turn my back on the power to control an army of ghosts? Far too much fun …'

Hardwick sighed, nothing had changed since the terrifying and disastrous encounter with the Technomicron and its demonic creator. Even such a close encounter with a force of ultimate chaos had done nothing to dent Darian's perverse delight in taking on the unknown and dangerous powers in the Universe. And yet again, Hardwick found himself in thrall to the prospect of shared adventure and riches and the challenge of creating new and astounding technology.

A few hours later after the ignominy of having to prepare a repast for the whole household including the ferocious little dragoncat nipping his ankles in impatience, Hardwick dutifully waited for Lewis to gather his tools and leave Darian's service. Lucky man. Uncomfortably aware that many unfriendly eyes were watching his dirigible leave Pleasance Square, Hardwick took the clockmaker to his new home before returning to his workshop to begin designing what he called the Ghostbinder. All his latest annoyance with Darian soon faded as the inventor returned to his drawing boards, his agile mind lost in the fledgling designs and complex calculations.

For the first time in months, he felt fully alive, back to his old, flawed but content, self. He remembered why he tolerated Darian and his errant, maverick ways. The man gave him the time, freedom and finance to create. This time it was working on something for the alchemist, but most of his inventions were Hardwick's to pursue without interference or undue influence. There was no better patron than Darian for all his shortcomings as a man.

It soon became apparent that the neat, precise device created by Michael Lewis would not be powerful enough for the task. Every day and night brought yet more spectres to Pleasance Square, it seemed the dying moments of the Technomicron had spread its malign influence far wider than London's restless dead. When some French victims of Madame La Guillotine joined the throng, Hardwick revised his design again. The Ghostbinder would need to be big, just how big became a concern.

Within long days, even longer nights and after numerable visits to his other workshops, an exhausted Hardwick had constructed a prototype. What a monster ... the only one strong enough to carry the device was Belial and the inventor had no intention of allowing the demon to wield it. The very thought triggered a shudder of horror and a fearful frisson of ice through his veins. Despite the creature's devotion to Darian, Belial was still a Fallen Angel, dedicated to violent mischief-making, mayhem and provoking humanity to wrongdoing

The problem was building a power source strong enough to create an ætherial field to encompass the ghosts but in a device a human could carry with ease. Hardwick realised he needed a missing, possible non-existent component, something incorporated into the machine that could amplify the ætherial field without resource to massive energy generation. Head in hands, the inventor slumped onto the workbench and fell asleep, mind and body exhausted.

23

Fury did not describe Major Stroude's reaction to the events unfolding in Pleasance Square or his discovery there had been a sniper positioned on the rooftop opposite Darian's house. Who had ordered this? And where was this man now? He, Stroude, was supposed to be in sole charge of the situation. Intelligence also told him of a disastrous crash through the barrier by a runaway steam coach and a gathering of armed Russian agents arriving at the barrier who had disappeared in mysterious circumstances. From the quantity of charred flesh and blood discovered in a side entrance close by, foul play had to be suspected.

The worst news had arrived via numerous reports of a powerful and fast dirigible making landings at Darian's home. No doubt he was planning an escape but as far as Stroude was convinced the man was still marooned in his home, a fact confirmed by the continued presence of the ghosts. There was little time left to try to persuade Darian to co-operate. He already sensed pressure from above, an impatience with the slow progress in reaching a satisfactory conclusion.

His superiors had good reason for their exasperation; the occupation of Pleasance Square was getting rapidly out of control with the ghosts ever increasing in number and the gawping crowds becoming larger and more unruly. There had been a number of violent altercations, one close to outright riot with the ever-present simmering bad blood between the public and the patrolling Mechmen, boiling over. It was time for a frank discussion with the Prime Minister.

Stroude was gratified to be ushered straight through to Sir Bowring on arrival at 10 Downing Street, which flattered his ego and quietened down his ire over the assassin ... a little.

'Ah Major, please come in,' Bowring greeted his visitor

without raising his head from a pile of official reports, 'I am expecting to hear good news from you over our ectoplasmic nuisance in Mayfair.'

This took the wind from the major's sails, he had nothing positive to relate beyond that Darian was still alive, not the words Bowring wished to hear.

'I might have been able to do this, Mr Prime Minister but my operation has been seriously undermined by some unknown outside source.'

He waited for Bowring to look up, watched the brief flash of guilty knowledge pass over the man's florid features before continuing,

'I cannot succeed without knowing what the hell is going on. Who commissioned a sniper to assassinate Darian? What are Russian agents doing getting involved?'

'I told you I wanted the alchemist dead,' Bowring answered, his fleshy lips pursed with determination.

Stroude knew he was on tricky ground but pressed on, 'Of course, sir, and he will be as soon as we know this is the best method of removing the infestation. But what if killing him does not work? He may be able to command the spirits from beyond the grave.'

Clearly this alarming concept had not crossed Bowring's mind. His small eyes darted between Stroude and the papers on his desk as he strove to find an answer. 'Cyrus Darian has made many enemies, any one of whom could have hired the assassin. As for the Russians, I am privy to top secret information from their government speaking for no less than the Tsar himself. Those men had no business with Darian and are of no concern to us. Dead or alive.'

Secret information you are not going to share with me, thought Stroude wishing he could shake the oleaginous little upstart until his rolls of flesh quivered with fear and he told the major everything he knew.

'If you say so, sir.'

'I do. Now find a way to rid the capital of these damned ghosts. And as for the greater campaign I have a gift for you.'

The Prime Minister reached into a desk draw to produce a brown envelope which he handed to Stroude. 'This contains all you will need to start up a small, elite team of special operatives. The men you will recruit and train to seek out all magickal practitioners and neutralise their malign influence on British society. It will give you the power and means to appropriate all their occult goods to destroy them.'

As a delighted, energised Stroude left 10 Downing Street, his departure via a waiting government landau was watched from an upstairs window. A man had joined the Prime Minister, as gaunt and aesthetic as Bowring was florid and corpulent. He wore simple, plain clothes in dark grey fabric, displaying no pocket watch or other adornment. The man's manner was commanding and showed no deference to the Prime Minister.

'Can you trust Stroude?'

Bowring joined him at the window, 'No, not at all. The major is a fearful snob, a son of old English minor gentry so he despises me and my humble origins, my hard-earned wealth and new title. He has no loyalty to me. But he is a patriot, every ounce of his being brims with loyalty to our Queen, country and empire. He is incorruptible and fanatical. That is good enough for me.'

The man pursed his thin lips in contemplation, 'I trust your faith in Stroude will be rewarded. If this country's apparent tolerance, even perceived allegiance to the unearthly and unholy continues, we could lose the Empire. Our brash ex-colonials across the Atlantic think they hold the high moral ground, they may use this to foment rebellion and a change in allegiance.'

Bowring puffed himself up like a threatened toad, 'I am fully aware of this danger, that is why I was elected to office. Do not forget I am the Prime Minister of this realm.'

Stepping away from the window and walking to the door, the grey-clad man replied without looking back at Bowring, 'Ah, yes. You are indeed elected. That makes you only a temporary holder of power. Today's man, tomorrow's nobody. This matter is too important to leave to someone of such supreme unimportance.'

He left the room with one parting remark, 'We will be watching.'

24

Two days later, Reggie agreed to meet the Indian fakir at an inn close to Smithfields at lunchtime. With so much danger for magicians, it was a curious time for a rendezvous with no protection from a cloak of darkness.

All around the inn, people thronged, busy with the daily business of the meat market, thankfully housed within a recently completed undercover area of some splendour. Reggie would never have agreed to meeting at Smithfields in the past, a stinking place of horror and filth still carrying the echoes of the bad old days of an open market where the poor, doomed beasts; cattle, pigs and sheep or broken down horses were brutally herded into far too small a space for so many animals. Close by, slaughterhouses had once been filled with cries of fear and pain and the streets were ankle-deep in blood, guts and ordure. Such places were Hell on earth for a sensitive soul like Reggie.

It was early afternoon when he found Haridas inside the Old Grey Cock, sitting on his own and tucking into a hearty plate of shepherd's pie.

'I thought you people did not eat meat?' A puzzled Reggie ventured, sitting down opposite him and ordering a portion for himself. The aroma from the dish of mashed potatoes and minced mutton was delicious, much better than the usual inn fare. Worth coming all the way to Smithfields on the overhead steam tram. At least it was a guarantee the meat was fresh with animals slaughtered and butchered close by.

'You people?' replied Haridas with a playful wink, 'it depends who my people actually are. And anyway, it isn't the flesh of a sacred cow.'

Reggie knew better than to pry, secrets of identity were closely guarded in their world. An air of mystery was sacrosanct. No one knew of his own humble beginnings as one of fifteen children of a miner in Wales. It would destroy his on stage image of an exiled European nobleman with special powers.

'What do you know of Randalfo Walpurgis and his museum of oddities?'

Puzzled, Reggie replied, 'Not much, beyond it burnt down destroying all the wax displays and cabinets of curiosities.'

'And of the Family of Others, Walpurgis' private exhibit of living human freaks?'

'I assumed they had lost their lives in the flames. I think we all did.'

Haridas sat back, let his companion tuck into the plate of food placed before him by the landlord's buxom and flirtatious wife. Trouble on two legs, no doubt. The fakir kept his eyes averted from her ample charms on display and was relieved to see Reggie doing the same.

'None of the Family, the live human exhibits perished that terrible night, they were saved by the intervention of one Cyrus Darian. Walpurgis and his weird crew owe the man a great deal. Enough for you to persuade them to help you reach Darian safely, knowing you mean the alchemist no harm.'

Reggie shook his head, hardly the straightforward solution he was expecting. 'And how exactly am I expected to track down these survivors?'

Smiling broadly, the fakir held out his arms in a theatrical gesture, 'By magic, my dear Reggie. As if by magic, I will conjure one of them.'

A tall, stooping form emerged from the back of the inn, a man who looked out of place in daylight and amongst normal people. It was Walpurgis himself, whose cadaverous features were partly hidden by a broad-brimmed hat pulled low over his face. He was dressed in a fading, once black caped coat of another era, adding to the strangeness of his appearance.

The man joined them at the table, keeping his head low. Reggie was relieved the freak show owner did not extend a skeletal hand in greeting or draw attention to himself by ordering food or drink. The temperature around their table appeared to plummet but Reggie put that down to his over-active imagination. For all his strange appearance, Walpurgis was just a man.

'I understand you have urgent business with the Persian,' Walpurgis had a voice as dry as a sepulchre, well-educated and aristocratic in manner. 'You have chosen a difficult time to contact Darian, with his spectral inconveniences.'

Reggie swallowed the last of his glass of porter and nodded. 'Our community is being threatened, people are disappearing. We hope the alchemist may shed some light on who and why.'

A curious sound like bones rattling in a bag emerged from under the wide hat, Walpurgis was laughing, 'And you think Cyrus Darian will furnish you with answers? A man so amoral he would sell his own grandmother, steal her back then sell her on again?'

'He helped you,' Reggie insisted. 'And this problem affects us all, even your people may be in line for a visit from these inquisitors.'

Again the bones rattled in their bag, 'My dear young man, what you see as an act of heroism was merely Darian safeguarding one of his assets among the Family. In reality, he wanted to save only her.'

Walpurgis stood up, 'I do not expect any problem with your enemies – we are not devotees of the occult or of demonic origin. Merely the poor unfortunates of the human race, cursed at birth.'

Before Reggie could stop him, the man strode out into the street to be lost among the throng. A wasted journey but for the excellent pie. The fakir had not given up. 'You give up too easily, Reggie. Find Walpurgis and make him listen. Use anything, charm, threat, blackmail. With no premises to continue his business, you will find the freak show travelling with a fair. One currently operating close by.'

'St Bartholomew's, the ancient fair the local people refused to have closed down by the authorities? I think at one point, the suggestion erupted into a riot, if my memory is serving me well.'

'The very one, Reggie,' the Indian had finished his meal and was also preparing to leave, 'I would see him today, now in fact, these people are secretive and are liable to flight at any sign of trouble.'

The sinking sensation that Reggie was no longer in control of his life deepened, only fear of being taken by the inquisitors, for want of a better name let him obey this Indian. Another time and he would have refused without hesitation or regret.

25

How quickly life returned to its old patterns, mused Darian as he took a rare moment away from his laboratory and workshops. Rubbing his curious lilac and silver eyes, aching from hours of close study, he relaxed with an old vintage red wine in his favourite chair. Misha the dragoncat was curled on his lap, purring with pleasure.

Hardwick, thankfully minus the lovely Athena, was curbing his true feelings as only a repressed, tightly wound English aristocrat could do while Belial took pleasure in goading him. Why? Probably his curse at work, dooming the Fallen Angel to endless fits of jealousy. Hardwick was fortunate the demon prince only taunted him with words. The quantity of torments available to the damned celestial beings was infinite in number and in the depths of cruelty.

With Lewis gone, they were stuck with the brooding, reluctant form of the Russian nobleman. A man only too aware that much as he hated remaining in Darian's home, he had no choice, at least until the Tsar's agents found the courage and means to cross the Mechmen guarded barrier and the ever present wafting phantoms.

Hardwick, having finally finished the Ghostbinder prototype, a mechanism far bigger and more cumbersome than anyone expected, was now living permanently at Darian's home, the better to fine tune and refine the design. It also needed the alchemist to fit it with the supernatural elements needed to entrap and contain the army of the dead.

Keeping busy did not diminish Darian's own problems, his claustrophobia, walled up and pinned down in his home surrounded by spooks and gathering enemies. Where in Hades was the Lady when he needed her? Surely the Emporium of Magickal Curios would be immune from these ghosts. He could use it to flee London, leaving its citizens to deal with the nuisance themselves. He doubted the accursed spooks could follow him while the Emporium was in transit.

But with no sign of his paramour and her itinerant shop, Darian had no choice but to concentrate on deciphering the fiendish Chaldean inscription on the thumb trap, support Hardwick's attempts to improve on the clockmaker's design and learn the secret Bartrev was hiding. No wonder Darian was suffering from nervous exhaustion, something that plagued a man of his mercurial and highly-strung nature. The Lady always knew how to diffuse such a build up of tension, damn it, indeed any skilful courtesan could. But here he was, trapped within his home with no access to even the most common street walker, for who would pleasure him surrounded by accursed ghosts.

He was aware of Belial's near silent approach, the ever so faint waft of brimstone that betrayed his hellish presence. Darian sighed as he allowed the demon to massage his shoulders and neck, feeling Belial's strong, hot fingers work their magic on his stress tensed muscles. A dangerous flirtation with the terrible consequences of such intimacy, should he give into Belial's infatuation. Darian would be destroyed, both in body and soul; he would literally cease to exist in this world and the next. A desolation that could so easily tempt the alchemist to provoke Belial into breaking the demon prince's own restraints. To seek a few moments of great pleasure then oblivion in the arms of a beautiful angel of the damned, cursing his friend to an eternity of the most terrible heartbreak and guilt beyond anything suffered by a human. After all, Darian reasoned, he would not be around to witness it.

Only a tiny, flickering flame of hope of being reunited with his wife kept Darian from giving in to all-consuming despair.

But despite the horror of the last opium's induced journey to his past, Darian's life continued on, his work at undoing a past wrong had not finished, however futile it now seemed. He allowed Belial to finish the much-needed massage, ignored the tight hug at the end and leapt to his feet, brisk and businesslike.

'You may be a Prince of Hell, old chap, but you are no use at working out this Chaldean word play. I thought you spoke the wretched language.'

Belial sighed, 'Speaking some jibber jabber from an extinct tribe of your primitive species is not the same as working out an insane jumble of letters. Why don't you conjure up a Chaldean mystic, get them to help you?'

Darian walked away, shaking his head, 'Don't you think I have enough ghosts plaguing me then to use necromancy to bring back another?'

'What's one more?' Belial reasoned. 'It's not as if you have counted the beggars.'

He did not answer because in truth necromancy was an exhausting act both in body and spirit and highly dangerous. Darian had nearly lost his life to a predatory Persian mystic last time he summoned an ancient spirit from *Beyond*. And there was no guarantee he could call up a long dead Chaldean who knew anything about the scrambled inscription … in fact it was highly unlikely. Just his luck to call forth some illiterate slave. Darian decided he had taken a long enough break and went back to his study of the thumb trap. There could be no shortcuts, just brainwork and patience; his least favourite virtues.

26

Shaken awake in its nest in a forgotten crypt, by a fearsome pounding the creature sprung to its feet. Snarling it paused, unsure. Normally there was no noise in this area of the cemetery, its presence had driven away the birds. Even the most curious of visitors disliked its aura and avoided the oldest part of the graveyard.

It chose a bird form – a kestrel – easiest to flee the den and discover what was making the noise of destruction. As the kestrel soared above gravestones and trees it saw a number of wagons hauled by heavy draught horses bringing gangs of tough looking navvies. A team had already started, smashing the old headstones with pickaxes and hammers.

With a relentless efficiency the gang levelled the memorials and demolished sepulchres and statues in an act of desecration that shocked the remaining humanity within the creature. Why was this happening? Why was there no one to stop this mindless destruction? Returning to the crypt, it could not break cover in human form so close, not without raising alarm within the invaders. Cambion took the form of a large dog and grabbing his clothes in his mouth, fled to the nearest place of good cover.

Changing to human form, an increasingly rare act, Cambion returned to the cemetery to seek the meaning of this obscene vandalism. It did not take him long. A wealthy property developer had bought the oldest area of the cemetery, ordering the clearance to build new homes on the site. Well, there would be no peace for the future inhabitants of those homes, thought Cambion with bitter satisfaction, not dwelling over forgotten, unmourned bones.

It was no longer safe to hide here and with the crypt likely to be smashed up that day, where could he go? Cambion was all too aware of the irony, the man he once served and betrayed would have always offered him a place of sanctuary, probably would still now if there was any advantage to Darian, the man was too unscrupulous to bear grudges. But his followers, that was a different kettle of fish, especially the besotted demon who would kill the traitor on sight. Slowly and painfully as possible.

There was one other solution, seek out the Family of Others, the shunned and forsaken outcasts of society. Would they take him in? He was only part human, would his demonic heritage bar him from their tight-knit and protective tribe? There was only one way to find out, direct contact and hope for the best.

Reggie found Lord Hector's Astounding Steam Fair easily. Once on the right road, he left the stench of the slaughterhouses and stockyards behind and followed the scent of gingerbread, steam and smoke, the sound of laughter and the wheeze and churn of the rides, the gaudy cacophony from many steam organs. And he joined the excited throng heading to the same destination, many being tugged along by over excited youngsters eager for thrills, sticky toffee apples and red stripped candy canes.

The magician had always enjoyed the jostle and overblown delights of funfairs especially their décor; heavy, gaudy gilding on the rides and panels of ill-executed but lively paintings of past heroes and mythical creatures on the steam organs. He loved the hoopla stalls and hooking cheery yellow wooden ducks using poles, games always harder then they looked. Bright strings of gaslights lit even by day pierced the London gloom. All was a blur of tawdry gold, green, purple and red, of jaunty sound, a razzle-dazzle created by wily showmen to part people with their money yet leave them with contented smiles on their faces. Even when their offspring brought up the overload of sugary confection on the way home.

He paused to shudder at the sight of a toothless old tiger hauled around the showground on a chain. Reggie did not like the menageries of caged pacing wild beasts with angry demented eyes or their human equivalent, the freak shows and he despised the hoi polloi who queued up to gawk and laugh. He tried to reason that the poor defenceless tormented unfortunates with nowhere else to go were at least clothed and fed and protected from the worst actions of the ignorant and cruel. But what a life! Now he had to face his prejudice head on and communicate again with Randalfo Walpurgis, the slave-master of a Family of Others.

Deliberately delaying the meeting, the magician took his time to sample some of the fun, enjoying a large piece of iced gingerbread and failing to win an exotic and expensive cocoa nut at the shy. He finally found the Family's tent, located between a larger than normal helter skelter, brightly painted in jolly hues of yellow and orange and a Dark Ride, an unsuccessful one from the total absence of a large queue waiting to be scared witless and no usual ear-piercing screams coming from within. Why pay for a ride with paper and plaster spectres when you could see and be terrified of the real thing for free in Mayfair?

This concentrated his focus on his unwanted task and he steeled himself to confront Walpurgis. Unlike the other sideshows, there was no noisy barker outside the freak show tent, bellowing about the attractions within in amusingly exaggerated terms. Setting the public up to be disappointed yet even this was considered part of the entertainment. This tent merely existed, to be entered or ignored as if it didn't matter either way.

As Reggie hesitated outside, a few people wandered into the Family of Other's tent, named the Curious Wonders of the Natural World on a painted sign above the entrance. As the magician finally found the courage to wander inside, Walpurgis himself was standing inside, 'I knew I didn't have long to wait, that you would come here today, no man with eyes so fear-filled would leave it long to seek help, however tenuous.'

'This is difficult for me,' Reggie mumbled, eyes down in case he should see a two-headed child or living skeleton and be sick.

'You fear my family? And despise me for exhibiting them?'

Reggie could see no point in lying, the cadaverous freak show owner appeared a man who could see through any guile or dissemblance, 'I do, Mr Walpurgis. I cannot imagine a more terrible existence for a human being. Better they had been ...' His voice trailed off.

'Smothered at birth?' Walpurgis' voice grew cold. 'Then you are a crueller man than I. My Family have the right to enjoy their life as much as any other. The gold I give for new exhibits at birth spares them the midwife's pillow and delivers them to safety and a new family. One where they will be loved and cherished for their otherness.'

Walpurgis beckoned him inside, thankfully to a side room within the tent away from the exhibits and continued with pride in his voice, 'It is we who pity your kind. Blessed with health and the normal pattern of a human being in body and mind, yet you waste these gifts to give us money to gawp and jeer. That, surely, is the more woeful existence.'

Sitting down behind a desk, Walpurgis did not offer the magician a seat or offer any hospitality increasing Reggie's discomfort at this encounter. 'Again, I must question why you think I can help you. Cyrus Darian is a man who lives by his own rules and the ties of past allegiance do not apply to him.'

Again Reggie decided to be honest, 'Desperation. Already our unknown enemies have abducted all the mages and sorcerers of high power and taken the tools of their craft ... all except Darian. They have started on the small fry like myself and I am terrified. Mr Walpurgis, I am nothing more than an illusionist, a flim flam man. Why take me?'

'Why indeed,' replied Walpurgis, a frown of concern stretched the thin grey skin of his forehead to an alarming tightness, 'and when they finish with you? Could our kind be next? This has the air of some religious fanaticism about it, powered by authority. It is well known that the new prime minister is a strict and humourless puritan by nature.'

Walpurgis paused to ponder on his dilemma, his Family had been nearly destroyed by a power-hungry industrialist seeking the Technomicron, the flames set to flush out and destroy Darian. Any further involvement with that young man was bound to endanger his people again. But if this peril could be stopped before it spread to the Family? Easiest option was to flee, they had done so before and survived. Perhaps they should head abroad and join one of the European travelling circuses that welcomed professional freaks.

Standing up to his impressive height, Walpurgis pointed to the entrance of the tent. 'I am sorry, there is nothing I can do to help beyond giving you this information. Tell the alchemist to seek out the Bane of Souls. That will help him with his ghost nuisance. Maybe then he will assist you and the other magicians. But I would not count on it.'

No longer the creature but in his human form, Cambion waited, hidden by the fairground crowds, he had seen Reggie the magician enter the Family's tent and leave shortly after in a state of distress. Sight of the contorted forms within had that effect on most people, himself included. He had no right to be squeamish of course, for unlike them, he was an unnatural monster infused with demonic contamination. They did no harm and did their best to live out their lives. He was a killer, a monster that rent human flesh and bone to shreds and devoured it. Cambion loathed himself but self-destruction was a grievous mortal sin, he still clung onto the hope that his human side could find redemption one day. But only after he cleansed the world of Darian and his demon partner.

But first he had to seek sanctuary.

27

Why had he come here? What could he do? Reggie had rushed straight from the funfair across London on the overhead tramway as far as he could before finishing the journey in a steam Hansom to the accursed Mayfair square. Here he remained, knees weak from fear as he saw the phantoms for himself. He tried to convince himself it was just an illusion, the use of *Pepper's Ghost* a trick of mirrors used by many of his fellows but on a far grander scale.

Illusionists in theatres throughout the land conjured up ghosts every night in front of rapt audiences. How could this be anything more than an elaborate hoax created by a master of the occult? He also tried to ignore the baleful cold wafting from the spectres as a trick of his overwrought imagination. It wasn't working. These ghostly forms were the real thing.

'Quite a spectacle, aren't they ...'

Reggie's already fraught nerves jolted with shock at a voice behind him, he spun around to see a familiar figure, Cambion. One of Darian's sidekicks. 'My god, man ... are you trying to give me a seizure?'

Cambion took the magicians arm and steered him through the silent, gawping crowds to a stall selling hot chestnuts and pies, 'Buy me some supper and I will help you.'

For the first time, Reggie could see the dreadful state of the small man, the dust-coated shabbiness of his clothing, his unshaven face, dirt-encrusted fingers. And his foul, feral smell, as if from the cages of the unfortunate beasts caged up at the funfair. Cambion's eyes were sharp and clear though, no alcoholic binge had brought him so low, instead they mirrored an alert and suspicious demeanour. Grateful to be away from the ghastly spectres, Reggie agreed and watched in wonder as the little man devoured four large and steaming steak and kidney pastries without a pause, he had never seen hunger that desperate. He waited until Cambion washed down the meal with a pint of mulled ale, then prompted him to speak.

'Why do you think I need help?'

Cambion wiped away the beer froth and pie crumbs from his unkempt moustache and gave a humourless grin, one nearly as chilling as the ghosts, 'I saw you, entering and leaving Walpurgis' Weird World of Ugliness, I followed you here. Something is making you frightened of your own shadow, Reggie, the 'Great Miraculus'. Something you foolishly think that blaggard Cyrus Darian can solve. Why else would you come here?'

Every instinct screamed at Reggie to get away from this man, the thought of Cambion stalking him across London was not conducive to his shattered nerves. Nor the open contempt the man showed for the alchemist. The last Reggie had heard was Cambion was a stalwart supporter. Clearly there was bad blood between them now. And with Walpurgis, why else use that offensive term to describe the Family of Others show?

'I am merely enjoying a day off from the theatre,' Reggie insisted, 'I availed myself of the many entertainments at the funfair, including the sideshow exhibits. I then decided to see these phenomena in Mayfair for myself.'

His voice hardened, 'I still want to know why you are following me.'

Cambion stepped back, considering his options to flee. He had made a clumsy approach to the magician and the already frightened man was more suspicious than ever. He cursed himself for such folly, aware that he had been apart from human society for too long, preferring the persona of a powerful beast to an insignificant and meek man. Perhaps only honesty would work now, at least a hint of honesty. It would only be a little sin to add to his growing tally awaiting atonement.

'I was not stalking you … .at least not at first. I went to see Walpurgis to seek sanctuary among the Family. I have betrayed Darian grievously and have nowhere to live, no employment, no income. Walpurgis told me to return later tonight. I then remembered your state of agitation and decided to use the time to see if I could help you.'

'Out of the goodness of your heart ...'

So, the magician was not convinced, Cambion did not blame him but with no other explanation, he could only press on. 'Out of guilt, Mr Reggie. I betrayed my friend most grievously and I do not expect him to ever forgive me. But I remember you are part of Darian's wider circle of acquaintances and helping you will be a small measure of recompense.'

Reggie had enough, there was something deeply wrong about this man, some deep, old instinct screamed out warning of danger. That all-pervading feral smell was not of unwashed human but something animalistic, something dangerous. Had Cambion not implied as much by wanting to join the Family of Others? Reggie bolted, using the packed crowd as cover. He had no idea, no plan just to put as much distance between himself and Cambion as possible. When he saw a gap in the barrier across Pleasance Square, he ducked under and fled towards Darian's house. There was nothing mirror-created illusions could do to harm him but his mind and soul knew Cambion could destroy his body.

All around him, people shouted out in alarm, the Mechmen bellowed amplified and ignored commands while the shapeshifter watched open-mouthed in astonishment as Reggie sprinted across the haunted square. Soon lost amid the packed throng of phantoms, the crowd argued among themselves, had he survived? Was he a lunatic? No one knew but Cambion raged at the loss of a means of gaining access to the alchemist. Unwilling to wait any longer, he transformed into a swift hawk and flew back to the funfair. Everything remained of Lord Hector's Astounding Steam Fair, every barrel organ, every ride, every hawker of sweet treats but of the Family of Others there was no trace. Rather than shelter an enemy of Darian's, they had packed up and moved on.

Cambion flew to a hilltop in Hampstead Heath, still a blighted wasteland since the Great Turbine Disaster. He alighted on the scorched earth and became a wolf, howling out his fury to the darkening twilight. What was it about Cyrus Darian that his allies refused to betray him as easily as he had? With yet another hope of shelter denied him, Cambion's rage against the alchemist grew. His course of action was affirmed. That man had to die before Cambion could hope to gain peace and forgiveness, cast out the beast within and live out the rest of his life as a human being.

28

'I am going insane from boredom living in this jail,' Darian paced the floor with the same manic intensity of a predator in a zoo, 'After this eternity of waiting, all I have is a clever but enormous gadget that can trap flies.'

Belial watched with amusement as the alchemist became increasingly agitated, with no access to Darian's usual distractions; magic shows, theatre, opium dens and brothels. Such stress would need a calming influence, one at least he would provide.

'I mean it, old chap, 'a genius of creating clockwork precision, the greatest inventor of the age and me, a master of the occult, all working together to catch bluebottles.'

Belial offered him a glass of fine wine but his companion refused with a curt gesture, a sure sign this tension was serious. The demon's amusement turned to concern.

'And what about our Russian and his mysterious secret? Any chance of *demoning* it out of him? I am being eaten up with curiosity.'

'Alas, Cyrus, the Count has furnished himself with the armour of righteousness, any mesmeric suggestion or threat of hellfire from me will fall on deaf ears. The man is determined to be Heaven bound, I cannot rattle him into revealing what he knows.'

Darian swore in colourful Farsi and grabbed the proffered wine glass, downing the contents in one swig, an insult to the quality vintage. 'That is all I need, another warrior for God. I am still livid at that close call caused by that little rat, Cambion. Nothing like nearly having my throat cut to discover who your friends are.'

A frantic hammering on the main door cut short any further discussion, whoever braved the ghosts was either desperate or dangerous or both but not to be ignored. As the household approached it, a voice high-pitched with terror shouted above the knocking.

'Let me in! In the name of all you treasure, I implore you, let me in, Darian.'

'Just when I thought my life could not get any stranger,' Darian announced reaching for the handle, 'I recognise that voice as one of my past assistants, Reggie the magician.'

'It might be a trick,' warned Hardwick reaching for his miniature gyroscopic-enhanced pistol. 'A shapeshifter or clever impressionist working for our enemies.'

The furious hammering and pleading began again. Ignoring the inventor's warning Darian pushed past his companions and bracing himself for the moaning incantation from the ghosts, opened the door. Of all people to impersonate, surely the not-so *Great Miraculus* would be last on the list.

As it opened, Reggie bolted through the door, falling on the floor in his panic, shaking as if pursued by a demon, which unknown to him, he was. He'd endured passing through many ghosts in his headlong flight across the square and the chilling, ghastly effects were still resonating through him. Hardwick grabbed an overcoat and threw it over the quivering form.

'Fetch him a stiff drink, someone,' Darian asked, helping the fear-stricken man to his feet, 'Reggie Dunne is either the bravest or craziest person to cross my threshold for many months.'

Once settled in a chair in front of a well-stocked parlour fire, Darian and the others waited for the magician to calm down and his hands to stop shaking. 'Thank you, Cyrus, I ran for my life, focusing on your door to take my mind of the ghosts, I knew you would let me in.'

'That was foolish, old chap, in these perilous and strange times, letting in any visitor would be a rash move.'

'I gambled on your curiosity,' Reggie gave a wan, weary smile. 'And I've known you long enough to know you are reckless and courageous by nature.'

The magician felt a caress of warm fur around his legs and reached down to stroke the dragoncat's head, rewarded by its curious loud purr.

Darian smiled, 'And of course, I have Misha, a better judge of character than any human born.'

The crackling fire casting dancing shadows on the cherry silk walls and the effects of the wine began to take its toll. Reggie's long and stressful day had caught up with him and his eyes became heavy with impending sleep. He also felt safe for the first time in days, surrounding by familiar faces to protect him. Indeed, he was content to never return home until all was well with the world again. Forcing himself awake, the magician related his meeting with the other mages and his encounter with Randalfo Walpurgis in careful detail. His mention of the Bane of Souls caused a ripple of interest, particularly with the newcomer, a big Russian of noble bearing.

'To be honest,' Reggie continued, 'I was too frightened of the spectres to seek you out, Cyrus, even trying to convince myself it was all an elaborate version of Pepper's Ghost.'

'I wish it was,' sighed Darian, 'I'd smash the scoundrel's mirror and be done with this vexation in an instance.'

'But my fear of the spooks was nothing compared to an encounter with a strange and threatening individual,' added the magician proceeding to describe his encounter with the scruffy little man and his curious aura of feral threat.

'Bloody Cambion, by Hades,' a furious Darian stood up abruptly, knocking over a wine glass, mercifully empty and no threat to the exquisite antique silk Persian rug beneath their feet. 'The bloody nerve of the creature. How dare its verminous shadow come anywhere near me or any of my friends.'

'Desperation?' ventured Reggie, 'He was in a pitiful and poor condition, bedraggled and unkempt. Maybe he is trying to ingratiate himself back into your favour and patronage?'

'That will never happen,' Belial's chilling voice ended any thought of reconciliation from the others. They all knew the limits of defying a demon prince. Absolute zero.

'That little bastard is a half-demon with shape shifting abilities. It could have changed into a wild beast in a heartbeat and devoured you. You were fortunate to have escaped. Do not be concerned, it cannot harm you here.'

His words were lost to Reggie, finally succumbing to deep sleep. Leaving him to his slumbers, the others walked to another room.

'The Bane of Souls, eh? Good old Walpurgis, coming up with a solution to my problem. Worth getting my best coat singed getting his Family out of that blaze,' Darian remarked, the old fire of adventure reigniting in his eyes. 'Now we have something to search for.'

In his excitement, Darian still did not miss the curious demeanour of his Russian guest, the Count was tense, hands clenching into fists, and he avoided eye contact with any of the others. Curious.

'Something demonic?' The alchemist asked Belial who shook his head. 'Sorry, not one of ours, my friend. Or anything belonging to dark deities either. Time to get back to hunting through all those dusty tomes and scrolls.'

Bartrev gave a mournful, soul deep sigh, what was the point now of holding onto a secret, one Darian would easily discover in one of his many occult books.

'There is no point wasting time researching, I know exactly what the Bane of Souls is. I know its precise location ... where I hid it before fleeing my homeland.'

The man's announcement created surprise and astonishment from all. Coincidence? Or the ever mysterious workings of Fate? Darian was a great believer in Fate and the complex interlinking of people's lives. The big Russian was always meant to come here; it was woven into the fabric of his destiny, just as Hardwick had escaped his strident wife in time to arrive with the *Dauntless*. What part Cambion's malign interference played in this new adventure was yet to be determined. Fate did not always deal you a winning card.

'You must tell me everything, Bartrev,' the alchemist urged. 'I can protect you and your secret in return for the use of this Bane thing.'

'Can you?' Bartrev was cynical and bitter, he had no doubt this Persian opportunist could not be trusted – the Fae mirror was yet another item for Darian to covet and steal. 'Can you return me to the favour of the Tsar and restore my lands?'

'Unlikely,' Darian admitted with a mock rueful grin, 'but I can eject you right now from my home into the army of ghosts and back to the threat of the Tsar's agents.'

29

A madman running through the dense crowd of spectres had been taken in by Darian's household. Major Stroude received this latest report from the ghostly siege of Pleasance Square with alarm. So the foreign beggar had yet more visitors within the beleaguered walls of his home. The large and high-powered dirigible had taken off and returned again shortly after. But as the spectres were still there, Stroude made the assumption that so was the alchemist. The man was clearly reaching out for help solving his problem. If he succeeded, Stroude would lose the army of ghosts for England and the Empire and all would be for nothing. What could be done?

Could Darian and his companions withstand an assault by a well-armed battalion of Mechmen? Would the soldiers working the mechanised suits of armour be protected from their weakening fear of the ghosts and their more rational fear of the alchemist's instant rust inducing potion? Despite these concerns, this strong-handed tactic was becoming more attractive, clearly reasoning with the man and appealing to his patriotic duty would get Stroude nowhere. Darian had no allegiance to anyone but himself.

At least his plans to seize all mysterious objects of interest were proceeding well. While the choosing and training of his young zealots was underway, Stroude already had made inroads into London's subversive occult community using his own agents – too few to make a big assault but still a promising start.

Stroude called for his aide and ordered the Mechman commander be brought to him that morning. The major had procrastinated too long, time for decisive action.

So, the Bane of Souls was a work of Russian Fae. Darian was relieved that the nobleman had confessed his secret, it had saved him many long hours of research. Darian knew many languages but his knowledge of Russian, modern or ancient was limited. He learnt from Bartrev that the Bane was a magicke mirror created by the *Bereginyas*, water dwelling nymphs who like all Fae were neither malevolent nor benign towards humans. They lived their own lives untouched by that of humans if possible. Any interaction with the otherworldly beings had to be done with caution and great skill. Not that there was any need to in this case, Bartrev had the mirror and soon so would he. One of the Russian's ancestors must have tricked a nymph into handing him the object which he then used to advance his power and wealth. Centuries passed and as Christianity spread across the land, local monks horrified at such an obviously unearthly object kept it hidden, apparently too superstitious and afraid of its influence to destroy it. The Fae did not take kindly to their possessions falling into human hands and were normally ruthless in getting them back. After so long, perhaps they had forgotten it existed, or maybe they no longer lived. Survival for such ethereal beings was becoming increasingly stressful in this time of human expansion into remote places and the relentless march of brash technology.

Darian just had to possess this mirror, it had to be the answer. Why else would Walpurgis through his unlikely messenger urge him to find it as the only way to control the ghosts? It meant embarking on one of the most perilous adventures of his life, a journey into the heart of Russia. Could he do this? By Hades, of course he could. Darian had a team already assembled whether they knew it or not. He had the stalwart and loyal Belial, who alone was worth an army of mere humans. He had the inventive genius of Sir Miles Hardwick and local knowledge and linguistic help from Count Nikolai Bartrev and now he had a failed illusionist and would be magician in the Great Miraculus … well, the best planned expedition had to have some cannon fodder. How could Darian possibly fail?

His elation was short-lived as the cold touch of reality

prevailed. Even if in principle his team could reach Bartrev's lands undetected, any plan was doomed for wherever he went, the bloody ghosts would follow like a spectral beacon. Darian cursed in several languages, he had never felt so trapped, so helpless.

Seeking solitude, he went up to the most useless feature in his stolen home, the roof top observatory. A victim of insanity or a wave of ridiculous optimism, probably both applied when he had this addition built to the Georgian townhouse after taking it over from the vanquished succubus, Bruxa. The curved glass dome had cost a fortune and had never been used, a magnificent telescope of polished wood and burnished brass remained poised, its precision lens looking up at a heaven it could never see. The wonders of the Universe hidden behind the permanent pall of London smog.

Darian slumped into the chair, pushing the telescope away, the instrument as futile as his knowledge in a situation that had no solution. Was he to live out his life walled into his home like some medieval anchorite? Unlikely, Stroude had made it clear Her Majesties Government would not allow him to live. A square packed with ghosts was never going to be a prized feature of London life for visitors to gawp at in wonder.

He was not alone for long. This time it was Hardwick who braved his displeasure by interrupting his meditation ... though depressed brooding was a more accurate description.

'I need to speak to you alone, Cyrus,' the inventor's voice was laden with intrigue, snapping Darian out of his self-pitying gloom. He spun the chair around to face Hardwick who sat on a wide, wooden window ledge opposite him.

'There is a way out, one both Belial and I realised two days ago ...'

Agitated, Darian leapt out of his chair and paced the observatory floor. 'Then why in Hades haven't you told me? So much for loyal companions, I'd be better off with Stroude and his minions.'

'Calm down, Cyrus, please. This is not easy. It involves the Technomicron and we know what happened with that accursed tome. We all nearly perished and a large area of London was laid to waste. I cannot bear to dwell on how many innocents died in the Great Turbine Disaster.'

'You are insane, the pair of you,' Darian's voice was cold as another brief spark of hope was extinguished. 'That bloody book evaporated in front of our eyes.'

Hardwick nodded, he would never forget the fear and horror of that confrontation with demonic evil, 'Yes, the book was destroyed but not the words. The incantation you were forced by Quibbe to read to activate the Technomicron and summon human souls. The book was gone before you uttered the next line, the one giving you control over the spirits.'

Hardwick was right. Quibbe had been a lower caste demon and the Technomicron therefore would not activate from his spoken words, it only obeyed a full blood human with arcane knowledge. He had threatened Darian on his life and that of his companions to utter the spell, ordering the summoned spirits of every human being that had ever lived and ever would to obey only Quibbe.

Darian thought the summoning spell broken but obviously enough remained to gather the earthbound ghosts to him. If only he could remember the next line of the incantation it might just bring them under his control. He sat back down, head in hands. 'I cannot remember any of the words. I just read them out under great duress and peril of imminent death. A brainwave indeed, old chap but a pointless one.'

'But you can, my friend. You have an extraordinary memory for this sort of thing. I've seen it in action. You recall facts from your old tomes that you merely glanced at many years before. The knowledge is there, locked into your brain.'

The alchemist nodded, that was true. 'So what are you going to do, Miles, invent a Cerebral Memory Extractor device?'

'No time for that, Belial sneaked out early this morning to check our surroundings. Something is afoot. More Mechmen have arrived, two whole battalions of the bastards. I fear they plan to end this siege by force.'

'Is the *Dauntless* ready?'

'As always ... but there is no point fleeing with that lot wafting in tow. You must endure mesmerism to release those words from your mind.'

Horrified, Darian returned to his pacing, the idea of anyone having control of his mind was abhorrent, what damaging secrets could be released? A Pandora's Box of past intrigue and betrayals at a time when he required his companions on his side. This situation with the ghosts brought them no promise of adventure and riches, just a fight for his survival. There was nothing to stop them walking, or more accurately flying, away, leaving Darian to his fate.

And the last thing he wanted brought to the surface was his true feelings for Belial, he had never needed his stalwart loyalty, physical strength and Hell born power more.

'I understand your concerns,' Hardwick interrupted, his voice calm, 'and I will ensure nothing is asked of you beyond remembering the Technomicron spell. You have my word as a gentleman and friend.'

That much was true: Hardwick was a weak man in many ways, unable to control his addiction to gambling that had lost his family's inheritance. But he was honest, raised on old English aristocratic virtues of chivalry and fair play.

'I don't want Belial anywhere near my brain, so who is going to pull off this feat of mesmerism?'

Hardwick smiled, 'Would you believe Reggie has trained in the art as part of his latest stage act?'

Darian did believe, how could he not? Yet again the yarn on Fate's spinning wheel stretched on, bringing the Great Miraculus to his door just when he needed him. Fate was neither friend or foe but She could be cruel. Even so, with no other choice, he decided to go along with her plans for him. But he would proceed with caution, one thing Darian refused to be was a helpless victim of Fate. She was just another authority figure to rebel against.

30

Both the tethered dirigible and the wafting ghosts were still in their places, reassuring Stroude his target was still trapped in his home. *Excellent*, he would have the wretched Darian in his custody by late morning. The area behind the barriers was clear of all but the Mechmen troopers. The crowds of onlookers and hawkers had grumbled to themselves but none openly argued with the constabulary, not with so many heavily armoured titans arriving, a menacing force clanking up to the barrier in tight formation.

Though their unease was palpable, the major had given the Mechmen battalions a severe talking-to. Any signs of cowardice would mean immediate expulsion from the squad and a spell in jail as a disgraced deserter. This was a potent threat. The Mechmen were universally loathed among the London populace. Stripped of their armour, these unfortunates would have a brutal if not fatal time in prison.

'These apparitions cannot harm you,' Stroude declared. 'They are nothing more than shades, faint outlines of past lives that have no power over the living. You will march through them as if nothing more than fog.'

It was impossible to gauge the Mechman's reaction to this command, their faces hidden by helmets with darkened visors, their body language behind their bulky armour and cumbersome weaponry. They waited behind the barriers in their ranks, still as statues, noisy as locomotives with their steam weapons and movement mechanisms powering up.

'Our mission is to capture Cyrus Darian alive, you have all been furnished with his image and detailed description. Anyone else in the house is a legitimate target. Do not allow that dirigible to leave but if it lifts off from its moorings, do not destroy it. Target the engine area only to disable it.'

If any pre-battle tension rippled through the Mechmen ranks, none showed so deeply were they locked into their armour. This made Stroude uncomfortable, he liked to know who he was leading into conflict, their mental strengths and weaknesses. At least beyond the insubstantial crowd of ghosts, there was a soft target, a few ordinary men armed only with swordsticks and pistols at worst.

With a snarl of fury, Belial sprinted down from his rooftop surveillance to discover the alchemist sitting in a parlour armchair, with Reggie Dunne waving a gold pocket watch in front of his face. Darian's eyes were unfocused, glassy despite their strange unearthly swirl of lilac and silver hues. Could this primitive nonsense be timed any worse? Growling with impatience, he grabbed the magician's arm, the heat from his grip causing Reggie to gasp in pain, 'Whatever you intend doing, human, you had better get a move on, every damned Mechman in London has lined up behind the barrier. We are about to be under attack.'

The magician nodded a curt agreement, at least Darian was succumbing to the trance easily, a sign he was willing for the mesmerism to succeed. Hardwick swore: the alchemist was nearly in a mesmerised state, so close it would folly to stop now but how could they hold off a Mechman siege? Never a natural leader despite his aristocratic upbringing, he stepped up to the breech now, he knew the bastard Mechmen would take no prisoners.

'Belial, grab every weapon you can, including occult stuff. Bartrev, you and I will make the *Dauntless* ready for flight. Reggie ... keep going, no matter what happens around you ... hold fast and don't stop.'

The magician's hands began to tremble, making the swinging rhythm of the watch joggle and jump about, nearly breaking Darian's concentration. This was bad, very bad, control of the spectres was vital to a successful escape. Reggie summoned every inner reserve he could muster, forcing out the sound of the demon crashing about the house seeking weaponry and the amplified shouts echoing across the square from the Mechmen leaders rallying their troops.

He forced his mind to shut off the sound of heavy furniture being thrown against the front door as a makeshift barricade, of the overhead thrum, shunt and hiss of the airship's engines engaging. All that matters was reaching Darian's inner mind, sending him back to the moment he read out the ancient Persian words written in human blood in a grimoire of spells, its old, old magicke boosted by vast steam turbine energy to become the dreaded Technomicron.

So well did he concentrate on his task, Reggie did not hear the ground shaking march of the Mechmen as they pushed through the barriers and into the square. Instead his voice, soothing and calm urged the alchemist to remember, 'Come on Cyrus, the book is in your hands, you have already spoken the words of summoning, read the next line, that is all you need to do. Just one more line … you can do it …'

As the leading line of Mechmen marched into Pleasance Square and into the throng of ghosts, Stroude was shocked to see the ranks halt and falter. Some Mechmen spun around seeking flight back out of the square. Clearly the threat of disgrace and imprisonment was not enough to overcome fear of the spectres.

The men were panicking but why? These were tough brutes of men, not chosen for their mental acuity but for their love of violence. The major ran into the square, ready to command them back into focus but as a ghost passed through him, the hideous sensation shivering through his being answered his own question. The armoured suits were no protection from the invasion of a dead but conscious mind. In this case the bitter, insane thoughts of a murderess who had hung for infanticide. This was the true horror of the ghosts, what gave such insubstantial entities their power to terrify the living.

Something was happening. For the first time since their arrival, the ghosts turned away from their determined staring at Darian's front door. As one, they moved to the barriers, forming a spectral wall across the square in front of the Mechmen ranks. Bloody things are defending the bastard, Stroude gasped. 'Ignore them, damn you all ... they are just memories, they cannot hurt you!'

He ran to the nearest battalion commander and shouted above the hissing jets of boiling hot steam escaping from the suit, 'Advance ... I order you to advance. For God's sake do your duty or all these suits will be melted in the nearest foundry.'

Under his breath, Stroude muttered, 'I haven't decided yet whether your men will be still in them.'

Turning his head with a whir of clockwork mechanisms, the commander addressed his superior officer with a weary air of resignation. 'That you can do, sir. Destroy our strength and throw us into jail, but you cannot expect the men do risk their immortal souls. They will die for Queen and Country without hesitation but not endanger their time in eternity.'

Stroude erupted into an outraged outburst, 'Cowards, all of you. There is no danger to your bloody souls from a wall of flimsy bloody wraiths.'

To prove his point, the major strode forward and walked through the nearest ghosts and into the most frightening experience of his life. A sensation of complete violation as other entities crowded into his mind, his body and yes, also into his soul. He felt their raw emotions, their rage, their fear, their greed and mostly their insanity. All the things that held them to this earthbound plain to fester. He experienced their memories, their crimes and the blood-chilling cries of their victims. Or the hopeless despair of the lost and lonely unable to move on.

Backing away from the line of spirits, his legs buckling, Stroude doubled over and vomited, the feeling of contamination too much to bear, enough to drive any man to madness. This public show of fear and weakness did nothing to boost the morale of the watching, appalled Mechmen. His gesture had been foolish and futile. The standoff continued.

Reggie gently brought the alchemist out of his trance despite the panic around him, it was too dangerous a procedure to rush. Dazed and confused, Darian remained seated, head in hands. There was no clue from his demeanour whether the mesmerism had worked. Count Bartrev ran down from the mooring point on the roof to announce the *Dauntless* was ready to fly. The urgency in the Russian's voice broke the spell, Darian shaking his head as the mists in his mind cleared demanded to know what was going on. It was not the news he wanted to hear.

'I have no intention of leaving here, allowing that barbarian, Stroude to help himself to all my things? My library? I refuse to go.'

'At least you will have your life, Cyrus,' Reggie urged, 'things can be replaced.'

Darian's voice was cold, determined, 'Some of my most precious things cannot. There is only one golden staff of Astrubin in the world and I have it. I own the only surviving copies of ancient histories and grimoires from the earliest days of mankind, from civilisations far older than Ur and Sumer. I possess crystal power orbs, gifts from a Fae queen and magickal living jewels from the depths of the ocean stolen from mermaids. Tell me how I can replace those, eh Reggie?'

The alchemist gave a melodramatic but heartfelt sigh, 'Without my treasures, I might as well be dead.'

'I'll stay,' Belial's voice cut through tension, 'I can hold those human bastards off, they are too afraid to pass the apparitions in any case. It will be easy. Even Misha could do it.'

The thought of fleeing without his demon companion appalled Darian but the plan made some sense. In the past, Darian could leave the house protected with anti-supernatural attack spells and devices and booby trapped against casual break in from humans. He also suspected his dragoncat was far more than a ferocious but small pet and capable of unknown powers.

But against a whole army of accursed Mechmen? The use of brute force and powerful weapons was a whole other story.

'So unless you can come up with that instant rust formula again in the next few minutes, I suggest you leave with the others and let me get on with what I do best, being a demon prince.'

'Er, just one thing, gentlemen,' asked Hardwick, 'where are we going?'

'Russia of course ...' Darian announced leaping to his feet, ignoring the outbreak of astonishment. 'You too, Reggie, it has been ages since you had a bit of fun in your life.'

'I do not think your definition of fun is the same as mine,' the magician answered, a picture of misery, if only he hadn't met up with Mesterior and the others, he would be safe at home now, practising his limited repertoire of magic tricks.

'Fine,' Darian replied lightly as he prepared to evoke the spell of control over the ghosts. 'Go home and wait for those mystery men to knock down your door late one night and make you disappear. I suspect not by magic either.'

He beckoned Belial to accompany him as cover and striding into the square began to chant words not spoken in three thousand years, their power resonating through the smoke-laden, filthy air and into the ethereal being of the apparitions. 'I command you to come here and to guard my home against all trespass until I return.'

There was a long, uncomfortable pause, long enough to cast doubts in Darian's mind. Had he remembered the words correctly? Did the lingering echoes of the Technomicron's power of the ghosts still remain? As one, the spectres turned away from the barrier and stared with their sightless voids at the alchemist. And as one, fury and resentment laden in their soundless voices, they intoned ... 'Yes, Master. We obey you.'

They moved away from the barriers and reassembled in front of Darian's town house, becoming an almost solid glowing wall of ectoplasmic malevolence as individual spirits merged and overlapped. What more could the locals want? He'd given them the square back, if they were brave enough to venture past his house, surely that would ease up the anti-Darian hatred a little? If not, well, damn them all to Hades.

Free at last of his entourage, Darian gave an uncharacteristic whirling jig of success and celebration before being grabbed by the demon, 'Idiot! There is no time for this! Hardwick and the *Dauntless* are ready. You must go before Stroude's brain engages and he organises an aerial attack on the airship.'

Recovering his senses, Darian ran back into his house and grabbing Reggie by the arm propelled him towards the stairs before pausing. He had not realised he'd feel such an emotional wrench leaving Belial behind, was he going soft and actually thinking of the demon as a friend and not just a useful addition to his armoury? He gave Belial a tight, fleeting embrace, 'Take care, old chap, eh? And don't give the beggars one item of my things ...'

Without waiting for a reply or observing the mournful glance of longing from the demon, Darian and his unwilling companion sprinted up the stairs to the rooftop mooring point where the *Dauntless* tugged at her ropes, eager for freedom. As the two men entered the luxurious, oak panelled cabin beneath the taut canopy, they found Hardwick and Bartrev studying a map of Europe.

'We will never make it all the way to Russia in the dirigible, Cyrus,' the inventor announced. 'Even with the engines at full steam and a constant powerful wind at our stern.'

'And anyway, we would have to carry so much fuel, the poor *Dauntless* would be unable to take off,' Hardwick added, shaking his head at yet another impetuous act from the alchemist.

'Of course not,' Darian replied. 'Do you take me for a complete fool, Miles? Do not answer that ... I intend to head for a safe haven while we plan our adventure into Russia.'

'So where do you suggest?' Hardwick asked as the two men prepared to unhitch the airship and take off into the London sky, 'Belial told me you have sold Wildewish Hall, so unless you have enough country estate hidden away somewhere?'

'Stop bleating, man. Let her free and let's see where the wind takes us ...'

31

The spectres had not gone but had reorganised their ranks and were now tightly packed around Darian's home. They left behind the devastation of the past weeks, the wrecked, burnt out steam Hansom with its charred corpse. The ground littered with smashed bottles thrown by the desperate living containing messages for their perceived loved ones among the ghostly throng. Broken wooden placards too, thrown by those denouncing Darian as the Anti-Christ, which Stroude thought too high a status for the maverick alchemist even at his most outrageous and ambitious.

At this new unexpected turn of the operation, Stroude's mind raced, had the alchemist gained more control over the army of the dead? Despite the sense of contamination and violation by the ghosts still infecting him. Stroude loudly cursed the weakness of the Mechmen, nothing more than tin soldiers with a weak human core. If only they had been true automatons, mighty titans of metal and steam at his total command. Such machines would show no fear of the apparitions and would smash into Darian's home with one word from him.

Alas, the government wanted no individual to have such power at their fingertips, even the Queen herself, and creating such machines were beyond the ability of English engineers at this time. Sir Miles Hardwick was probably genius enough to make them but was too much in Darian's pay. And the man had the inconvenience of a lingering conscience. So, what now?

His backup plan had been an aerial assault, utilising Her Majesty's Sky Corps of heavily armed dirigible warships but they were already assigned to Dublin to quell a rebellion among the troublesome Irish seeking to break away from British rule. Stroude was astounded at such folly, why would anyone not want to be part of the greatest Empire the world had ever known?

He snapped out of his musings as a cry went up from the Mechmen, their amplified hearing had detected the sound of an engine being primed for steam, the dirigible was being readied to leave. There had to be something he could do, in a feat of mental discipline, Stroude forced the invading ghost thoughts from his mind and focused on the task of stopping Darian from leaving. He needed airships and weapons ... damn it, the Mechmen had the armoury and London was full of dirigibles. All he had to do was commandeer the closest craft and pursue that bloody man across the skies.

'Take this, old chap, you look like you need it the most.'

Darian had opened up a cabinet in the cabin and poured out a large measure of cognac into a lead crystal balloon glass. He had insisted on a high degree of comfort when Hardwick first designed the *Dauntless*, the alchemist could travel like a gentleman even if he was far from being one.

His hands still shaking, Reggie Dunne took the glass with a nod of gratitude. Relying on the wind for propulsion to save fuel, the dirigible had risen swiftly and smoothly at first but was now buffeted by thermals rising from the many chimneys of foundries and gas works as they passed through London's toxic skies. Reggie's pleas to be let off somewhere had fallen on deaf ears ... at least on Darian's. He could see the other two men were not best pleased to be taking an unwilling passenger on their flight from authority.

'Come on, Reggie ... you are a young man, urged Darian. 'This is the time to have wild adventures. Outrageous tales to bore your grandchildren rigid on long winter nights. Anyway, Fate brought you to me, who am I to throw away Her gifts?'

'Somehow, that does not sound reassuring,' Hardwick added, not looking away from his controls. The Russian was at his side, proving a useful and diligent trainee navigator.

'It is all right for you, Miles, you have spent weeks gallivanting around the sights of Europe by day and bedding your eager and energetic new bride by night,' Darian replied, enjoying the inventor's blushes – who would know better of Athena's amorous ways then the man who had her first –, 'while I have been trapped like a rat in my home.'

'Come on, gentlemen, Darian continued, 'let us celebrate our freedom first. Even you Miles, the wife will never know. Let us seek gaiety, bright lights and merry music. Let us drink and laugh and have the delightful company of beautiful, willing women.'

Bartrev broke into a rare smile, 'That does sound wonderful. I too have known no relief from my loss and the perils of pursuit. Some carefree recreation will do us all good.'

'Then it is settled, Miles ... take this craft to Paris.'

Commandeering a large, public airship full of businessmen was never going to be a popular move. Ordering the indignant passengers off the craft with a number of heavily armed Mechmen at your back was at least going to stifle any vocal complaint. Stroude did his best to quell the passengers in their silent but obvious alarm – this was not an everyday event for any Englishman about his rightful business.

'I must apologise for the inconvenience, gentlemen. At least the Freedom of the Skies Company is efficient and there will be another airship along soon. I must take this extreme measure as a matter of great urgency, to safeguard the good citizens of London against a foul and dangerous enemy of the State.'

Pleasantries dealt with, Stroude and his clanking, hissing retinue boarded the craft, the weight of the Mechmen causing it to dip and sway on its mooring in Green Park. The pilot and his young navigator were terrified as they struggled to control the dirigible. The major ordered the Mechmen to stay still and to everyone's relief the craft found a new equilibrium.

'There is a large private airship that has just left Mayfair under wind power and heading east. You should easily be able to catch up with it under steam power. It is vital you get me and my troops alongside it.'

His eyes never leaving the Mechmen, the nervous pilot nodded and replied weakly, 'I'll do me best, sir. Some of these rich gents own craft that can easily outrun one of these old chuffers once under power.'

'Then it is fortunate this particular rich gent is not expecting an attack from a humble passenger airship,' answered Stroude, settling himself in a seat near the controls. 'So you had better make haste before he realises he is being followed.'

Paris! Hardwick's gloom thickened to match the roiling, polluted air his beautiful craft had to fly through. A wildly hedonistic city where Darian could be as outrageous as he wanted and be feted for it by the locals. The alchemist would be in no hurry to leave once he was reacquainted with the Green Fairy and the delights of the courtesans. At the back of Hardwick's mind was the nightmare of meeting up with Athena in Paris. It had been their first port of call at the start of their honeymoon but there was no reason to think she may not return with the Pringles. How could he explain his presence at the Opera or some other of the city's wonders? So, he was on an urgent mission to save London from an invasion of phantoms? With a glass of wine and a *jolie fille* on each arm? Hardwick shuddered, imagining the confrontation, just as a metallic clang and snap resounded from above the cabin and the *Dauntless* jolted, veering off her wind-borne course.

'Have we been hit?' shouted Bartrev as an uncontained part of the canopy billowed noisily over their heads.

'Unlikely,' Hardwick snapped fighting to control his craft, 'there would have been a considerably larger bang followed by our immolation. One of the rigging supports has broken, damn it.'

'Fool! Incompetent heap of mindless metal!' Stroude's pale face coloured up in his fury as one of the Mechman shot at the gondola beneath the airship but missed, 'I ordered you to take out the engine, not hit the canopy. If Darian dies, so do you!'

Fortunately the wild shot had bounced off some metal rigging, had it entered the airships canopy, the resulting explosion would have been catastrophic. The troopers incompetence had also destroyed their only edge over the *Dauntless*, that of surprise. Any lookout on Hardwick's dirigible would not have been alarmed at the sight of a humble passenger liner approaching, the London skies were full of the lumbering craft. Now, Stroude expected to hear their boilers engaging, building up a head of steam to power up the engines ready to bolt, the *Dauntless* would be too fast to give chase. There was still time for one good, well aimed shot at the craft's full canopy.

'Get this old windbag alongside the *Dauntless*, use everything you've got to reach her.'

The pilot was outraged, no one insulted his craft. 'Windbag? My Nelly is an honest workhorse unlike that floating gin palace. She'll do her best. I'll not risk pushing her to destruction.'

Stroude pulled out his pistol and levelled it at the pilot's head, 'You will tear out this craft's guts if need be. Do it now!'

With its crew still unaware of the sudden attack on the Dauntless, the damaged rigging was now lose and moving in the wind, threatening to pierce the canopy.

'I urgently need someone to get it soldered back,' Hardwick shouted as the dirigible became increasingly harder to steer. It was time to engage the steam engines to bring her back under his control but Hardwick did not want to add greater risk to whoever was chosen to repair the damage. A task the demon would have done with ease, Belial was agile, strong, had his own heat source and had the advantage of immortality. Hardwick never thought he'd miss the sneering celestial being.

'I'll do it,' Bartrev volunteered immediately.

'Meaning no disrespect, Count,' Darian lied, 'but your sturdy physique puts us all at a disadvantage. Reggie, your nerves and shaking hands will get us all killed. I will go.'

No one argued with him.

32

Firmly harnessed to a safety cable, Darian climbed out of the gondola and scrambled up a rung of metal steps onto the roof. Fighting the buffeting air and struggling to keep his feet firmly on the wooden roof, he was grateful the *Dauntless* was not under steam power. Though the wind created uncertainty in the airship's movement, her veering impossible to judge, the slower speed was a bonus. Darian had no trouble locating the broken rigging, it waved at him, a sharp tear in the metal rod flapping perilously close to the canopy, stretched tight with Zephyron gas in preparation for the journey to France.

Reaching the damage, Darian produced a portable Luxcite Extremis Intensifer from his inside coat pocket, one of Hardwick's inventions for his personal use, it was a tool more than capable of reuniting both pieces of the broken metal with enough precision not to ignite the canopy gas. Unless his hand slipped.

Total concentration on the task was vital, so much so, Darian was unaware of a passenger dirigible approaching swiftly as if to overtake. If he had seen it, the alchemist would have ignored it – the sky lanes above London were always overcrowded with craft about their daily business. Gritting his teeth, Darian engaged the device, waiting as the Luxcite flame grew in intensity to the required brilliant turquoise blue, a sign it was at its hottest. He began work, painstakingly fusing the broken rod, keeping it taut but keeping the flame from touching the canopy. Something Reggie with his infamous unsteady sleight of hand, a distinct disadvantage for a magician, would never have succeeded.

The join was complete, still hot and glowing with vivid blue metal. Darian relaxed, waiting to see if the repair held. He heard a loud sound, felt hot air rushing towards him and something slamming into his right shoulder. By Hades, he'd been shot. And the beggar had ripped through his new Siamese silk coat, damn their eyes. For the first time he noticed the passenger airship, now alongside the *Dauntless*. The main door was open and a Mechman stood, aiming his weapon at Darian again. Commandeering public transport, an airship-load of businessmen, now that was bold and underhand. Darian's respect for Major Stroude grew.

With no time to return to the gondola and warn Hardwick, the alchemist had no choice but to deal with this threat himself. Darian knew he was bleeding profusely, shock and weakness from blood loss would soon set in but he had more time than a normal human. The venomous bite from Bruxa the Succubus had strengthened him, allowed him to heal quickly and so far not age. He would need every enhanced minute to survive this assault.

A gust of wind lifted the *Dauntless* higher than the much heavier pursuing craft, this could be Darian's one and only opportunity now he was out of the Mechman's line of fire. The easiest solution would be to drop the Intensifer onto the liner's canopy and hope the resulting explosion did not reach the *Dauntless*. A terrible loss of life, but bad things happened to good people too, Darian reasoned. As the liner rose to catch up and come alongside the *Dauntless,* only the danger to himself stayed his hand.

The Mechman still could not get an accurate shot at his target, there was still time to do something. At least Darian thought there was until he could feel vibrations build beneath his feet and hear the dirigible's engines begin to engage. Hardwick had decided the risk from the attacker was too great and was readying to outrun the slower craft. Idiot! That Mechman would bring down the *Dauntless* long before she had built up enough head of steam to make her run.

As the liner swung even closer, Darian prayed the cable harness would hold, leapt from the *Dauntless* towards the other craft. For a few ghastly seconds, he remained suspended in the open air between the airships, all too aware of the city spreading so far beneath. One that for once would welcome him with open arms, should he fall. Forcing such thoughts from his mind,

Darian focused on the liner's canopy.

He reached the side of the canopy and clung onto the rigging, again only with his left arm, wrapping it around the metal rod for greater purchase. He hoped Hardwick and the others could see him and not accelerate away now, the speed would yank at his harness with such force, he would be pulled apart. Messy. And no handsome corpse for his many conquests to weep over. Darian let out a savage growl as a white hot stab of pain wracked his body, he had to use his right hand to pull out a knife from his coat and force his fingers to take a firm hold. Simple in concept but near impossible to carry out.

'Cooperate, damn you,' he berated the pain-wracked and now freezing cold digits, curled into a rigid fist. There was no more time, the *Dauntless* let out a loud unladylike belch of steam. Grimacing, Darian wrapped the protesting fingers around the knife hilt and tore into the liner's burgeoning canopy, ripping through the canvas and releasing a satisfyingly large whoosh of air. He pulled free of the crippled craft and flung himself back into the sky just as the *Dauntless* sped off. Mercifully, he was unaware of the harsh buffeting as he dangled helpless, like a spider behind the speeding craft, the pain had won and left him in a dead faint.

No longer threatened at the point of a gun, Norman Frederick Turnbull, pilot of the Nellie relished the panic among his unwanted passengers. It was his ship again and he wanted them to know it. Insult his dirigible? Wave a gun in his face? Turnbull would show 'em.

He watched with quiet satisfaction as a white-faced Stroude clung to a metal rail, his knees buckling from the twisting, spiralling descent of the airship. The arrogant git and his monsters thought she was out of control? Good. Only Turnbull and his crew knew different. That the years of experience and thorough training for a canopy tear were paying dividends and the ship's trajectory was carefully monitored and designed to bring her down safely. Time to enjoy his return to power.

'It's no good,' he yelled above the rushing air and loud hiss of escaping gas, 'she is far too heavy. We need to lighten the load. And don't think of ejecting any of my men. I will need every one of them to get Nellie down in one piece.'

Even before Stroude was able to issue a command, the leading Mechman booted one of his men out of the open door, oblivious to his screams and the gasps of shock from the other troopers. 'That was for the two badly aimed shots that got us in this nightmare'

None of the others protested.

Darian came aware into a world of pain, lying in a berth on the *Dauntless*. His right shoulder was on fire and his stomach and chest were badly bruised as if he lost a close battle with an enraged elephant. Had he still held onto the liner's rigging as the *Dauntless* sped off, there would have been no awakening in this world. Beside him, a stricken Hardwick waited for him to awaken, his relief at the sight of Darian's curious eyes opening was palpable.

'My god, Cyrus ... what the hell were you playing at? I could have killed you.'

'The thought had crossed my mind, old chap,' Darian replied with a groan: talking hurt too, 'but you were too busy trailing behind the fragrant Athena like a little dog to invent a long overdue communications device.'

'But leaping from one dirigible to another? That was insane.'

'Not even the first time,' Darian replied, this time in a less painful hoarse whisper, 'it is becoming a habit. Remember, I jumped from that bastard Crimm-Smyths's airship onto the canopy of a passing liner to escape his Mechmen. I did tell you at the time.'

'I thought it was a tall tale,' Hardwick confessed. 'Let's face it, Cyrus, you and the truth are not close allies.'

'Well, I have no intention of making it a third.'

Darian did his best to relax on the berth, made up with pure white Egyptian cotton sheets, well, almost white. A spreading blood stain leaked from the impromptu bandaging around his injured shoulder. At least the bullet had gone straight through leaving nothing behind to fester and poison his blood. Those accursed Mechmen needed to be dealt with, permanently, Darian decided. But now his immediate concern was reaching Paris safely.

'Did I succeed in eliminating our pursuer?'

Bartrev stepped forward with good news. 'I saw her go down, Darian but the descent was survivable. You do not have the fate of those innocent passengers on your soul. We are on our own over the Channel now, with France in view.'

'Well, isn't that just wonderful,' Darian's reply was laced with sarcasm. He had no lingering qualms about the liner's occupants, innocent or otherwise. And his dreams of sauntering down the rue du Fauburg Poisonierre to the L'Alcazar to hear the saucy songs of the celebrated chanseur Theresa fading with his consciousness as his head spun in another impending faint. Nor could he expect to enjoy the company Madame Arlette's most beautiful and charming courtesans under the influence of *la fee verte*, all these dreams disappeared as the gunshot wound stepped up its assault of white hot pain.

A wave of nausea overcame the alchemist sending Reggie flying across the cabin armed with a large ceramic bowl. With Hardwick needing the Russian Count to help him fly the *Dauntless*, the magician had drawn the short straw and was assigned to nursing the stricken Darian. Something told him, the man would make a dreadful patient.

33

Any defeat was always a personal insult to Major Stroude, he never met it with any sense of gentlemanly grace, something the aristocrats seemed to imbibe as infants, no doubt fed to them with the apocryphal silver spoon. Stroude was a middle son to near penniless minor gentry, his older brother would inherit the dilapidated manor and two struggling tenant farms, he was duty bound to enter the military and his younger brother the clergy. Only Rafe, the black sheep, fled at the thought of a dog collar to the Americas and became a wealthy riverboat gambler along the Mississippi. Lucky Rafe.

The major was convinced that Darian had somehow found a way to keep the ghosts in one place and had fled in Hardwick's dirigible. Pleasance Square was more open and the terrible debris of the last weeks began to be cleared at last but the continued presence of the phantoms crowded into the entrance to Darian's home was a nightmarish as ever.

Would the alchemist return? Stroude believed he would, he doubted Darian would abandon a lifetime's worth of valuable occult possessions without a fight. There was someone … or something still living in the Georgian townhouse. His intelligence agents reported seeing a strange, winged creature on the roof and a blond youth at the window. Darian had left his house guarded by two of his monstrous cohorts.

Plans to storm the house were put on hold until the major learned what he was up against. He refused to endure another humiliating defeat after the debacle with the Mechmen. To think he owed his life to the flying skills of some working class airship pilot after the clumsy and disastrous actions of Mechmen. Tin-brained idiots that could have destroyed both dirigibles and claimed all their lives in a mid-air inferno.

A more esoteric and subtle approach was needed to breech

Darian's defences and allow the major access to the alchemist's goods. Leaving a trusted sergeant in charge of the continuing surveillance of Pleasance Square, Stroude needed to concentrate on recruiting and training his new squad of military-minded clerics and researching who best to tackle his on-going frustration at thwarting Darian.

Watching in the shadows unseen in the form of a glossy, pampered black cat, Cambion wondered if his ploy to slow down his enemy had worked. A desperate plan born from his unbridled fury and frustration. How did Darian live such a charmed life, seemingly able to escape from any threat using his natural wiles and the backup of a powerful demon? He was still only human and therefore ultimately fallible. Cambion's raging need to physically rip the man to shreds had to take a step back when he saw Hardwick's damned dirigible arriving in Pleasance Square. It meant Darian would try to escape the Mechman siege in the *Dauntless*.

Cambion had to be patient, unable to prevent him leaving, he had to yet again bide his time. He was comforted by the knowledge that the alchemist never left London for long, seemingly joined to the toxic city he loved by an invisible umbilical cord. Though Cambion loathed even the thought of their company, the shapeshifter visited the secret haunts of London's demonic inhabitants, raucous, hidden inns where they mixed with his fellow half-breeds and unsavoury human occultists. All the beings he'd struggled to avoid in his attempt to lead a God-fearing, normal human life.

Using gold he'd stolen from the many victims he'd killed as the beast, he sought some foul being willing to trade with him. It had proven difficult. For many years, Cambion had already earned a bad reputation among the unearthly denizens of London's night. Firstly by his refusal to be one of them, openly despising them and seeking redemption and the sanctuary of the Church. Later his betrayal of Cyrus Darian and by association the earthbound prince Belial had created a ripple of loathing and distrust that would continue without end. Despised and feared by humans, shunned by his erstwhile friends, rejected by Walpurgis and his freaks, Cambion was also hated by the supernatural.

A pariah to all, he was truly alone, but gold always smoothed the way past any difficulties and the night before Cambion had trotted down a stinking Lambeth back alley, blending in with the other large brown rats. Though they paused to investigate the picked clean carcass of a stringy old chicken, Cambion continued on, seeking a basement to an abandoned smithy. Following the pungent stench of brimstone, he found his prey, squatting in the cellars, devouring a foul lump decomposing flesh of unknown origin. Dubrub, a toad-boggart, one of the lowest forms of demonic life above blaggers and breeth.

With some haggling, Cambion was able to obtain a viscous yellow-green potion made from hydra entrails from the demon, a vile slime-coated monstrosity who usually shape-shifted into the form of a genial grocer named Albert Bottomley. The potion could not undo the succubus venom coursing through Darian's bloodstream keeping him young and strong. But it could make him very ill, weak enough to return home, back to his demon paramour and back to Cambion's waiting sharpened fangs and claws.

It had not been difficult to wait until the Mechmen preparing to enter Pleasance Square were distracted or resting, coating their bullets with the toxin was easy. No one suspected a member of Her Majesty's Constabulary about his business.

34

Hardwick took the dirigible on a slow circular route above the clearer, cleaner skies above Paris, a city where all heavy industrial works were banned. Darian had slipped in and out of consciousness throughout the journey and was clearly in a bad way with a dangerously high fever. The alchemist was suffering from terrifying nightmares and vivid hallucinations but what they were remained a mystery to the others, he only raved, screamed and whimpered in Farsi. A language no one on board spoke, though Hardwick recognised some curse words the alchemist had frequently used.

Their original plan was to land in the official dirigible docking area in the spacious Parc de la Villette. But the risk of customs officials and local gendarmerie discovering a man with a serious gunshot wound and therefore possibly a felon escaping British justice was too great. Darian may have known an alternative landing point but he was either in pain-free oblivion or murmuring incoherently.

'We can't do this indefinitely, my friend,' Bartrev said in an even tone, aware that the inventor was feeling both guilty and stressed, no doubt berating himself for taking off in the *Dauntless* and putting Darian in such peril. 'He is getting worse. Would it not be better to risk the curiosity of the French authorities to get him urgent medical help?'

Hardwick nodded, the Russian nobleman was right of course. If he felt bad now, how could he live with Darian's death caused by his indecision?

'Bartrev, as always everything you say makes sense. Reggie, could you do your best make your patient as comfortable as possible, we are going in to land in the official park.'

'Bugger that!' the alchemist's weak but coherent oath startled the others, 'Head for the Avenue Foch, Palace de Dauphine and the private dock of the Princess Cosenza.'

The sudden interjection of reality exhausted him and Darian sank back onto his pillows, once more in a fevered trance.

The Princess Cosenza, formally Lady Arabela Grayshott, formally Miss Libby Jenks, successful, wealthy adventuress, one time travelling companion of Lady Athena Hardwick and occasional bed mate of Darian's. Despite his delirium, it was a sensible suggestion. The pretty little minx was made from the same mould as Darian, a shameless, untrustworthy outsider who exploited the foibles of society for her own ends. She would most definitely take him in.

The final stage of the journey was uneventful, the city's gracious new layout and reasonably clear skies made navigation easy and the *Dauntless* touched down safely at the Palace's airship dock, surrounded by its large, formal gardens. Situated in one of Paris's most exclusive districts, the palace like others in the street, had high walls and tall, metal gates to keep the city's riff-raff separated from its most wealthy inhabitants. A perfect place to keep a low profile, no nosy official would dream of making waves among such influential inhabitants.

Libby had done well for herself – again. Hardwick wondered who the next besotted fool would be, he doubted being a princess of minor Italian royalty would be enough for her restless ambition. As he closed down the airship's engines, a few servants from the palace household were already standing in a formal line ready to greet their visitors and attend to their needs. Hardwick hoped this meant Libby must be at her extravagant new home, for she would recognise the *Dauntless* from past escapades. Hopefully she was alone. He remembered encountering her ailing, aging husband, a man of great arrogance and seething jealousy. Not one who would welcome four much younger men arriving at his palace.

As Hardwick alighted first, the lady herself ran to greet him. Other than her glamorous Worth-designed silk gown and array of new sparking diamonds, she was the same impish beauty he'd last seen in Italy on the arm of an elderly and frail widowed prince. Avaricious little she-devil that she was, Hardwick could not help liking her. In fact, everyone liked her, she had the rare gift to dazzle and charm men and women alike. Men wanted to protect her, women wanted to be her friend.

'Miles, my sweet darling friend. How wonderful to see you again so soon. Where is Athena? We have so much ladies gossip to catch up on.'

Embarrassed, Hardwick was relieved to see her interest switch instantly to Count Bartrev as he alighted from the dirigible, saving him the trouble of making some excuse for abandoning Athena into the company of that humble industrialist and his wife. 'Princess Cosenza, may I introduce you to Count Nikolai Bartrev, exile and friend.'

Interrupting the Russian's formal bow, Reggie ran down the ramp from the *Dauntless*, 'Sorry Libby, gentlemen, but I am really worried about Cyrus ... I think we may be losing him.'

Libby gathered her skirts and outran the men into the dirigible's gondola, dropping down besides Darian.

'Poor baby, how did this happen?'

Darian was unable to answer, he had slipped into a dangerous unconscious state, his face chalk-white, bloodless.

Without taking her gaze from his stricken form, she interrogated his companions, her voice demanding from concern, 'Why is he like this? He is protected from succumbing to such sickness by the succubus bite. How long has this gone on for?'

Hardwick felt foolish, helpless, 'So sorry, Libby ...'

'The Princess Consenza to you ...'

'*Principessa, mie scuse,* my sincere apologies,' the inventor corrected, this was no time to argue niceties of protocol and there were servants within hearing range, 'he was shot two days ago by a Mechman, a flesh wound, normally of no concern.'

Bartrev continued, 'Your highness, I am a military man, well used to battlefield injuries and I can assure this was a minor wound, one Darian himself was unbothered with. Until he was overcome by this fever.'

The princess sprang back to her feet and ordered Darian's companions to carefully carry him into the palace.

'This is not a good situation for me, gentlemen. My husband is away on family business in Rome but he has left behind many of his spies … in other words, his Parisian servants. But I will not turn Cyrus away in this pitiful state.

Once outside the airship, she commanded her staff in rapid and fluent French to prepare a room for her poorly guest. She called his condition dirigible sickness, though who would believe such passing nausea would leave a man on death's door. It was clear to Hardwick, she was out of her depths, a pampered songbird trapped in a gilded cage, surrounded by jailors. But what else could they do with Darian dying before their eyes?

Libby ensured the patient was as comfortable as possible in a quiet back room, appointing two maids to assist Reggie in his care.

'I know Cyrus will not welcome the assistance of a doctor,' she remarked, stroking his fever-tousled hair, 'not with the strangeness of his metabolism. We cannot get through this alone.'

'I wish I knew what to do for the best,' admitted a crest-fallen Hardwick. 'He is always so strong, so resilient, that I have taken his immunity from illness for granted. And now this …'

His voice trailed off as the hopelessness of the situation hit home.

The princess walked away from the bedside and seeking some writing paper and a quill on a nearby bureau, began to write in a rapid, agitated hand.

'We are fortunate in one thing. There is another visitor here in Paris who knows and loves Cyrus. A woman with an exotic past and great knowledge of the world and its strange ways.'

She handed Hardwick the paper, 'This is the address and location of the Rani. Seek her now and plead for Cyrus's life.'

Hardwick's mind raced, could this Rani also be Darian's paramour, the Lady?

'I know wot yer thinkin' Lawd 'ardwick and the answer is no,' Libby broke into his puzzled thoughts, her voice slipping into her original Cockney accent, 'this laidee is all 'uman. Now stop bloody wasting time and find her!'

35

Too lost in their own thoughts, Hardwick and Bartrev were not concentrating on their route through Paris in one of the princess's fine landaus, drawn by four pure white Arab stallions. The red velvet upholstery and gilded fittings meant nothing to them, trapped in a foreign country with Darian close to death.

Expecting to meet a gracious aristocrat in a gilded sari surrounded by servants and residing on her luxury ocean-going yacht, to their astonishment, the carriage drew up alongside an abandoned and derelict wharf.

'This cannot be the right place,' Hardwick announced, 'the driver has made a serious mistake. Libby told us to meet a Rani, what would an Indian queen be doing in such a dreadful location?'

Bartrev, as all Russian noblemen spoke fluent French, alighted from the carriage and questioned the driver before returning to his companion. 'Sorry my friend, but it appears we do have the correct address. Gaston told me we must head down to the river side and seek out a brown –painted warehouse still in use. He told me to follow the sound of metal work and unladylike oaths.'

With the mystery deepening, the two men left the carriage and walked through the broken glass and twisted metal debris strewn across the wharf until they reached the dock on the Seine. The only craft moored there were a couple of rusting hulks, stripped of anything of value. All the buildings were in a sorry state of decay, windows gone, metal rusting and wooden sides rotting. A thin wind blew dust and scraps of yellowed paper around the broken stone cobbles. What woman – aristocratic or not would want to spend a minute in such a bleak place?

They soon had their answer. As the driver suggested, a vile oath voiced by a female in some unknown language rang out from the only building that seemed halfway viable. At least it still had windows and a roof. Puzzled, the two men walked towards the warehouse, pausing as a slim, but unmistakably female, figure stepped out of the only entrance, clad in an engineer's overall suit, a blow lamp in hand, a large wrench tucked into a wide leather belt and eyes hidden by green glass and brass goggles. On seeing that she had visitors, the woman pulled the goggles away from her face, revealing young, beautiful features marred by copious smears of engine oil. Alarmed by the intrusion, she also produced a curious and complicated-looking weapon from her belt which she aimed at their heads.

'The woman of your dreams,' whispered Bartrev with a grin.

Hardwick silenced him with a glare, this was not time for levity. They were being threatened by some sort of augmented pistol wielded by a clearly deranged female. Why else would she abandon womanly dress and seemly female nature to indulge in the indecorous machinations of the working man?

'Madam,' the Russian was first to break the uneasy standoff, 'we mean you no harm but were told this was where we could seek audience with the Rani. Is your mistress close by?'

The young woman removed her goggles and head-gear revealing a glorious tumble of bright copper hair. With her dark gold skin and vivid, large green eyes, she was a remarkable beauty, most likely of mixed race. The musical lilt in her speech suggested origins in the Indian subcontinent.

'First, who in damnation are you? And who the hell sent you?'

No lady then, Hardwick confirmed to himself at the shock of her course language reached his offended ears …

'Our business is only with the Rani,' he announced in a pompous attempt to gain authority, 'so be about your business and let her know Sir Miles Hardwick and Count Nikolai Bartrev are here to speak to her.'

'Ah, Hardwick,' she replied with a dismissive shrug, 'Cyrus Darian's pet inventor. Never heard of you, Count. Not that I give a stuffed fig.'

She began to walk back into the warehouse, oblivious of Hardwick's gasp of outrage. 'Oh and there is no Rani,' she announced without turning around, 'that is a nickname, Libby ... I mean Princess Consenza has labelled me with. I am Tiamat Marina Dakkar and you are trespassing on my property.'

'Tiamat, an angry Babylonian goddess of salt water and chaos ... you were well-named,' murmured Hardwick backing off, hands up with his palms facing her in a gesture of surrender.

'I would not insult a lady armed with such a fearsome looking weapon,' Bartrev advised, intrigued by the young woman and Hardwick's open hostility towards her. A feisty female at home with a blow lamp and a wrench? A soul mate, surely? He was evidently not well versed in the innate snobbery and underlying misogyny of the English upper classes where women were meant to know their place and keep to it.

'I'll speak to Darian, but not his lackeys,' she added as a parting shot before disappearing into her warehouse, firmly shutting and locking the doors behind her.

'Well, that put us in our place,' Bartrev said, suppressing a desire to laugh at the inventor's expression of outrage, colouring his cheeks with a florid blush.

'Cyrus is welcome to that shameless, little hoyden,' Hardwick grumbled, returning to the carriage, 'if he pulls through.'

On their return to the palace, they were met not by the usual retinue of fawning servants but by a tearful and distraught Libby who could see the concern in their eyes at her appearance.

'Please, do not be concerned, Cyrus is still with us ... just. But you must all leave now for your own safety and for mine.'

Gathering up her trailing silk skirt and petticoats, she ran up the many sweeping stairs and through the endless corridors to reach the suite of rooms where Darian lay. Puzzled, the two men followed close behind. Once safely inside, she closed and locked the doors, beckoning Reggie over to join them.

'My husband's servants in Paris work purely for their salary and have no abiding old family loyalty to the House of Consenza or to me. I can trust only Nora, my personal maid and friend from London. This morning, she overheard the others plan to report your arrival to the French and Russian embassies in return for generous rewards. Nora's ploy to pretend not to speak French or Italian has served me well in the past.'

She gave a sorrowing glance to where a gaunt and fever-stricken Darian lay, 'You have to leave and take him with you. Today ... No, now.'

'Impossible,' pleaded Reggie, 'he is barely hanging on to life as it is.'

'Don't you think I know that,' cried Libby wringing her hands in anguish, 'but what else can I do? My husband would throw me out on the street, penniless, at the first whiff of scandal.' Gesturing to her surroundings and jewellery, she added, 'I've worked too hard to get all this.'

She walked over to Darian and stroked his hair with genuine affection, 'I do not understand why he is so ill. That bullet must have been coated with some noxious substance. Bruxa's bite made him so strong but that poison is stronger. I hate myself for doing this but my only comfort is he would do the same to me in a heartbeat.'

'I'll help you get the *Dauntless* ready,' Bartrev said to the inventor, eager to put some distance between himself and the Tsar's persistent agents, 'I do not think it will make much difference to Darian whether he recovers here or on the craft.'

Libby sank down on a settle and wept into her kerchief, 'You cannot leave in the airship. Not today. Some of the staff have sabotaged it, to prevent you from leaving before the authorities get here.'

'Then we are trapped like rats,' Reggie was perilously close to outright panic.

'I told you to seek the Rani,' pleaded Libby, 'she can get you all out of Paris from right under your enemies' noses.'

Hardwick's laugh was cold and laden with bitterness, 'A highly unlikely scenario, *Princess*, that tempestuous little madam would not give us the time of day let along assistance. Anyway, I have no intention of abandoning the *Dauntless*.'

Libby stood up and summoned the inner core of steel that had made her such a successful adventuress, turning her from common streetwalker to a princess living in gilded palaces around Europe.

'The *Dauntless* is no longer here,' she announced and waited for the inevitable resulting furore to settle before continuing, 'as soon as I found out she had been damaged, I had her canopy deflated and hired a heavy draught wagon and crew to take the craft straight to the Rani's dockyard. It should have reached there by now. Your airship awaits you, *Lord* Hardwick.'

The princess leant down and kissed Darian on the lips then walked with a purposeful stride to the door, 'I want you all to leave now, Gaston is waiting with an old carriage. Everyone in Paris knows my white Arabians.'

This was too much for Reggie, already tipping over the edge into complete fright. 'So that is your plan, Libby. Scupper our escape and deliver us to an ambush. I know what will be waiting at that dockyard and it won't be the *Dauntless*. I suspect you have been paid well.'

In a frantic scramble, he gathered up his hat, coat, cane and bag and made for the door, 'I do not need to be involved in all this. I am not a wanted man, anywhere. I have done nothing wrong. I can step out and find a way home from Paris.'

'Anyone leaving the palace will be under surveillance,' Libby replied, 'you'll not get far on foot ... but it is up to you. You are not my prisoner.'

Bartrev gave the magician a reassuring pat on the shoulder, 'Maybe you would be safer with us, my friend. I have successfully escaped the clutches of the Tsar and his cohorts for some time. I see no reason for that not to continue.'

The Russian then turned to Libby, 'Why should we trust this *Rani*? And how on God's good earth can she get us out of Paris unseen?'

Libby's anxiety was growing, why were these men so stubborn? They needed to leave and not hang around debating with her. 'Did you not see the Xantho? Tia has invented a subaquacraft. A ship that can move unseen beneath the waves.

36

Hardwick refused to abandon the *Dauntless* and attempt to flee Paris by other means. He decided to accept Libby's assurance that there was no waiting ambush of gendarmes or Russian agents at the abandoned docks. He agreed to be smuggled out of the Palace and into horse-drawn transport, parked by Gaston some streets away. The rarer steam driven vehicles always drew curiosity from onlookers. Reluctantly with no better plan, Bartrev and Reggie had to go along with the inventor. Any plan, however farfetched, was better than none.

Wearing well-worn and dirty working man's clothing smuggled in by Libby's maid, Hardwick and Bartrev placed the unconscious alchemist's arms around their shoulders and carried him through the narrow, secret corridors, an escape route known only to the aristocratic owners of the palace. No one alive remembered the French Revolution at first hand, but the tales of the old horrors ran deep in the minds of all Parisians. No more so those of the new nobility created in the now overthrown French Second Empire.

Reaching the street from a basement in an alleyway, Hardwick recognised Gaston's dour, lined face. He no longer wore the smart dark green livery of the House of Consenza but a frayed draught driver's coat and floppy hat pulled down over his eyes. The carriage was little more than a glorified open farm wagon pulled by a pair of aging, sway-backed Ardennes mares. Nothing that would draw any undue attention on the busy streets of Paris. As carefully and discreetly as they could, the men placed a blanket-wrapped Darian on the floor. Reggie took off his coat and folding it, used it to cushion Darian's head and with a sharp crack of the driver's whip, the old mares trotted off towards the Seine.

On arrival at the dock, unsurprisingly, they saw Tiamat

Dakkar standing in front of a cumbersome dray vehicle pulled by four heavy horses, berating the nonplussed driver and grooms, waving a letter in their faces.

'The lady is not best pleased,' murmured Bartrev with a rueful grin, 'I have drawn the short straw again to try to make peace with her.'

'I have never regretted my inability not to speak anything but the Queen's English,' Hardwick replied with a grin of his own, 'and this encounter with that tigress confirms I was right.'

Bartrev leapt from the wagon and approached the female engineer with his palms open in a gesture of appeasement. She was in no mood to be polite.

'I take it you know about the princess's outrageous demand of me? To transport a gaggle of strangers and this pile of junk out of France in my ship?'

'That was the idea,' Bartrev confirmed, 'and this is not something we would have gone along with if it was not from great need and urgency.'

Tia paced the dock, kicking at any debris in her way before returning to the Russian nobleman. 'And did I not say I would not speak to anyone other than Cyrus Darian in person?'

'You are welcome to try, he is in that shabby excuse for a carriage.'

The woman strode over to the vehicle and gasped in shock on discovering Darian lying on the filthy carriage floor. She climbed in and cradled his head in her lap. Hardwick sighed, did every female they encountered have to be a past conquest of the wretched man?

'How long has he been like this?'Tia demanded, her green eyes flashing in anger.

'Days,' Reggie replied, 'and far too many days. Whatever brought him to this sorry state is not natural. Cyrus is too strong to succumb to normal ailments. I'm worried to distraction that he will not overcome this.'

The woman glanced up at Reggie, 'Whoever you are, I like you. The others, well …'

Her voice tailed off, as she considered her options. It would be simpler and safer to just take in this earnest young man and Darian, leave the others and their dirigible to take their chances. A weak groan from the stricken man cut off her thoughts, Darian had regained consciousness.

'Is that you ... little Tia?' Darian's eyes flickered open, struggled to focus, he spoke a few words further, addressing her in a flow of rapid Hindi, leaving the others nonplussed.

'Yes, it is I, Cyrus, all grown up and full of concern at the terrible state of you,' she replied in English, wiping away a stray tear as he sunk back into the dark world of fevered delirium.

Though still anxious about his continued poor health, Hardwick was relieved, this girl was not a conquest after all but it appeared Tia was once a child of the alchemist's acquaintance. Damn the man for all his many secrets, how could he have not mentioned such a remarkable, if annoying, female before?

'Carry him into my warehouse straight away,' she commanded Reggie and Gaston, 'you, Hardwick and the big Russian. I want you to supervise unloading your big bag of wind in there. The sooner you are all out of sight, the safer we will all be.'

It was clearly not prudent to object to her demands and the men obeyed her without question, visibly relieved when the carriages departed, their handlers, including the dour Gaston, rewarded with more gold and the big doors closed behind them. They soon realised Tia lived in her workshop. One section was furnished as gracious living quarters and she directed Reggie to carry the alchemist to her own bed. The mahogany four poster was draped with long swathes of gold embroidered sari fabric in vivid jewel colours of red, fuchsia and pink hues, further embellishing her exotic Eastern origins.

'The princess gave me much appreciated financial help for my project to build the Xantho but she has too much faith in its progress. The ship is not finished and it has no crew.'

Tia's announcement was not the news they wanted to hear.

'Can we not be your crew?' Hardwick suggested, desperation in his voice, 'Just to get us away from Paris ...'

The woman did not answer, too concerned over Darian.

Frowning in intense concentration, she boiled up a kettle of hot water, poured the steaming contents into an earthenware jug and added drops of pungent tinctures from a selection of blue poison bottles from a crowded shelf.

'Kill or cure,' she said, adding to their anxiety. 'Whatever has got hold of him needs complete purging from his system. Young man,' she addressed Reggie, 'I hope you are not squeamish, your role as nursemaid is about to get a great deal worse.'

Young man? She was considerably younger than him, a mere slip of a girl barely out of her adolescence. Optimistically expecting the young woman or one of her maids to take over nursing Darian, Reggie nodded in resigned acceptance of his role in an adventure he'd found himself embroiled with. Tia kissed Darian's forehead then turned her attention to the inventor and the Russian.

'If Cyrus had you on his payroll, Hardwick, I suppose you must be a reasonable engineer. I do not know what you can do, Count Bartrev but you look half intelligent for a Russian serf master. Come with me ...'

Bartrev did not bother correcting her, serfdom had been abolished a decade or more before in his mother Russia, indeed he found Tia's impudent manner amusing. Unlike the poor, confused Hardwick, raised in a strict society where no youngsters would be so confrontational and disrespectful to their elders and betters.

Once back in the warehouse, Tia pulled down a large brass lever which engaged a steam powered generator, powerful enough to send vibrations through the floor. The thrum and pounding hammer of mighty pistons engaging was sweet music to Hardwick's ears and for the first time since leaving England he found himself smiling in appreciation.

'Think that sounds impressive, wait until you see my darling Xantho,' the young woman declared, knowing the subaquacraft would astonish them.

Pulling another lever, the floor beneath the *Dauntless* slowly lowered on hydraulic chains into a lit chamber beneath.

'That is your windbag safely stored in the hold, it just about fits. Now it is time to introduce you to the lady herself.'

She led them to a corridor unseen by the outside world by a secret panel hiding a pneumatically sealed brass door and took them down a steeply sloping passage. It was purely functional with damp, concreted walls and dimly lit by a line of basic gaslights but it opened up to an underground world of wonder. Hardwick all but swooned in astonishment as he walked into a cavernous chamber and saw huge glass panels keeping it safe from the muddy waters of the Seine. He had no idea glass sections could be manufactured so large and so strong.

It was only when he neared the windows did Hardwick notice there was a vessel beneath the surface of the river at the other side of the panes. His hand hit his forehead as he struggled to believe his eyes, at the size of a large craft, her metal sides covered in curving mirrors that hid her from the prying world by sophisticated camouflage. A clever ruse, using the reflections of the surrounding water to hide her from the casual observer. Extraordinary, miraculous, the Xantho was sleek and elegant, a thing of great beauty. Hardwick was in total awe of her craftsmanship and the genius of her inventor.

'You could not have done this ...' Hardwick murmured. 'At least not alone.'

Predictably, Tia bristled at his words, what a pompous, condescending and typical male. 'I will have you know, the Xantho is all my own design,' she bit back with great pride. 'Of course I had to have sections of her structure manufactured elsewhere. The mirror glass and power system were invented by my father. But the design and construction of her workings and controls are all mine.'

37

While his companions discovered the wondrous subaquacraft, Reggie Dunne discovered Tia's predictions over the effect of the tinctures were not exaggerated. In horror, he did his best to keep Darian clean while his body convulsed in one messy flux after another. Reggie could see the distress and humiliation on the alchemist's dulled eyes but there was nothing he could do but murmur soothing words and deal with the outpourings as quickly and efficiently as possible. Tia's exquisite bedroom now looked like a battlefield hospital, with filthy and bloodied sheets strewn around the floor.

Would this ever ease? No mortal however strong could survive this brutal purging for long. Ten minutes later he had his answer, Darian doubled over and tried to vomit but there was nothing left. He collapsed back on the sweat-rumpled, ruined silk sheets with a low groan and closed his eyes. Resting or dead? Reggie forced back his panic as he reached for Darian's wrist to seek a pulse ... struggling to find any recognisable throb. Nor could he feel any heartbeat. The magician ran to Tia's dressing table and found a small, gilt-backed mirror, returning to hold it close to Darian's mouth. After what seemed an eternity, a slight mist confirmed his patient was still alive, but only just.

Reggie sank onto a nearby chair, wiping his forehead with the last clean piece of linen, his own kerchief. There was nothing more he could do but wait. Exhausted by his efforts, the magician feel into a deep, dreamless slumber in the chair.

'I do not think they sound too friendly, old chap ...'

Startled awake by the sound of furious hammering and Darian's voice, Reggie leapt from his chair. Someone was trying to break into the warehouse, his mind whirled as he strove to concentrate and shake off the remnants of heavy sleep. This was bad, very bad. He could not understand what the intruders were saying but he recognised the language ... Russian. They'd been found by the Tsar's ruthless agents. He hauled Darian to his feet, an easy move as the sickness had stripped his lean frame of all surplus weight. Reggie dragged his patient to the cargo pit, the only open aperture to Tia's underground world and bellowed for help.

Praying his companions had heard him, Reggie winced in fear at the sound of battering hammers and axes assaulting the warehouse door. It was stoutly made but nothing could withstand such a battering for long.

His heart skipped a beat at the sound of someone approaching, had the bastards found another way in? He spun around to see the others running from a door in the warehouse wall ... an escape route?

'Your highness,' a determined and curt Tia addressed Bartrev, 'help Reggie take him down to the lower chamber and your lordship, help me close up all the doors and hide the evidence of my occupation. I want them to discover nothing more than a near derelict warehouse.'

'We do not have much time,' said Hardwick stating the obvious, splinters of the warehouse door already fell inwards from the assault.

'Then I suggest we run,' Tia snapped, already sprinting to disguise her workshop and living areas behind cleverly wrought false walls. Remembering how she operated the winch system, Hardwick was able to close up the cargo bay and grabbing an old hessian sack swept dust and debris over the floor. He noticed she had opened up a nondescript wide door at the back of the warehouse that led only to the docks outside, a simple, clever ruse suggesting they had already escaped.

'That will have to do, now run for your life.'

Hardwick needed no encouragement, head down he sprinted beside her through the last remaining open door as the first section of warehouse door was breached. Once inside, he helped her turn a large brass wheel connected to an array of cogs and levers that sealed up the door and pulled more camouflaging wall in front of it. Only the most perceptive observer would discover the secrets behind the decrepit warehouse walls but there was no time for complacency. Whoever was battering down the outer door meant serious business. None of them had done anything to engage so much interest from the French authorities. It had to be the Russians.

Tia gave a little smile of pride as she witnessed the magician go weak at the knees in astonishment, first at the chamber and then at the craft. Creating the Xantho, named after one of the Sea God Neptune's daughters had been a secret project for so long and one that must continue to be unknown to the world but she had to admit to enjoying sharing her masterpiece with these men, all outsiders to normal society like her. Not trustworthy maybe but far more so than any so-called honest men.

They were safe beneath the river for now but it was time to break the bad news. Tia cleared her throat and made her announcement.

'Gentlemen and Cyrus. This may be as far as we can get. The Xantho's drive has never been engaged or tested. She has enough minor power for lighting and a rudimentary steering system and so far has been watertight but not under power or out into the rough waters of an open sea or ocean.'

'With her steering operational and the slow flow of the Seine, could we at least drift out of Paris?' ventured Hardwick, 'Then between the two of us, we can get her main engines running at Le Havre.'

A loud explosion reverberated down through the concrete from above followed by two more in quick succession. Concussion waves sent alarming cracks along the chamber roof and threatened the integrity of the glass panels. Frustrated at not cornering their quarry, their enemy was destroying her warehouse. *'Bahincut,'* Tia swore violently in Hindi, she had to endure yet more loss in a short life time of losses. Hardwick was right, it was time to take her beloved Xantho on her maiden voyage whatever the outcome. Trapped in this sanctuary turned burial chamber, they had no choice but to try.

As she operated the mechanism to unseal the airlock leading to the Xantho, another resounding explosion sent a lump of concrete crashing from the roof, allowing a pall of choking, oily black smoke to invade the chamber. The shock wave from the blast created an ominous crack down one of the glass panels, a trickle of water already seeping through the fissure. With seconds left before that trickle became a flood, Tia could do no more than wait. As the door finally swung free with a wheeze of hydraulics and grinding of engaging cogs the adventurers rushed through, with no time to reseal the door behind them. The window panel gave way in a sharp crack of shattering glass and with river water surging towards them, they threw themselves into the Xantho, dragging Darian along like a broken marionette. Grateful for Hardwick's help, Tia closed the doors with just a sluice of cold, dirty water getting through.

She busied herself starting up the auxiliary power to release the docking cables and unwind the Archimedes screw anchor fixing the craft firmly to the river bed, it was too heart-breaking to witness the destruction of her workshop and only home. The Xantho was now all she had left in the world.

With the subaquacraft appearing watertight and now brightly lit by curious glowing tubes emitting a warm yellow light, her passengers could see how beautiful the Xantho was and what a miracle of modern technology, putting the *Dauntless* into shade in comparison.

'Stunning,' Hardwick gasped overawed. 'Simply stunning.' He struggled to take in all the ingenious design, the sinuous grace of her form, the richly polished wood and brass fittings of her panelled interior and wide screen of curved glass at her helm. Objects of beauty and great antiquity and occasional use of stained glass panels in luscious, rich shades of the sea completed the exquisiteness of her interior décor. But Hardwick's main interest lay in what propelled her, what manner of engine and power source kept the miracle of the Xantho water tight, full of breathable air and moving beneath the surface of the river.

Settled in one of the sleeping chambers, Darian awoke and to Reggie's relief, the alchemist's curious eyes had some of their old sparkle back. Reggie propped up some pillows allowing his patient to sit up unaided while he explained where they were and narrated the nerve wracking flights from the Consenza palace and underground as Tia's warehouse exploded around them.

'So this beautiful marvel is the Xantho, eh? Tia is most definitely her father's daughter. I bet Miles is the darkest shade of green possible'

Reggie gave an impudent smile as he nodded agreement, 'A green so dark it could be mistaken for black.'

Darian tried to laugh but it turned into a choking cough, he accepted a glass of water, his throat was a raw mixture of ash and fire as if he had tried to inhale the burning air above a volcano. As he settled back onto his pillows, Darian became aware of his condition, growling in disgust and humiliation at the state of his sweat-soaked and filthy clothes.

'So sorry, Cyrus, I changed you so often, I ran out of clean clothes and I also did my best to keep you clean but Tia said we needed to purge the poison from your body to save you. There was so much ...'

Darian took the magician's hand and gave it a firm squeeze of gratitude, 'Thank you my friend. There are few if any humans who would do that for me. But I need to ask one more favour ...'

'Of course,' Reggie answered, the worse was over and his patient had beaten the odds, 'if it is within my power.' It was always prudent to add a caveat when it came to Darian.

'Can you find me some decent clothes?'

38

Lady Luck was once again on their side though the fugitives doubted this beneficence could last much longer. An uneventful short voyage brought them to the outskirts of Le Havre, the ship utilising the steady but gentle flow of the Seine. Tia was able to bring the Xantho close to an abandoned small fishing village, the harbour recently destroyed by a massive storm. Anchoring off shore and close enough to the surface, Reggie and Bartrev disembarked in a small dinghy to seek out food supplies and fresh clothing for all the men.

While Darian stayed on board to recover, Hardwick and Tia laboured on the mechanics of the craft's new engine, a task made difficult as the mistress of the subaquacraft refused to say what fuelled the Xantho's mighty heart. Tia knew she had divulged far too much already but this was something she was determined to keep secret, following in her father's footsteps. Like him, Tia had decided the modern world was not ready to have such a power source, one which they would inevitably misuse for war. Something he had a great abhorrence for.

So devastating was the coastal storm, which destroyed many harbour-side homes and taken lives, no one in the locality had returned to the site of such cruel destruction. Anything worth salvaging had already gone. For now at least, the Xantho remained unseen on the surface, long enough to be well stocked up and the engine started up on two successful trial runs. Determined not to push their run of good fortune to breaking point, Tia released the great craft and took her into the deep water of the English Channel.

At first there was tension and silence, as the craft entered the turbulent waters. Tia stood at her helm, a slight figure, hands gripping the wheel too tightly with concentration. The Xantho idled at first, veering at the whim of strong currents and under tows, her steering basic only on auxiliary power. Tia took in a deep breath, steeling herself for the big decision, should she engage the main drive? What would happen? It was now or never.

Cyrus approached, put his arm around her waist with the familiarity born of long acquaintance since her childhood days. 'Her heart is like yours, Tia *mere kimati*, strong, young and fearless. It will not fail ... let us see what this beauty can do.'

Grateful for the dubious yet still reassuring presence at her side, Tia pulled down the great central lever that triggered the Xantho's main engine to come on line. The ship paused as if drawing breath, then pounded with vibrations from its massive pistons, truly like the deep, drumming heartbeat of a leviathan, a giant of the open oceans. She surged forward, her speed beneath the waves phenomenal, causing Darian to whoop with exhilaration. He could hear cheers of glee from Hardwick and Bartrev echoing up from the engine room. Even the nervous Reggie joined the excitement, clapping and dancing with relief and delight.

Once safe from detection, Tia secured the Xantho on her deep sea anchor and joined the men as they sat down for an evening meal in a candlelit galley to celebrate the success of the subaquacraft's first undersea journey. Again, the décor was luxurious and reflected Tia's Indian connections. The plates and cutlery were pure gold, part of a hoard from a shipwreck in the Caribbean. Tia explained they were from the Spanish treasure ship, *Espiritu de Curacao*, on a homeward voyage from the Americas, brought down by a rather over enthusiastic pirate captain who'd been too robust with his cannon fire.

'His loss, my gain,' she smiled, raising a beautiful, emerald studded gold goblet in a toast to her new companions once again clad in clothes befitting their status. Cyrus had baulked at the boring cut and traditional style of his new outfit but was slightly mollified by being the only one decked out in an expensive silk and wool mix.

'So, gentlemen, what happens next? Do you wish to be taken to Dover?'

Their silent lack of enthusiasm for her suggestion was all the answer she needed. They were on a mission, a dangerous one from the close encounter with ruthless Russian agents. Tia was intrigued and wanted to be involved. 'I take that as a no, then,' she remarked. 'So, where do you fine gallants want to go?'

Darian reached over and kissed her hand, 'Tia, *mere thora priya,* is there any chance you could give us a lift to Russia?'

'I suspect you could persuade *your little darling*, but first Cyrus, I want to know why you have half the Tsar's secret services on your tail and why are you going to Russia?'

She took a deep swig of ruby red wine before fixing Darian with a cool, knowing gaze. 'And don't bother lying to me or it is a long, cold swim home.'

Darian related the wild tale, starting with inheriting the ghost army from the last dying moments of the Technomicron and the need to find the Bane of Souls in Russia. If she thought it strange Count Bartrev had arrived in the alchemist's life with intimate knowledge of the very curious object he needed, she kept quiet. The man seemed straightforward enough but her short time alone in the world taught her to distrust people on sight. This had kept her safe but lonely. Ironically, the only man she could trust was Darian because he was so devious. At least he never disappointed her.

Reggie waited until Darian finished narrating their adventure so far, still uncertain why he was now part of it, before posing what seemed an obvious question. 'Count Bartrev's estate is deep inland, right in the middle of nowhere. How can we reach there in the subaquacraft? Unless the Xantho has the power of flight?'

Bartrev laughed, giving the startled magician a hearty pat on the shoulder, 'My dear Reggie, worry not. This lovely vessel will be able to navigate through the Turkish Straits into the *Chornoye more,* what you call the Black Sea and onto Russia along the mighty Dnieper river.'

The Count raised his wine glass towards Tia, 'And with this extraordinary young lady's expert navigating and a helping of good luck on our side, we will travel undetected right under the Tsar's long nose.'

Tia joined him in the toast, 'To adventure and a filthy pox on the Tsar.'

The others raised their glasses with less enthusiasm. They were heading for open seas in a new, untested craft to go into the heartland of Bartrev's mortal enemies. To a strange, hostile land where time had stood still and where new technology would be regarded as bizarre and demonic. This would not be plain sailing.

As if to reinforce their fears, a loud klaxon screamed warning sending everyone leaping to their feet. Tia grabbed the tool belt hanging on the back of her chair. 'She's sprung a leak, nothing to concern yourselves about. I'll soon knock her back into shape.'

39

They waited for him in the courtyard of the newly built Chelsea Barracks, seeming oblivious to the summer rain storm that battered them with sharp hail while above apocalyptical thunder and savage lightning raked the skies. Twenty young men, all clerics in various stages of their journey to priesthood, now nominally soldiers for Prime Minister Bowring's crusade against the occult.

Relaxing inside, enjoying the comfort of the officers' mess hall, the new squad's leader, Major Stroude enjoyed another strong cup of tea and a plate of his favourite Cornish Fairing biscuits. He'd spent a pleasant time reading a copy of the latest *Morning Post* which now lay folded on the table. No mention of missing occultists which was to be expected. Their lives were secretive, solitary and most would not be missed.

He had remained in the dry for over two hours while his men stood to attention during the height of the storm. A toughening up exercise, one to test their mettle and discipline, things they would need in the months to come. Taking his time, he finished the last of the ginger based treats and strode out to talk to his men.

Ignoring the lashing sting of the hail and rain, a last feeble attempt of old forces to disrupt his cause, Major Stroude glanced along the line of rain-drenched yet still fervent young men – his hand-picked soldiers of God – and smiled with pride at his achievement in a matter of weeks. That idiot of a Prime Minister had chosen him badly, the man expected Stroude's agents to destroy all discovered magickal objects on sight? It would not happen. Nothing that could potentially help protect the Queen and the Empire would be lost.

Stroude's squad knew and understood this. All had to swear a solemn oath of secrecy on the Bible when first recruited. Any that showed signs of wavering were immediately cut from the training program. Many had fallen by the wayside but it left the major with a small but elite corps of fanatics: young men who had already proven their mettle with nightly raids on addresses throughout London. Swiftly and efficiently using the element of surprise, they had captured many of the capital's most notorious and powerful mages.

Now housed in a remote prison on Dartmoor, any attempts at escape by these sorcerers using malicious magickes was prevented by the use of holy relics and prayer and the robust guarding of Stroude's armed men with instructions to shoot to kill anyone foolish enough to break free. The major saw no moral dilemma over this order. The security of the country and empire was under threat from these dabblers in unnatural practises. They had forfeited the right to be treated like a law abiding citizen.

To add to the occultists defeat, their goods had been seized and taken to a Fenland convent under the supervision of their Abbess. If she had a name, Stroude was yet to discover it. He learnt the other nuns addressed her as *Mother Superior*. The major would call her *ma'am*. If that term was good enough to address the Queen of England, it must be sufficiently respectful to some cloistered female. A stern, taciturn female by all accounts who did not suffer fools or mistakes. It would not be pleasant to cross her when the time came. Which it would.

It was Stroude's desire that many more schemers and dabblers in the occult would join their fellows in the jail, a dank, bleak building in an even more bleak setting. The moors were a wilderness, dangerous with hidden crevices, bogs that could swallow a man swifter than quicksand and weather that could kill from exposure within minutes.

To Stroude's annoyance, his greatest prize still eluded him. Cyrus Darian had survived an unauthorised, botched assassination attempt and the disastrous failed siege by the useless Mechmen. The major had survived the near disaster of the stricken commercial airship and watched on the ground in helpless fury, surrounded by the resulting wreckage of the Nellie as Darian fled the country with a group of adventurers.

His only comfort was that the alchemist had not taken his ghosts with him, leaving Stroude with hope he would one day gain control over them. The continuing presence of the wraiths did nothing to calm the frayed nerves of the people of London or the Prime Minister's temper. The spectres remained, though no longer blocking the entrance to Pleasance Square.

None of the householders in the square returned home save one doughty old dowager and her two timid Indian maid servants. A survivor of the Siege of Cawnpore during the Indian Mutiny in 1857, Lady Blunt-Hoare was not going to let a gathering of apparitions permanently drive her from her home.

Stroude could afford to be patient, the man never stayed away from London for long. The capital was like a lodestone to the alchemist, always drawing him back to its seething pit of intrigue and mixed fortunes.

By the time Stroude had finished his mission, Darian's London would have disappeared, all contamination from the occult purged from its streets. A brave new London with no ghosts, demons ... or alchemists. An honourable capital from where the British Empire would spread out and flourish, going boldly from strength to strength until the whole world lived under its beneficent guidance. There was nothing so noble, so chivalrous, and so God fearing than an Englishman, the ignorant savages of the world would show nothing but gratitude for the great gift of enlightenment and citizenship of the Empire.

Another sky-raking bolt flashed across the afternoon sky, the leaden pall of clouds turning day into night. Stroude could feel the reverberating thunder echo through his body. 'Rage all you like, nature,' he snarled to the angry heavens, 'I will have you tamed too.'

He finished his inspection of the line of young men, none had slouched or appeared dejected during their long wait for him. None showed signs of resentment or anger at their treatment. Their eyes burned only with fervour and dedication to their righteous cause. Human beings turned to well-oiled, obedient automatons by their patriotic pride and deep faith. They were perfect.

'Gentlemen, you look truly splendid. There is no greater cadre of men today under my command. You are England's finest examples of pious and brave young manhood. I am bursting with pride. What you have achieved so far has been admirable, an efficient and successful rout of our enemies.'

Stroude's words were met with further straightening of backs and the occasional quick smile of satisfaction. 'But that was the easy part of our mission. Our foe knows we exist now, the rats are scurrying underground and fleeing the city through the sewers. Some will be enlisting the assistance of demonic beings to thwart us. It will get brutal, there will be casualties among our rank.'

He looked along the line of young men, none had wavered, if anything looking more determined. Good.

'I have a short and seemingly easy mission, but one that could be ambushed by the forces of evil and darkness. I will need four volunteers.'

As one, every man took a step forward in unnerving unison.

40

Tia's enchanting and impudent presence was difficult at first for the gentlemen on board the Xantho. Feisty, beautiful and clad in her boyish garb that only accentuated her slender, lithe figure, it would take some time to get used to her free-spirited nature. They were men accustomed to the fairer sex clad in protective layers of skirts, petticoats, bustles and decorum. Even the racier company they'd enjoyed in houses of ill-repute stayed clad in their undergarments at all time. Tia had only to lean across a control panel to set their pulses racing.

Darian of course had no difficulty in relaxing in the company of the Xantho's mistress. He'd known her since a dreamy doe-eyed little girl with a mighty crush on him, something he intended to shamelessly exploit on the long voyage to Russia. After all, once you have seen one shoal of darting silver fish or a giant squid pass the window, the novelty has long gone. The dangerous seduction of Tia Dakkar would pass the time most agreeably.

Yawning in boredom, Darian lay on his berth and watched another day dawn as sunlight rippled through the sea in a scintillating spectrum, igniting flashes of light on the glistening scales of fish as the subaquacraft passed through their territory. The sea's beauty was lost on an increasingly restless Darian, recovering well from the poisoning and needing some distraction.

With the vessel set fair on her course, her passengers sat down to breakfast, one usually enjoyed in relaxed near silence ... there was plenty of time during the long hours of travel ahead that day for conversation. Hardwick and Bartrev at least had the shared crewing of the Xantho to occupy them. With the alchemist on the mend, Reggie once again felt surplus to requirements on the voyage.

Amused, Darian noticed the magician's gaze turn with longing to Tia's trim form, fetching though unconventional in male dirigible aviator's garb. The tan breeches and short, brown leather coat showing off her slender but feminine curves. The young man was smitten.

Darian was not conflicted, as was expected in a man of so little conscience and absolutely no morality. Didn't they say all was fair in love and war? Reggie was old enough to make his own play for the young woman's tender affections. It was not Darian's concern that the magician was too shy and too much of a gentleman to make a move.

Nor did it matter to Darian that he'd known Tia in the past as a coltish young girl who hero-worshiped him. At the time, Darian had been old enough to be her adult brother. Her father insisted Tia call Darian, Uncle Cyrus to the alchemist's considerable dismay.

Her father had turned his back on the land and all the laws that governed mankind. But when it came to his daughter, he was as fiercely traditional as any from his cultural background. Honour was all, guarding his daughter's virtue as a precious treasure made him a dangerous man to anger. Tia's father would flay him alive and throw him into the agony of salt water and hungry crabs if Darian made a scandalous move on his precious girl's virginity.

But, the alchemist reasoned, life was precious and short, every drop of joy should be squeezed out of it like a delicious ripe fruit. Darian knew the young woman had adored him in the past, seducing her would be so easy. There was nothing so invigorating to his male ego than the eager, agile and joyous response of a lovely woman discovering erotic pleasure for the first time. He owed it to Tia to be her first lover. It was the least he could do to thank her for her assistance. Indeed, so would Reggie in time, should his infatuation with Tia be reciprocated. The young man would reap the rewards of Darian's tuition by inheriting a lover who knew how to please her man and not some teary, fearful virgin.

That morning, Darian began his campaign of seduction,

skilfully applying well used and successful tactics. The occasional glance that lingered just long enough to intrigue, the slight but compelling smile. The frisson of his hand accidently touching hers and pausing just long enough before disengaging.

His assignment did not go unnoticed. It was inevitable that Hardwick could see what was going on. The inventor had also inherited a wife *broken in* by Darian and the shame and humiliation still festered like a sore that would not heal.

Choosing a time when they were both alone, Hardwick grabbed the alchemist's arm in a tight grip and dragged him into a quiet corner of the galley.

'No, Cyrus. Not this time and not this girl.'

'Old chap,' Darian drawled, 'I have no idea why you are so animated.'

'Of course you do,' Hardwick continued, his pale face becoming flushed with anger, 'I have known you too long, so do not play games with me. You mean to have the girl, ruin her honour just for your selfish pleasure.'

'Any pleasure I take is never selfish. No lady has ever had cause to complain on that score.' Flirting with danger as ever, he added, 'the enthusiastic Athena included.'

'Insolent cur! If we were not deep under the sea, I'd call you out on that,' Hardwick thundered, rising to the alchemist's bait.

'Pistols at dawn? How very old fashioned,' Darian shook his head in amusement, 'and over what? I did not take the former Miss Dedman against her will. Quite the opposite in fact, she was on her knees on the floor begging me for it, I recall.'

Hardwick swung a punch, a wildly inaccurate haymaker that Darian was able to avoid with ease. He knew he deserved it but was still too weak and sore to take the blow and make Hardwick feel better, more of a man. Another time perhaps ... more likely not. Hardwick would get over his resentment eventually, he always had in the past. But Darian had misjudged him, today the man's anger was not so easily diffused, years of past mistreatment had reached boiling point and needed venting.

'Not this time, Cyrus. You will leave her alone, do you hear me! Tia is little more than a child, one that trusts you. I will not stand by and see her ruined. You leave her alone, you cynical, heartless bounder.'

Cyrus shrugged and gave a slight, wicked smile, 'But old chap, you know I find forbidden fruit the most delectable, the sweetest on the lips.'

He found himself pinned up against the nearest wall, one of Hardwick's hands around his throat, the other a threatening fist close against his face. The physical work of engineering had made this aristocrat's arms strong, hurt made him passionate breaking years of upbringing, the relentless conditioning to be emotionally repressed, stifled.

'So much fire,' Darian continued, as if oblivious to his precarious position. 'The delights of your honeymoon and travelling around Europe has certainly loosened your stays.' He managed to sound nonchalant, unafraid, 'Anyone would think you were not an Englishman and a gentleman.'

Hardwick growling in disgust, released the alchemist and pushed him away, 'it is precisely because I am an English gentleman that I will not soil my hands on you. You are nothing more than a thieving, foreign guttersnipe, Cyrus and always will be.'

'And Miss Tia Dakkar is captain of this fine vessel,' Darian replied, rubbing his throat, there would be bruises even his silk cravat may not disguise, 'and very much her father's daughter. A man who would brook no dissension to his command. I have no wish to become luncheon to the fish should I deny her orders.'

Hardwick's face darkened in fury again, as if that would ever happen, no doubt Tia had an unconventional upbringing but virtue for a young lady was the same whatever their background and wherever they dwelled. Before he could reply, Count Bartrev appeared and could see the signs of a heated argument ... more than that, a possible fight between the two men.

'Is everything all right?' He ventured, encased in a metal box deep beneath the sea and many miles from shore was not the ideal place for a feud. Hardwick remained, rigid with rage, fists clenched, his indignation unabated.

'My dear Bartrev,' Darian sauntered away, heading for the

nearest stiff drink, 'of course it is. We are all one happy band of adventurers, aren't we, Miles, old chap …'

'I sincerely hope so, this is neither the time or place for bad blood between us. We face a difficult expedition among many enemies, let us save any aggression for them, gentlemen.'

Bartrev doubted either men had listened to a word he'd said but he knew he had to watch the situation between them carefully. They would stand no chance of success if old allies fell out.

41

Bleak did not do justice to the landscape. Major Stroude watched the flat fenlands pass by his window as he traversed across eastern England in a first class carriage pulled by what he deemed the slowest locomotive in history. His companions, four of the best of his private army appeared equally unimpressed as field after endless field of the black, sodden soil passed by, a landscape so flat that even a wind-bent hawthorn bush seemed an interesting feature. Stroude wished he'd brought a book or a news sheet to pass the time, certainly there was no scintillating conversation with the others. Watching the tedious landscape was preferable to a religious debate.

No doubt over-awed by being with their commander, these young churchmen though dedicated were as dull as the water filling the fenland ditches that spread for miles across the gloomy landscape. Stroude knew little about the area beyond the fact that it was populated by a fiercely independent people, the fen tigers, sullen, still brooding about the forcible draining of the region from 1820 by wealthy landowners. Changes that forced the marshland to become these wide arable fields that robbed many of the wildfowlers and thatchers of their livelihoods. They were all welcome to it.

Certainly not his choice of destination to store the confiscated occult items but one chosen for its remoteness. Who would want to come here? Their destination was first the market town of Wisbech then on by private coach to the little known Fursey Abbey.

'I suggest, gentlemen, we take advantage of any meagre fare on offer in the town before travelling on. I believe the nuns may well follow the ascetic life of their founder saint.'

'Should we not also follow their example?' urged Bayliss, the most earnest of the young men, 'to strengthen us against temptation.' The man glanced uneasily at the sealed boxes on the floor as if the weird and potentially dangerous objects they contained were somehow reaching out to corrupt him. Which was in truth quite likely.

Stroude sighed; he was no religious zealot but a man who loved his country and its empire with a passion that superseded all other. But he was also tired, bored and hungry. 'We need to be strong in mind and body, gentlemen, so a bowl of hot, meaty broth and a mug of ale will do no harm to our immortal souls.'

He turned back to look out of the window, nothing had changed, just identical field after field of ploughed earth waiting to burst into life, unless the drainage engines failed and the sea reclaimed its stolen territory. It was also welcome to it.

The sun had long set before Stroude and his party finally arrived at the Abbey. The young men burst into prayers for their safe deliverance. After the hearty lunches in Wisbech, which unsurprisingly all had indulged in, even Bayliss, their coach had followed a narrow, dirt road parallel to long, deep and well filled ditch. An uneasy journey as it would only take one of the carriage horses to spook to end up with the whole vehicle overturned in the deep water. Such accidents were one of the highest causes of death in the region, their dour, local coachman had been at pains to inform them with dark pleasure.

The abbey was small, ancient and built on what had once been an island of higher ground, surrounded by treacherous bogs and flooded marshland. Its dreary and dangerous location and vows of poverty from its nuns had kept it safe from the ravages of history. Now all its grounds were on dry land, it remained, a stubborn survivor and the only high building for miles. Stroude was grateful for the thicket of tall, old poplars that shielded it from distant view. The nuns did not want to be disturbed by straying visitors.

It was a plain, stone and wood building, very old, mostly likely a rare Anglo-Saxon survivor designed with a chapel leading off from the main body of the nunnery. Once monks had lived and toiled here but now it was the home of a secretive order of nuns.

As they approached, it was apparent the nuns had done their best to make the sombre old building as welcoming as possible. As Stroude and the others stepped through the main door of the abbey, they encountered a hallway lit by a blaze of candles, surely far more than the apparently austere nuns would normally use. Indeed, he suspected they would normally rise at daybreak and retire on sunset. Only one nun approached, a tall, slender form in her all black habit, the woman must have been beautiful once but her strict regime had left her face gaunt and lined. Her eyes were granite grey, sharply intelligent and declared a character who would not tolerate fools. Her authoritative air gave no doubt she was the formidable Abbess of Fursey.

'Welcome, Major Stroude, gentlemen. Your presence here must be brief as we do not allow males within our cloisters. I will take you to deliver the boxes into our storage area, then Mr Gomm, the coachman will take you to the nearest village for food and lodgings.'

Observing the crest-fallen expression on one of the young clerics, already exhausted from the day's long and stressful journey, the abbess continued, 'I do not mean to be inhospitable but our holy vows dictate we cannot have males staying at the Abbey, even young men of God like your companions. I cannot promise the rooms will be of the standard and comfort you are used to in London but they will be clean and the food fresh and wholesome.'

'Thank you ... er ...' Stroude struggled to find the right term of address but the nun had already moved away, moving through the corridors in that serene, floating and near silent way of the sisters. She led them down a series of winding stairs, becoming less and less well lit until they arrived in a crypt-like chamber.

'Please, I must request you turn your backs until requested not to.'

Mystified, the men obeyed, aware of the jangle of many keys and the complaining groan of something heavy opening. Once they were able to turn around, they saw an opening in the stone wall. Inside the hidden doorway they discovered a narrow, barely lit corridor, a labyrinth of unknown dimensions, a seemingly endless passage way of twists and turns, steps both down and up and branches off to dead ends. Only following the Abbess with one oil lamp and her knowledge of the route kept the men from becoming hopelessly lost. It had clearly been there for many centuries, there was no disguising the musty smell of passed ages, but Stroude was pleased to note at least it was clear of noticeable vermin. Rats were a particular loathing for the major.

'This structure is very old, ma'am. Why was it built?' Stroude ventured, fascinated by the complex corridors beneath such an insignificant little abbey.

'Our founder saint was known for his miracles both in life and death, so much so, his relics were always under threat from the rich and greedy. It is our duty to protect them as it will now be our duty to protect innocent people from the evil you have brought us.'

The Abbess led them on a long and circular route, no doubt to confuse them, finally arriving at the entrance to a claustrophobic chamber.

'Put your boxes in the centre of this room,' the Abbess announced in a grim tone, 'this malevolence will never be touched by human hand again.'

That is what you assume, Stroude thought with quiet satisfaction as they entered the secret chamber. Lit by a single, spluttering torch mounted on a wall, the Abbess and her sisters had prepared the depositary well. Every surface of the surrounding stone wall was set with crucifixes, icons and other, far older symbols against evil, a collection made of carved stone, precious metals and jewel studded wood.

A narrow inner circle surrounded the storage area, a precise circle of highly polished clear quartz inset into the stone flagstones, a curious touch of old earth magicke amongst the holy symbols. The young clerics put down the boxes where directed with a palpable sense of relief that their duty was done.

At least until next time there was an appropriated collection of occult artefacts to bring to the Abbey.

The Abbess intoned some interminable Latin prayers, ignored by Stroude and the whole transaction was over. All that long and tedious journeying for an operation lasting less than an hour.

42

Until now, the Xantho was able to cruise not far from the surface of the Atlantic Ocean, avoiding detection and close encounters with shipping by use of an ingenious device Tia called the Horizoscope that projected above the craft and was able to take a 360 degree view of the surrounding seas.

That morning, the distant skyline ahead roiled with approaching black, low clouds, growing larger at alarming speed. Even at its distance from the Xantho, she could see the clouds lit by tremendous sheets of lightning in an almost continuous light show. It was the largest storm, Tia had seen in these waters and inner alarm bells sounded a warning. For the first time on the voyage, she had to risk a deep dive, take the craft lower than the storm tossed waves and surging undercurrents.

Gathering them together, Tia warned the others that the next few hours could be dangerous, the outcome of a deeper voyage unknown. The craft had already sprung a few leaks at near surface level, which meant the pressure at a lower depth could prove catastrophic.

'How deep can the Xantho go?'

Hardwick asked, ready to help but as he expected her answer was vague, again not willing to divulge any of her ship's secrets to outsiders, most especially the English inventor. Like her father, Tia had a horror of a powerful government discovering her subaquacraft's technology and what government was greater than that of the British Empire? How much stronger, more tyrannical could it become with a fleet of vessels like the Xantho?

'She is most certainly designed to go deep enough to avoid such a fierce storm,' Tia answered, 'but like everything on this voyage, her operation under more pressure has not been tested.' Putting on a confident expression, 'But needs must, so Sir Miles, are you ready to man the engine room?'

Hardwick bowed in assent and taking the Count along to help him, left Tia at the helm. Her fingers curled around the polished wood and brass wheel, its touch still new and unfamiliar. As the Xantho surged forward, she tilted the wheel, dipping the subaquacraft's nose downwards. Too fast! The ship bucked and veered like an angry wild horse, sending its passengers and loose contents flying about within the cabins as the front of the ship tipped downwards at an acute angle. Tia felt someone step close to her back, cover her hands with his. Cyrus.

'You must be gentle yet firm with the Xantho, she is still a young virgin, unsure of her own ability and skills.'

Tia allowed him to take command of her hands, bringing the ship level once again before taking the Xantho to a deeper depth at a less sharp angle of entry and a slower speed.

'It is frightening to take a plunge into the unknown, *janu*,' Darian's voice was soothing yet erotically charged, 'sometimes it is best to ease her gently at first until the unfamiliar becomes a welcoming, pleasurable place to be. The world she was born to dwell in.'

He levelled the ship off and sent her forward through the deeper ocean, a darker world enveloped them away from the filtering light of the sun. The haunt of the ocean's leviathans and monstrous unknown forms of sea life. Her metal sides made a few groans of adjustment to the high pressure then settled. The Xantho had passed another test.

Exhausted, the makeshift crew retired to bed early, the Xantho resting at last, sea-anchored in calm, shallow coastal waters. With the men all sound asleep with the chorus of loud snoring to prove it, Darian sought out his prey. He found Tia still awake, fully dressed in her chart room. Spread before her, many maps and charts, some of great antiquity lay over a large 17th century olive wood table, taken from the admiral's quarters of a Spanish Man o' War. On hearing his approach, Tia did not look up but murmured in a sultry tone, 'Lock the door.'

Darian obeyed and stood behind her again, close enough for

her to feel his presence, his breath on the back of her neck, without touching. 'What are you searching for?'

'The answers to many questions. I have had no one to ask up until now. Not anyone I wanted to help me, that is. Questions with no answers in words but only from experience and feelings.'

'Like this?'

Darian ran his fingers down her back in a light caress, rewarded by her giggle and shiver of delight. The game was on. He paused long enough to make her crave more then did the same but with more sensuous pressure and movement. When she did not resist, he reached around and lightly stroked her neck, her youthful small, firm breasts, then down to her stomach where he lingered. Tia took his hand and guided it lower … she was a quick and eager learner. Darian allowed her to take control, not wishing to frighten her by progressing too fast, too aggressively.

At his firm but gentle touch of her most intimate secrets, she began to sigh, needing more. He pulled away, stood back.

'I think that must end today's lesson.'

Tia spun around, her vivid green eyes aglow with rising pleasure, 'Don't you dare stop, Cyrus Darian …'

He silenced her with a chaste kiss on her lips, rewarded as she parted them, hungry to experience him. Darian gave a sigh of his own pleasure, she tasted so sweet, so young, so genuine. No matter how youthful a form his shapeshifter paramour the Lady could put on, her kiss betrayed her identity and experience. A timeless supernatural being of unknown origin and form, the Lady's creations were illusion, however desirable. Tia was as fresh and lovely as an untouched dew-kissed rose bud and a better man than Darian should have backed away. Indeed, for once he tried to do the right thing. At least the appearance of the right thing.

'Tia, if we continue like this, then we will end up fucking. Your father values your virtue more than his greatest treasure. There will be consequences … most likely fatal ones for me.'

His choice of crude language was deliberate, to shake away any romantic notion of what would happen if they carried on.

She answered him by taking his face firmly in her hands and kissing him again, an even deeper, longer embrace. When he appeared to remain unresponsive, ready to disengage, her hand began its own journey of discovery, finding him hard and ready. Though innocent herself of sexual congress, Tia had seen the erotic statues on temples back home, she knew what his readiness meant and had no intention of stopping.

Pretending to give in with a groan of reluctance, Darian took over the initiative again, kissing and caressing her neck and breasts until she moaned with rising delight, her body quivering with need. He lifted her onto the table, gently unbuttoning her shirt and pulling down her breeches. He took his time, almost teasing, building up her desire but not giving in to her pleading demands, allowing her to feel his heat and hardness at the soft, pliant entrance to her inner core.

Again he paused. 'We do not have to go too far, *preciosa*. I know many ways to give us both great pleasure yet leave you intact. No doctor in the world could prove otherwise.'

She put a finger on his lips to silence him and wrapping her legs tightly around his hips, pulled him closer. Her voice was low, slurring with desire, 'I may never get this chance again, I want you Cyrus. And I want you now.'

Darian could never refuse a lady and relaxing her with another long, lingering kiss, took her in one firm thrust. If Tia felt any pain, it was fleeting, she welcomed him in eagerly, pushing forward her hips to experience him deeply as possible.

Delighted by her enthusiastic response, Darian remained passive at first, the young woman was lithe, athletic, working her hips to reach her own climax in a frenzy of enjoyment until she cried out, not caring who heard, hugging his neck, her tears of joy and pleasure on his face.

'No wonder, my father's people celebrate this amazing act on their temples,' Tia gasped, laughing and crying at the same time. 'What a waste ... all these foolish Westerners believing making love is a shameful sin.'

'Luckily I am not a Westerner then,' Cyrus grinned, still hard, 'time for lesson number two.'

43

His mission had certainly brought him to some ghastly places, Major Stroude travelled alone in a brougham across bleak Dartmoor. Jennings, the driver was the only one to know his destination but not its purpose. One that would lose the major all authority with his squad should it be known. The swaying, bumping carriage crossed a wind-carved landscape so intimidating it made the fens around Fursey Abbey look like the Garden of Eden.

The team of sturdy but fleet black Friesian stallions, normally used as hearse horses were ideal for the task, battling a mean-spirited northerly wind that drove ice-spiked wind into their faces. They arched their powerful necks, dropped their noble heads against the assault and bravely trotted on. Stroude thought himself as good a judge of equines as of people. Their driver had served under Stroude in past military campaigns, proving himself loyal and valiant. Jennings asked no questions but firmly urged on the horses as they battled the elements and the harsh terrain.

That it was summer meant nothing up on Dartmoor where all four seasons could be experienced in a matter of hours. Lonely, desolate and dangerous, only the most suicidal and foolhardy would dare leave the narrow, muddy tracks that crossed it. Many who had, met their death to hyperthermia or sucked down into a quagmire, the moor was a vast unmarked graveyard of lost bones. The perfect location for a Madhouse for the criminally insane built in the 17th century and abandoned at the start of this century with the growth of more humane, official asylums. Stroude had utilised the abandoned edifice and rebuilt it to house his prisoners.

It was impossible not to be intimidated by the grey, slab of granite that rose from the moor like some temple to dark, crazed gods. Haytor House was built to be a fortress, holding in the dangerously insane and only a madman would want to escape its grim walls. Stroude read in the Madhouse records that none who had fled the institution had survived to find freedom. This made it perfect to house his unique prisoners, men who lived beyond the natural laws of God and nature.

Without the homicidal rage of the insane or weapons of the criminal, they were dangerous in their own, occult way. Now he was forced to negotiate with the most dangerous of all, to strike a deal with a diabolical but very much all human individual. The prospect was deeply unsavoury but Stroude believed it vital to gain control over Darian's demon and ghosts to allow his squad to strip Darian's home of all its treasures. Bring the arrogant bastard to his knees, pleading for his miserable life. How the major would relish housing the decadent hedonist within these forsaken walls.

He could feel the carriage sway as the horses picked up speed, their hooves had touched the firmer ground of the driveway to their destination, their disposition along with their driver's rising as they both saw dim lights ahead, somehow piercing the relentless lead grey wall of rain. Stroude wiped the condensation from his window and looked up towards the building, he'd been there before but its power to intimidate and depress the human spirit remained as potent as ever. A lookout opened the heavy oak doors as the carriage approached and closed it as soon as the team clattered into the cobbled courtyard. Stroude was a free man, in authority over this establishment, yet the closing of the doors sent an uneasy shudder of dread through him. He felt as trapped as the inmates.

The head warder approached holding up a lit lantern though it was barely mid-afternoon, reaching out with a hard calloused, sinewy hand in greeting. 'They are all behaving today, as if they sense the approach of a visitor.'

'Hope is a difficult emotion to quell, Mr Banes,' the major replied after shaking the man's hand. Banes was approaching 70 but was still strong as a young ox, in body and mind, 'a visitor could be a messenger of release.'

'I've prepared your guest,' Banes said, ushering his employer to a nearby door, 'but first you and your driver will need some refreshment after your long journey. The cook has prepared a good hot beef broth and baked fresh bread for you.'

Grateful for the hospitality, if only to delay his meeting with the prisoner, Stroude nodded his gratitude but added, 'I will take my repast alone, Mr Banes.' The less Jennings knew of the mission, the less burdensome to his conscience. A good man deserved that.

Stroude took his time over the broth, followed by cups of strong tea and a rich fruit cake. He was weary from the journey and the fatiguing effect of his stretched nerves from what he was about to face. But it could not be put off. Sighing, he called for Banes and asked to be taken to the prisoner.

Rivulets of rain water ran down the leaking high walls of the cell, adding another layer to streaks of green coated damp. The cell had the atmosphere of an abandoned sepulchre, musty, grave-cold and mildewed. The prisoner was seated, hands manacled to a solid stone table, his legs were shackled and a blindfold hid his eyes. A harsh but necessary arrangement, his hands could weave spells, his eyes mesmerise. There could be no chances for Dragor Magerian to regain power. His name was real as was his occult abilities, Stroude thought he was destined to become a sorcerer to live up to his ominous name. He took a seat opposite the prisoner with his nerves stretched to breaking point. The major had never felt like this facing an enemy army on the attack, why was a heavily shackled man making him so nervous?

Magerian was a striking, tall figure, even in this forlorn, vanquished circumstance, his presence transcending the filthy grey prison tunic and loose trousers with no buttons or laces in case of self-harm. Though a man in his forties, Magerian's once distinctive snow white hair was greasy and unwashed, hanging in long, yellow rat tails down his narrow back. His pallor was as grey as the rain lashing the moors. To the casual observer, he looked like a broken man, but Stroude was wise enough not to trust appearances. There was an intensity of power radiating from the sorcerer that added to Stroude's growing discomfort at such close proximity. At least it reassured the major he had the right man in front of him, Stroude needed the best, the most powerful mage in his custody.

With a deep, almost seductive voice, Magerian spoke first, his head inclining down to the unseen shackles. 'At least allow me to see my jailor, as you can see, I can do you no harm.'

'Perhaps, later ... if you co-operate.'

Stroude liked to think he was beyond the power of mesmerism. That was something only the feeble of mind and character would succumb to but was not ready to prove his point of view.

'And why should I co-operate with my enemy. A man who has stolen my freedom, my goods and keeps me in conditions no rabid cur should be subjected to? I have not faced a trial for any crime, this is not the way of British justice. '

'Because, Magerian, you are more dangerous than any mad dog,' Stroude answered. 'Our society needs protection from the likes of you. But the conditions of your incarceration can be improved ... greatly ... if you collaborate with me.'

'I want freedom or you will get no help from me.'

The major shook his head, a futile gesture in front of a blindfolded man, 'Death or imprisonment in greater comfort. That is all I will offer you.'

Magerian laughed, a hollow sound like an icy gust passing through a graveyard, further chilling the major's blood, 'I suspect I would prefer the freedom of death. I would join Darian's legion of spirits that are so vexing you. I would enjoy that.'

Shuddering, Stroude stood up in a move abrupt with rising panic. There was a time, a recent time, where he would dismiss such a threat as the futile ravings of a madman. But the major had now experienced the full horror of contact with the earthbound spirits haunting Mayfair. He could only imagine the terrible power Magerian's ghost would possess.

'My offer is final, there will be no other.'

Stroude rang a brass bell on the table, summoning the guards and walked towards the cell door.

'There is no need for such haste,' Magerian's voice halted the major's steps, 'I will at least listen to your proposition.'

Stroude quelled his disappointment at having to get close again to the sorcerer but returned to his seat. 'Go on.'

'But I must have this infernal blindfold removed first. No sighted man should be forced to dwell in unnatural darkness.'

The major had planned for this, he had Banes and three trusted, stalwart guards on standby should Magerian attempt any mesmerising trickery.

'I agree to your terms, Magerian. You will have your sight back while we negotiate a mutually beneficial arrangement.'

The sorcerer gave a deep growl of displeasure, 'And after that?'

Stroude stood up again, 'That will depend entirely on you, on how successful and co-operative you can be.'

44

With Banes and his men in place, the major ordered Magerian's blindfold removed. It did not take the man long to adjust to the cell's gloom. The tiny high window, reinforced with narrow iron bars allowed only a measure of the afternoon's grey light. An untimely darkness had fallen as the storm clouds outside thickened. Approaching thunder rumbled along the horizon. Further heavy rains would make the moorland tracks an impassable quagmire. His depression deepened as Stroude realised he and his driver would not be crossing back over Dartmoor until the next morning.

Released from their binding, the sorcerer's eyes were compelling, shards of glacial blue highlighted by deep, dark shadows. Magerian fixed his intense gaze on the major, a cobra ready to strike. Stroude decided to do away with any small talk, get this over with quickly and get the man out of his sight.

'I want access to Darian's home.'

Again the chilling, hollow laugh, 'Best of luck with that, Major Stroude.'

Magerian shook his head at the idiocy of the man's aims, 'Your agents caught me unawares as an innocent man about his legitimate business. But that blaggard Darian's home will be well protected in ways you could never imagine.'

Stroude nodded in agreement, already knowing there would be problems beyond his comprehension as a straightforward military man.

'That companion, servant whatever of his. I suspect he is not fully human ... maybe of demon blood?'

This statement produced a snort of derision from the prisoner, his baleful eyes looked up to the ceiling in disbelief.

'Of demon blood? You really have not got a clue, have you Stroude. You are talking about Darian's bedfellow, a full blood demon in human form. And not just any old demon. That is none other than Belial, one of the seven High Princes of Hell.'

Stroude swore, this was worse than he could ever have imagined as the sorcerer continued, 'In his human form, Belial can cause great damage to the area around the square. In full demonic mode, he can destroy the planet.'

'I need him eliminated or at least contained, maybe sent back to Hell. Can you do it?'

Magerian's thin lips split into a rictus like grin, exposing recently broken, yellowed teeth, more evidence of the brutal degradation of his imprisonment. 'Of course. There is no one in this country, maybe in the world that can. But it will take more than an untrustworthy promise of better living conditions. Nothing less than my freedom and the return of my possessions will do.'

The major stood up again, 'I need time to consider this.'

As he left the cell, the image of Magerian's eyes still burnt into his retina, Stroude heard the sorcerer whisper.

'I will do what you want, Stroude, but if you betray me, you will suffer torture day and night for the rest of your life and dwell in torment for eternity.'

Easily to dismiss as the raving words of a madman but all Stroude's past certainties had been dashed to pieces at the arrival of the ghosts. Insane as that curse sounded, Stroude believed it.

45

The Xantho succeeded in reaching the busy, crowded waters of the Mediterranean without detection or incident. The change in marine scenery was a source of as much fascination with her crew as it was with boredom from Darian.

Reggie in particular, appeared to be relishing the clearer seas, more numerous marine life and intriguing wrecks and ruins on the sea bed. It was a tiring and complex route to navigate safely, Tia was grateful the young man was keen to help her and learn to use the sonic devices that warned of nearing impediments. That he was seated beside Tia and engaging with her an added bonus for the smitten magician.

With the help of his cane and a strong dose of determination, Darian used the time to explore the subaquacraft. His interest was not in her astounding design, far ahead of any contemporary technology, he'd seen something similar on her father's craft. Darian was more fascinated by the many beautiful objects that graced Tia's craft. So much treasure taken back from the sea and painstakingly restored to its former splendour. He recognised wonders from many ancient civilisations around the world and some from unknown, lost cultures. These were the ones that fired his imagination and the wiles of his inner thief.

Common sense screamed from a well-suppressed part of his being that this was not the time or place to be light-fingered. Tia's father would not approve of any theft, his punishment swift and brutal but Darian reasoned he had already transgressed too far already by taking Tia's honour, what more could he suffer from this family's hands beyond a watery death?

Again, it was the ever-vigilant Hardwick who stopped him in his tracks, cornering him as Darian studied a curious small obelisk of carved rainbow quartz, etched with gold inlay hieroglyphs of unknown origin.

'I know what you are planning, Cyrus and I strongly advise ... no ... I order you to stop it immediately.'

'But it is so pretty,' teased Darian. 'See how it sparkles in the light.' He tossed the artefact between his hands like a juggling ball. 'And so small. Who would miss such a trinket?'

'Betray a remarkable young lady who saved your life and brought us close to our mission? One who has known you since childhood? Even you would not stoop so low.'

Darian reluctantly returned the crystal to its plinth, 'Miles, old chap, surely you should know by now there are no depths too deep for me to go. I am an utter cad and bounder ... Totally without boundaries or remorse.'

Hardwick shook his head, somehow never letting go of the hope a decent man lay at the heart of the alchemist's soul. The faint hope was something he needed to keep alight, how else could he go on with his friendship?

'Control your guttersnipe urges, Cyrus, please. We are nearly at our destination. I for one, do not want to be ejected from this craft to drown or be devoured by sharks.'

Within days, the Xantho began the most perilous part of her journey, where she left open seas and began to navigate the Dnieper River. Reggie grew increasingly despondent, soon his underwater adventure would be over and he would lose sight of the enchanting Tia Dakkar. His mood was not overlooked by the object of his devotion and when the subaquacraft could no longer travel in safety along the river, she called the crew together and made an unexpected announcement.

'Gentlemen, your lift into the heart of Russia ends today. I can moor the Xantho in this deep part of the river, hopefully safely and unseen. But the next bridge along the route is too great an impediment.'

She watched the disappointment cross their faces, they would miss the protection of the hidden craft, to travel on exposed to constant danger and the threat from the Tsar's ever-vigilant spies.

'However, I am having too much fun to just drop you off

here. I will continue the adventure with you ... if you will have me.'

The men reacted with mixed emotions, delight from the lovestruck Reggie, grave concern from the chivalrous Bartrev, Hardwick was more distracted by the fate of the Xantho should any harm befall her mistress. And Darian envisaged more amorous encounters in secret beneath the vast Russian skies.

'Good, well that is settled then,' Tia announced without waiting for an answer. 'We will wait until nightfall and unload the *Dauntless*. This is going to be fun.'

46

Midsummer meant little to the passengers of the *Dauntless*. The air high above the Russian steppes had a razor edge, a chill reminder that winter was the true ruler of this land of grass oceans. Darian remained in the galley, disinterested in the endless rolling landscape below. City born and bred, he suffered from agoraphobia and preferred the enclosing surroundings of dark oak panels and access to the wine cabinet.

His mind wandered to the stolen moments, he'd enjoyed with Tia on the Xantho, trysts that were not repeated in the crowded space of the airship. Indeed, Tia had lost all interest in flirting in secret with him since arriving on land and floating high above it.

All lascivious thoughts drained away at the sound of furiously grinding gears and the scream of distressed metal clashing against metal. The Dauntless revealed more of the damage she'd endured at the hands of Libby's servants and with the deep sigh of a wounded leviathan began to slow down. With the canopy full of gas, it should have been a simple matter to cut off the engines and drift onwards under wind power but the *Dauntless* was not listening to her commander anymore.

White-faced, Hardwick wrestled with the controls to no avail, he'd lost steering and the airship had become a runaway. 'Bartrev, hold the helm, she's not responding but we must do something.'

Without needing any prompting, Tia was on her feet and running beside Hardwick to the engine department. Helpless, Darian and Reggie watched as the others wrestled with the wounded ship. Minutes that seemed like hours later and an oil-drenched Hardwick and Tia returned into the cabin.

'There is nothing we can do mid-air, we will have to cripple her steam engines by force and bring her down with the canopy alone. This could get messy, I suggest you all hold onto something firm. And Darian, please lock those damned wine bottles away.'

'I'd never risk losing so much fine vintage,' Darian returned, affronted by the suggestion, 'and wine stains are deuced difficult to get out.'

A combination of great piloting skill, raw courage and an overabundance of continued good fortune brought the dirigible to a bumpy, difficult but successful landing. The craft's gondola lay tipped at an awkward angle which meant its passengers had to climb upwards onto her side to disembark. The canopy billowed forlornly but was intact, missing some tearing thorn bushes and sharp boulders by yards.

The *Dauntless* had been brought down on a rare hilltop surrounded by the ocean of steppe grassland, its flat landscape broken only by stands of wind-bent trees and snaking rivers. A land heartbreakingly familiar to Bartrev, though not his estate, his stolen lands looked very much the same. He busied himself by volunteering Reggie and Darian to join him seek out fresh water and dry fire wood, leaving the two engineers behind to begin work on repairing the dirigible's engine.

For once, Darian did not argue with someone else giving orders, the count knew his own homeland, lack of cooperation was pointless and idiotic. This would remain a hostile land, reports of the airship crossing it would inevitably get back to the Tsar's agents. The adventurers were on borrowed time.

Hardwick ignored the palpable impatience inevitably rising from the alchemist, too busy concentrating on the recalcitrant engine. Highly-strung and eager for action in the form of a quick escape, Darian paced besides the stranded dirigible, scanning the horizon for signs of trouble with one of the inventor's long range, vision-enhanced telescopes. The longer the airship remained grounded, the more likely they would meet danger head on. Though swift up until now, the progress of a large, steam driven bag of hot air above the steppes, like a yellow, purposeful cloud, would attract astonishment from all who saw it.

Many fearful serfs and nomads would put it down to a visitation of demons or the side effects of too much badly stilled crude vodka. But there would be others, more world-wise who sensed such a sight would be of interest to the authorities ... it was information too potentially lucrative to be ignored.

At least the inventor had a good team on hand to help him, Tia was a godsend, when they were not arguing, inevitable, with her great knowledge and understanding of things mechanical, rivalling Hardwick's. The Russian nobleman was not too proud to roll up his sleeves and get his hands dirty, doing what he could to help Hardwick. Reggie Dunne made himself useful, keeping the workforce supplied with liberal and regular pots of strong tea and the occasional bottle of fortifying ale. Only Darian himself did not toil on repairing the *Dauntless*. Not because fine silk brocade and engine oil did not mix but his weakness from the poisoned bullet had left him still fragile, he tired easily and there was crippling pain in all of his joints. How did Stroude or a mere Mechman know how to concoct such a toxin, one powerful enough to hold back the healing effect of the succubus venom? He doubted they could, some other enemy was at their nefarious work, but who it was impossible to know at this point, he had so many.

A cloud of dust rising above the flat horizon caught his attention. Why did that wretch of a shapeshifter have to turn traitor? How useful it would have been to send Cambion to check this out in the form of a swift raptor. Thoughts of his companions reminded him of Belial, the alchemist had surprised himself at the depth of his emotions over the demon: he really missed his company ... not that he'd ever admit that to anyone, alive or dead. Forcing his mind to concentrate on the matter in hand, he looked again at the dust cloud. It was not a natural phenomenon, the air was stifling and still and this cloud had direction and purpose ... and was heading their way. They had company.

Running back from his vantage point, he was nearly breathless by the time he reached the dirigible. Darian went straight to the armoury within the cabin and unclipped all the weapons. He threw an Accelerated Momentium Fragmentiser, towards Tia, not doubting for a moment she would have the skill and courage to use the powerful weapon, 'Help me arm everyone with AMFs, we will soon have uninvited guests,'

Darian went straight to the inventor, 'I don't suppose for one minute, Miles, that you can get the old girl airborne?'

'Not a chance,' Hardwick shook his head and gave the *Dauntless* a pat. 'Those bastards in Paris knew what they were doing. We are trapped, Cyrus.'

Borrowing the telescope, Bartrev had gone up to the vantage point to see for himself and returned with more bad news. 'There are too many, all armed to the teeth and they have got heavy artillery. Professional soldiers from the Tsar's elite guard and not just a rabble of curious locals.'

Darian beheaded some tall bulrushes with his sword stick as he thought for a moment, his agile mind creating a mad scheme but usually they worked the best.

'They are looking for the Count, me and an aristocratic Englishman. The last thing they are expecting is a female aviator and you, Reggie. If the rest of us are out of sight, they may be confused enough to move on.'

'I will not allow Tia to be used like that,' Reggie thundered. 'That would put her in terrible danger. Your plan is insane.'

At last, the young man is developing a backbone, maybe I have competition after all, Darian was amused by the evolving hero but not threatened. The magician did not have Darian's charisma and worldly experience. That won over gauche heroics every time.

'That was only the first part of my scheme,' Darian continued, 'the ruse will buy us enough time to mount a successful ambush – should hell forbid, we need it.'

'Madness!' Reggie was clearly still not convinced.

'I can do this,' insisted Tia, 'I have looked after myself long enough to cope with a few hotheads on horseback.'

Hardwick walked away from the *Dauntless*, arms folded, head down in total defeat, 'We may need those horses if our journey isn't to end here. I cannot get her flight worthy before those soldiers get here, I need more time and access to a workshop and forge.'

Tia's estimate of a few hotheads was wildly inaccurate. The Tsar's men had brought a veritable army with them, including laden gun carriages pulled by hard-straining teams of horses. Heavy artillery against five people and a stricken dirigible. Time to even the odds, thought Darian, those ghosts of his would be useful now, knowing if he summoned them to leave London, they would come in an instance. Spectral travel recognised no limitation of time or distance. The downside to this plan was most vexing, it would leave his home vulnerable to Stroude and his fanatics. Would Belial and Misha be enough to defend it?

Noticing the alchemist was deep in thought, Bartrev addressed him, 'Whatever you are planning, Darian, I suggest you share it with us, now. Those heavy guns will be in range any minute.'

Darian nodded, his mind made up. Belial had kept his home safe in the past with no difficulty, what danger could an English army major and a few bible thumpers do? He stood on the highest promontory close by and held out his arms to the sky ... more for dramatic effect then necessity. He began a solemn incantation in Farsi, again for effect ... the apparitions would obey him regardless of language.

'Ghosts!' Reggie cried out from below in disbelief. 'You are going to use spectres against explosions and mortar shells?'

Relaxing his stance, Darian shook his head and returned to his companions, 'No, old chap ... I am going to use them against easily spooked horses and men ruled by old superstitions.'

'What in God's name is that?' Reggie whimpered, catching sight of a curious and unnatural disturbance in the sky.

Darian smiled, success. Looking up to the near cloudless firmament, he raised his arms in welcome as a silent streak of glowing energy appeared high above them. It became a dense spiral, collecting and coalescing before descending in front of the alchemist in a cloud of seething spectral forms. Darian's army of the dead were a reality.

47

'They've gone ... all of them?'

Stroude's mind reeled with the news. According to his aide, at some point during that afternoon, all the phantoms outside Darian's Mayfair home had vanished. There was no time to ponder on the veracity of this welcome news or speculate whether the vile spectres would return.

It could mean their master, Darian was dead but whatever caused them to disappear, Stroude knew it was time for some direct action. He must activate Magerian to overcome Darian's demon and gain access to the alchemist's home.

Leaping to his feet, Stroude grabbed his bowler and caped tweed coat and ordering his men to follow, ran to the barracks courtyard. Magerian was imprisoned in the brig, in the comfort, if not the freedom he demanded. It was time the sorcerer earned his reprieve from the grim internment on Dartmoor. He found the man sitting at a desk, piled high with notes written by scrawling, impatient hand. Magerian had not been allowed grimoires or any other tools of his occult trade, a limiting but necessary move to curb a man so dangerous.

'Are you ready?' Stroude demanded, again trying to avoid the scorn and mesmeric power of the man's eyes. 'Darian's ghosts have disappeared, we may only have a short window of opportunity.'

'That is all I will need,' Magerian replied in little more than a whisper, rising to his feet. Stroude was convinced he saw a curious, cold light gleam in the sorcerer's eyes but he pushed such fanciful thoughts aside, the man worked hard at spooking him, that was all. An elaborate act to weaken the will and sew doubt. Magerian may be skilled in manipulating people, but Stroude was above and beyond such machinations.

From its high vantage point on a chimney pot, the beast in the form of a jackdaw watched events unfold in the square beneath. The grey bird's black cap of feathers tipped to one side as it heard the gasps of surprise then cheers from the crowds behind the barricades as word spread that the spectres had gone. The barricade remained, as well guarded by fearsome Mechmen as ever.

Did this herald the loss of its quarry? That the spirits had left as Darian's own soul had departed his body? Disappointment and curiosity were too many emotions at once for the corvid mind, the beast swooped down as close as it dared to Darian's home and waited for news of the alchemist's fate.

Before long, the clatter of many hard-pressed horses signalled some action, the beast watched intently as the barriers parted and three military coaches trotted into the square, pulled by animals no longer spooked or balking. A group of armed civilians, all young men in sober coloured suits leapt out of the vehicles and surrounded Darian's home. An upright middle-aged figure with greying sandy hair and moustache was in command, a man the beast recognised as Major Stroude.

'Ah, so they meant to take Darian's home. Well, best of luck with that,' the beast gave a squawk of mocking amusement. The alchemist's house was well guarded by both magickal and mechanical means, and by two ferocious guardians, the demon Belial and that curious, unearthly thing Darian called a dragoncat. They'd soon learn the folly of this mission.

There were no lights or sign of movement inside the townhouse but the beast knew sharp, cold eyes would be aware of Stroude and his team and preparing to repel them. The major signalled to one of the men and two other vehicles entered the square, both armoured prison vans pulled by sturdy draught mules. Stroude himself opened the back of one of the vans, the watching bird shivered, alarmed. Magerian! A powerful, wicked man feared by all the occult community ... other than Darian of course. But then he had a demon prince as his right hand man.

Once renowned for being a fastidious, dark clad dandy, the sorcerer was now clad in stained prison issue, his once luxuriant long white hair straggly and unwashed. To the beast's horror, Magerian stared straight up at it, his gaze freezing the bird into immobility. The jackdaw could not move or transform but remained as animated as a stuffed feathered exhibit beneath a glass dome. Only the rapid pounding of its small avian heart let it know it was still alive. It had never been so vulnerable or so frightened.

Magerian looked away but the jackdaw could not move, it was in a helpless limbo until the sorcerer made his intentions known. Intentions, the bird knew would not be benevolent. All it could do was listen.

'Clever … ingenious even. Much as I expected,' Magerian turned to address the major so quickly, Stroude was unable to hide an instinctive shudder of repulsion. The sorcerer if he noticed ignored the reaction and went back to studying Darian's townhouse.

'It is difficult not to be envious of a mage so skilled and yet so young. Darian understands and utilises arcane matters, esoteric practises and dark enchantments that have taken me many decades of study and experimenting to learn. Not always successfully.'

Magerian lifted his manacled left hand and pulled back his prison tunic exposing a livid area of scarred and seared flesh in stark contrast to the fish belly white of his skin. An injury that appeared to be caused by both fire and raking talons. Stroude did not wince or look away, he'd seen worse on the battlefield. His customary impatience erupted, 'I only want to hear one answer, can you do it?'

'Well, of course, my dear major,' Magerian's confident, sly smile was so much worse than the damaged stomach, 'Darian is a clever man but with a butterfly mind, skimming the surface of so many interests. I however have concentrated my studies and know them in far greater depth. I will gain entrance to the alchemist's home and I will bind Belial in my snare.'

Nothing could be done until the demon prince was subdued and entrapped. To Stroude's great consternation, the sorcerer had warned that his assault on the townhouse would be a long drawn out affair, necessitating closing up the square again to the public, hardly conducive to keeping this collaboration with the enemy away from the Prime Minister's attention. Stroude knew he must endure with distaste the spells and evocations, the arcane rituals needed to diffuse the many supernatural barriers guarding Darian's treasures.

To protect human life, Stroude was reluctantly forced to stay with his squad behind the barrier, a protective ring of sacrificial Mechmen around them. Magerian had warned of the chaos and bloody, burning carnage to come if he failed to contain Belial. The sorcerer strode into the square alone and raising a copper staff mounted by a large black crystal orb, began a whispered incantation of the oldest, dark earth magicke spoken in a tongue extinct for many millennia. A spiral of dark radiance seeped from the ground, one born in the lowest depths of the planet, enveloping the sorcerer in a protective shield of baleful rays from an unknown spectrum.

The watching Stroude gasped in fright as Darian's companion, burst out of the door, pale eyes gleaming with malice and fury. A streak of flame shot from those demonic eyes towards Magerian, bouncing harmlessly off his protective shield. Belial roared in anger, his attention turning to the helpless humans cowering behind the Mechmen's living barrier. Frozen in defenceless disbelief, a cowering Stroude watched as Magerian raised his staff and aimed it at Belial. The demon fell to his knees, unable to raise his head.

This was the most dangerous part of the plan, Magerian had warned his conspirators about this crucial moment. If Belial chose to reject his human form and become full demon then all would be lost, including their lives and possibly all those of surrounding London. Magerian gambled that the prince's obsessive devotion to his human beloved would be enough to keep him from transforming. The gamble appeared to be working.

There was no time to ponder on this success, Belial needed to be bound further. Magerian raised his staff high and chanted again, this time summoning assistance, not from the living but from spirit forms. All around him swarmed swirling black smoke with hideous, tortured faces filled with hatred and spite. They were Wraith, the spirits of evil magicians who tried to extend their lives by unnatural means and had become little more than malice incarnate. More powerful than any normal human shade, these malign forms were pure concentrated evil. The angel Belial fell from grace and was cursed to demonic form from his rebellious pride. The Wraith willingly chose to be evil, that choice gave them their strength.

Wrapping their spectral forms around the stricken demon, the wraith became chains, tight supernatural bindings that kept Belial frozen in a form of stasis. Magerian did not know how long the Wraith could hold their powerful prisoner, but supernatural matters had a different time scale to human affairs. A brief time for a demon could be many centuries on Earth. All he needed was enough time to deliver Darian to his enemies and once defeated, take all the confiscated occult possessions from Stroude for himself. Magerian smiled, the blind stupidity of the major knew no bounds, if he was powerful enough a sorcerer to capture a Fallen Prince, how could a mere military stooge and his young, naïve cohorts stand in his way?

Magerian dreamed of a new era, a time when he would be the true ruler of an England and Empire submitting to his arcane might. With Belial disarmed and Darian dead, who in heaven or hell could stop him?

48

The Count had done well, choosing a hiding place so nondescript, the agents of the Tsar would waste many lifetimes finding it, if at all. Bartrev steered his horse across a flat stretch of open grassland with no discernible notable features such as trees or rocky outcrops. There were a few scrubby, wind-bent bushes blending into the monotony of the surrounding steppes but nothing beyond that. He rode with a relaxed confidence and familiarity with the sun-dried ocean of grass terrain though he was still far from his own, stolen lands.

He paused only once and that was at the site of his concealment of the Bane of Souls. Alighting from his mount, Bartrev took out a long knife and dug deep into the dusty soil to remove an object protected by a wrapping of humble sackcloth.

This astonished and angered Darian, how could such a priceless and potentially dangerous thing be left buried in the ground like a root vegetable? There were no circles of protection, no spells, no physical booby traps to catch out the unwary and impatient. Just a damned hole in the ground. He felt curiously insulted on behalf the precious object and its Fae creators for such cavalier treatment. Bartrev did not deserve to have the Bane of Souls in his possession.

Curbing his tongue for the first time in his life, Darian rushed forward, eager to see at last the reason for their quest but Bartrev tucked it in a deep inner pocket of his coat, aiming a pistol at the alchemist's head.

'I will honour my agreement and allow you to use the Bane to trap and contain your ghosts but it must remain in my protection at all times. Is that understood, Darian?'

'Of course, I agree,' lied Darian easily, 'and you have my sincerest gratitude for this.'

Remounting, the men turned their horses around and

retraced their journey back to the stranded dirigible. For once the fickle steppe weather was benevolent and with the brief summer sun warming their backs, all of nature seemed to celebrate the season. Hawks and eagles wheeled in the sky riding thermals, spiralling so high it must have been for the sheer pleasure of flight and not hunting prey. Deer appeared relaxed and unafraid, this spring's fawns already grown to independence and the grazing rich and plentiful, allowing them to fatten up before the all too swift return of winter. Darian was saddened when the count took advantage of the animals' content, bringing down a fine young buck with one clean shot to the head. But he would not refuse venison cooked on the campfire later that night.

Three days relaxed and uneventful travelling brought them within sight of the *Dauntless*, still moored on the hilltop. The alchemist reined in his horse on the higher ground above the valley and took his time surveying the scene below. If there had been a disaster during his absence, he could turn his horse's head and ride away. First impressions were not good, there were no signs of life near the dirigible. Perhaps his companions had been captured or killed? Then the slender form of Tia appeared, draped in leather tool belts and clambering up the rigging with lithe ease to check the canopy's vital metal support structure. Darian grinned, the little hoyden had impressed Hardwick after all, only days before, the inventor would not trust anyone with the safety of the *Dauntless* let alone a chit of a girl. There was hope for Hardwick yet, thought the alchemist, a man who lived beyond the foolish strictures of modern society.

He turned his attention to the wider scene. Apart from the crashed wrecks of the overturned gun carriages, there was no sign of the Tsar's army. Curious and worrying, Darian doubted they would give in so easily. Apart from the deep, circle of motionless phantoms, the *Dauntless* and its crew were vulnerable to attack. Could Stroude have been right, that the Army of Ghosts was a powerful weapon that spread fear and pandemonium through an enemy force? Darian was not convinced. Not all armies needed horses and a long distance canon feared no apparitions.

Neither was Bartrev fooled by the peaceful scene below, 'This isn't right, those troops' fear of the Tsar would be greater than that of spirits. I suspect an ambush, later, when the airship is on the move. They think they know our route, straight back to England.'

'Then it is fortunate that we will be going the opposite way, to the Dnieper and the mighty Xantho,' replied Darian, digging out his Fractal Enhanced telescope from the depths of his coat. The device was perfect for long-range viewing in broad daylight, its lens and metal work had been treated with a substance that prevented any betrayal by sunlight glinting off it. Something the enemy did not possess. Within seconds, Darian's observation was rewarded by tell-tale glints and furtive movements in the valley below. The Tsar's forces had spread out and thought themselves well hidden. It was almost a shame their hard work would not yield any reward, mused the alchemist, the Dauntless was not a toothless bag of wind, the dirigible was well armed, he would quite enjoy giving the Russians a pasting from above.

Greeted with an enthusiastic show of relief from their companions, Darian and the count rode down to the airship, her canopy taut and engine already stoked up and ticking over, ready for flight.

'It appears we have to congratulate you on a successful repair,' Darian's smile was genuine as was his pleasure at Tia's eager kiss and embrace. Despite his pang of jealousy, even Reggie shook his hand with ardent warmth. The two travellers' safe and successful return meant perhaps, everyone could finally go home.

The mood snapped to instant dismay when Darian announced a slight change of plans. 'Sorry to be the spectre at the feast but we cannot leave straight away. The count has most generously allowed me to use the Bane of Souls once but he does not intend to return to England. I must do the ceremony soon if not now.'

Before they could answer, a loud detonation sounded from the hidden army, some fool had accidently set off a canon, giving away their enemy's ambush. The shell landed within fifteen feet of the *Dauntless*, exploding with a deafening blast, showering earth and rocks over a wide radius. One large stone caught the airship's gondola but left only a dent in her metal side. The blast inevitably spooked their stolen horses, sending the terrified animals careering down the valley in a flat-out bolt.

'Too damned close,' yelled Hardwick. 'Whatever you intend to do, Cyrus, it must wait. We need to leave now. Everyone, get on board while we still can.'

The others scrambled for the *Dauntless* and the fragile safety of her cabin but Darian remained on the ground to untether the airship, he was the fastest and most agile of the team. Having unleashed an accidental mortar, their enemies must have decided they had nothing to lose. Another screaming fireball shot up from the valley, exploding barely feet from the craft. Darian swore and wound the large brass flywheel at the side of the dirigible that released the tether lines, shouting, 'Go now Miles, by Hades, get out of here!'

Grabbing hold of the now loose metal cable, his feet on the ballast block, Darian hung on with grim determination as the airship lifted swiftly away from the ground, its engines on full steam powering it away from what was now a full on barrage of heavy artillery fire. Choking cordite smoke rose from the flaming ground, mud, sharp stones and metal shrapnel exploded upwards, Darian twisted and turned on his precarious lifeline trying to avoid the flying shards of hot metal.

Forcing himself to concentrate on the Chaldean enchantment, he summoned his ghosts to follow, tempting though it was to leave them on the steppes. They had proved too useful to abandon with the adventure far from over. Dutiful, the obedient souls became a glowing ribbon of interwoven spectral forms and followed the dirigible like a nightmarish flock of geese.

'I am still here,' he bellowed up to the cabin, unable to be heard above the deafening detonations and the *Dauntless'* chugging, hissing engine, 'I would appreciate some assistance.'

49

Easily outrunning the Tsar's land-based forces, they found the Xantho's mooring place in the hidden cove, thankfully safe and undisturbed. Under an alarming cloud of roiling ghosts, the companions deflated the *Dauntless'* canopy and stored her in the subaquacraft's spacious hold.

Count Bartrev stopped the alchemist from boarding.

'I am not returning to England and you know I intend to keep the Bane of Souls. Therefore now is the time to entrap your unwanted spirits.'

The Russian removed the package from his coat and unwrapped the mirror, keeping the reflective side hidden. Darian sighed at its beauty, his eyes glowed with acquisitive need, this was most definitely the work of a Fae master craftsman, the deceptively fragile working of precious metals, moonstones, a filigree decor of natural forms, willowy boughs, stars and creatures of ancient legends.

'I have kept the mirror surface hidden for a good reason,' explained Bartrev to the intrigued companions. 'Among its many powers, the Bane will show you the true, primal nature of your soul, exposing your hidden vices and thoughts.'

'None of my vices are hidden,' Darian returned. 'And my soul has been bought, resold and damned so many times, I am long beyond caring.'

Bartrev was adamant, pulling out a pistol from his belt and aiming it at the alchemist. 'But I will not let any of you gaze into it, triggering unknown harm. These are my terms for its use. I will allow you to trap your ghosts, Darian, but then the Bane of Souls must return to my care.'

His curiosity disappointed, Darian had no choice but to agree and while Tia primed her craft for departure, he fetched the Ghostbinder and prepared to capture and contain the army of the dead. With Hardwick's help, the device was started up, a complex routine of switching levers and turning dials in a pattern that had to be in an exact, precise order for the mechanism to function, droning into life in a blaze of inner Galvanised light and engaging metal gears and cogs. Within its structure, a labyrinth of chambers and lenses opened, setting the Ghostbinder's inner traps.

Finding his balance as he wielded the cumbersome device, Cyrus took a deep breath. This was an untried device, a combination of two men's ingenuity and now an ancient object of Fae design. He directed the nozzle towards the wafting wall of resentful apparitions and called for Bartrev to insert the Bane of Souls into the spirit trap. As the Russian lifted up the Bane, wan moonlight flashed off the mirror's delicate, twisting design and ignited its spectral power in a shimmer of hundreds of silver lights dancing in the air before joining with the frame.

Not wanting to see their true forms, the core nature of their own souls, the companions averted their gaze until the Bane was firmly in place deep within the structure of the Ghostbinder. No point in delaying, thought Darian, controlling his shaking hands and squeezing the trigger. The device began to vibrate, its entire form glowing with a silver light and a discordant sound of unworldly ethereal singing emanated from it in ever louder waves, floating through the night air towards the spectres.

Something was wrong, even with the use of Fae magicke, the Ghostbinder's emanations seemed too benign and had nothing of the nature of a trap about them. Darian's suspicions grew as the light reached the ghosts circling above, bathing them in the deceptively delicate silver light. He heard them sigh with longing and hope then watched in horror as they entered the light and disappeared without entering his trap.

Frantically, he tried to disengage the Ghostbinder. Unable to remember the precise order to switch it off, Darian was helpless, only able to observe as his army of phantoms sought release from their earthly prison, moving onto a higher celestial plane of existence in the eternal *beyond*.

He threw down the Ghostbinder in disgust.

'You lying, worthless son of a cur,' Darian shouted. 'Damn your eyes for eternity for your trickery.'

Count Bartrev was unrepentant, his sense of righteousness keeping him calm in front of the alchemist's futile rage. The ghosts were gone, sent forever to a higher celestial domain by the Bane of Souls.

'No trickery, Darian,' he answered with calm authority. 'Just doing the right thing by the earthbound souls and for the world of the living. No one, especially not a scheming rogue like you, has the right to command the army of the dead. They have gone to eternal rest at last.'

The others stepped forward, Hardwick taking the initiative to defuse the overwrought situation, 'He is right, Cyrus. Whether you wanted to or not, you did the decent thing by destroying the Technomicron. Now the Ghostbinder has finished the job. This nightmare is finally over.'

Darian was far from convinced. Over the past months, he had enjoyed possession of two formidable occult devices and so much power at his command. Now he had nothing ... well, apart from a lifetime's worth of mysterious acquisitions back home. And a loyal demon companion and a beautiful shapeshifter lover plus an obscene amount of wealth, dashing good looks that would not decline or age and a body that healed quickly. Apart from that he had nothing.

He felt a small, firm hand take his, 'Darling Cyrus, don't think of this as a defeat but a lucky escape,' Tia reached up and kissed him on the cheek. 'Having all those angry, resentful and insane ghosts bound to you was a curse. It would have destroyed you.'

She led him along the river bank towards her ship, 'It is over *Jaan*, I am going to take you home.'

Tia anchored the Xantho close to the shoreline well beyond the busy harbour city of Zonguldak. This was not Count Nikolai Bartrev's homeland, not his beloved Mother Russia. He had decided to finish his adventure with Cyrus Darian and begin another in Turkey.

Bartrev made his farewells abound the subaquacraft. Tia had embraced him with an exuberant and sweet-scented hug, the first expression of genuine affection he had experienced for many years. He'd shaken hands with Reggie and Hardwick, good men despite their allegiance to the notorious alchemist. Cyrus Darian stayed in the background. Darian had offered him gold to set him up for his future life, but the count had refused, curbing a rising anger. Anything from Darian would be tainted, blood-money. Bartrev had survived with nothing but his honour before.

A light skiff waited, bobbing above the Xantho on a tether; a parting gift from Tia. He gave a curt nod to Darian and returned to his life of solitary exile and wandering. Once on dry land, he patted his coat, reassured by the weight of the Bane of Souls against his chest. It did not belong to humanity, especially to anyone in power but only to its Fae creators. Bartrev knew the only way to keep the world safe from its disastrous powers was to return it to them and undo the wrong perpetrated by his distant ancestors.

The count gave a final wave of farewell to the departing Xantho and her crew and strode up the beach and on towards his unknown future. In the distance along the shore line, he saw a group of local fishermen, maybe they could buy the skiff from him? Even a handful of coin would help begin his new life. As he secured the boat, his eye caught a shimmer of fuchsia and embroidered gold sari silk crafted into a purse, partly concealed beneath the rudimentary bench seat. Tia! He opened it and poured out a gleaming stream of perfect, large pearls into his hand. A generous farewell gift gleaned from her beloved ocean. These treasures he would not refuse.

As Bartrev strode up the beach, he knew his dreams of returning to his family estate could only be that ... hopeless dreams while the Tsar held power. Nor did he know how to contact the mysterious and elusive Fae, if they still existed beyond myths and legends. Darian would know. The wretched man could no doubt summon them but Bartrev had more than enough of that man's wiles and connivances. He wanted more honourable comradeship, indeed the further away from Darian's company, the sweeter the air seemed to be.

'Er ... Tia, *tesora*. How fast can this beauty travel?' Darian queried, 'I am getting a curious warning sensation something is very wrong back in London.'

A total fabrication, in fact he wanted as much distance as possible between him and the big Russian. It wouldn't take long for the count to discover the sacking wrapped parcel in his coat pocket held nothing more exotic than one of Tia's gilded Indian mirrors.

50

The adventurers disembarked from the dinghy and stood on a narrow expanse of wet shingle. Tia had taken her craft as far as she dared along the wide Thames Estuary, arriving at London's dockland region in the early hours of the morning at low tide. Even then the area was busy, with cargo ships and Thames barges bustling along the waterway bringing the wealth of the Empire into the city.

'I cannot linger,' she said with a sad smile. Tia had enjoyed her adventure with these men - the craft would seem empty in the days to come. 'Once day breaks it will be harder to remain unseen in these busy, shallow waters.'

Leaving the Xantho had fallen hard on Reggie and Hardwick, both had fallen in love, the inventor with the subaquacraft, the magician with its captain. As he disembarked, Hardwick had glanced around the beautiful, extraordinary wonder that was the craft, knowing his own engineering skills could never have achieved such a feat. There was so much he wanted to know about her, the origin of her propulsion, how she kept the air so fresh for long periods beneath the waves. The mystery of her construction that resisted the crushing weight of pressure deep under the ocean. What weapons did she possess to defend herself? Who was her mistress's father? But Tia had made it clear, the subaquacraft's secrets would remain a mystery and she had a mission to fulfil. Hardwick had to accept that the Xantho may never reach the shores of Great Britain again.

No less bereft was Reggie, his unspoken adoration of Tia remained locked in his heart, the thought of not seeing her again tearing him apart. But why would she be interested in a nobody? A penniless failure and the laughing stock of all his fellows in the entertainment trade. Tia Dakkar was a freedom loving, exotic creature with a strong, wilful mind of her own, one that could never endure the subjugation of domestic life on land. He loved her enough to never suggest such a crime against her. He recalled his distaste at the chained and caged tigers at the funfair. Tia was no less a wild soul, one needing the world's oceans to roam free.

He fought back a stab of jealousy as Darian took Tia's arm and led her away to talk to her in private. A situation made worse by the strange language they both used with each other, a lilting, lyrical tongue redolent of the Indian subcontinent. It suited them, two beautiful, glamorous people who kicked back against the strictures of modern British society. They looked right together and made him feel shoddy and worthless.

'Are you sure you do not want to finish the adventure with me? See the escapade through to the end?'

Darian caressed the subaquanaut's soft tumble of curls and for the first time openly gave her a lingering, sensuous kiss, oblivious to the hurt in Reggie's eyes. Tia was another conquest that would cause serious repercussions in Darian's future. It was worth it, she was adorable and an eager, pliant pupil in the delights of the bedroom.

'No, Cyrus. It was good to test out the Xantho with an exciting caper in good company but my mission has not changed. If my father is still alive out there, I must find him.'

She gave the muddy shingle a derisive kick. 'I have spent too much time on dry land. Mankind's laws and social restrictions are not good for my soul. I was raised in freedom. The deep ocean has always been the only home I have known or wanted.'

Tia gave an impudent wink and squeezed Darian's hand, 'Don't worry, *priya* ... my darling ... I'll never tell my father of our little dalliance. We both know how badly he will take the news. He never forgives.'

'Is that all it was to you?' Darian was expecting avowals of undying devotion from one so young. The first time was always so intense, so emotional for young women. He'd expected tears and declarations of love at the very least.

'Of course!' She laughed, a throaty, sensuous sound that stirred Darian's desire for her again. 'You are nothing more than a notorious womaniser, a heartless philanderer and liar of the very worst kind. But who better to teach me the art of making love?' She reached up and gave his face a playful tap, 'Most of all, you are not a repressed, shame-filled Englishman but one fully in touch with sensuous, erotic delights. You were useful to me, *Uncle* Cyrus ... nothing more. No man will ever touch me again unless he is the love of my life. And that will never be you.'

Little minx. Darian shook his head in wonder and grudging respect, once again on this adventure the player had been well and truly played.

'Oh, and one more thing ...' Tia's hand went straight for his breast pocket and retrieved a crystal and gold object, which she held up to his eyes with a look of mock disappointment and reproach, 'I'll have that back. Oh Cyrus, you are incorrigible, you only had to ask.'

She turned her back on Darian and strolled back to the dinghy, saying her goodbyes to the others, noting the sense of loss in Hardwick's eyes, not for her but for the marvel of engineering that was the Xantho. A craft he would never see again if her plans succeeded.

As Tia stepped back into the little vessel to row back to the Xantho, she beckoned Reggie over to her. 'Mr Dunne, you are a failed illusionist, an utterly hopeless magician. How about becoming a damned fine and expert subaquanaut and navigator?'

Astonished and delighted, the young man waded through the gathering surf and eagerly climbed aboard the dinghy without a backward glance.

51

London at last. Cyrus watched from a window of the dirigible as the clear air of the flat, rolling Essex countryside gave way over Hackney Marshes to the dense soot grey and filthy green miasma that hung over the capital in a perpetual pall that no strong wind could ever scatter. His adopted home in all its dysfunctional, filthy and dubious glory and was to Darian the best place in the world to dwell.

Hardwick did not risk attracting attention to the *Dauntless* by flying her straight to Mayfair but moored her in the expensive dock for private airships in Green Park. There, deliberately tucked in behind larger, showier dirigibles, she blended in with the dozens of other rich men's toys, well protected by high fences and an army of security guards. It was then a small matter to hire a horse-drawn Hansom to finish the journey. Though Darian hated adding to the workload of the industrious beast, a horse-drawn vehicle drew less attention than the more showy steam cabs favoured by the wealthy.

'I will drop you off first at Mayfair but then I must head straight home.'

Darian laughed, 'Poor old Miles, having to face the music at last. No doubt Lady Hardwick will be waiting well-armed with a sharpened parasol, a weighted handbag and for back up, her cook wielding a heavy rolling pin.'

The inventor did not reply to Darian's predictable show of ill-mannered ribbing but was pinning his hopes that Athena was still on her tour of European cultural treasures with the stalwart and generous Pringles. But in truth, the meeting would be tempestuous whenever he was reunited with his wife. In Athena's eyes, for her husband to have any further dealing with Darian was a hanging offence – if she was feeling merciful.

With no ghosts to spook it, the carriage horse happily trotted into Pleasance Square and came to a halt outside Darian's home. Straight into a new nightmare for the alchemist – his elegant front door had been broken down and replaced with a slab of wood protected by iron bars. Falling out of the cab and onto his knees on the pavement, Darian let out a soul-deep howl of horror. Someone, some *thing* had broken through his many defences, leaving his home open to this shocking violation. He did not need to look inside to know the house had been gutted. Hardwick hastily paid the Hansom driver and dismissed him. How could he go home and leave Darian distraught on his knees and crazed with loss?

'It must have been that bastard Stroude and his cronies,' the inventor murmured, stating the obvious as he helped Darian back to his feet.

'How?' Darian's voice was subdued, clouded with disbelief. He had placed so much faith in his own occult skills, Hardwick's engineering ingenuity and the fearsome power of Prince Belial. Yet still the bastards had broken through and robbed him of all he cared about. All the precious items gathered for many years in the desperate hope for a means to turn back time and rescue his wife. Their loss and what it meant to his aims felt like a mortal injury, as if his heart was slowly torn out by blunt, rusty weapons.

'Not by Mechmen, that's for sure,' Hardwick replied, supporting the deeply distressed alchemist, preventing him from collapsing again, 'Stroude has conjured up some powerful help, that's for sure.'

'Belial?' Darian's confusion and anxiety grew, 'Where in Hades is the prince?'

He always had sole control over whether the demon stayed in human form or was thrown back into Hell. Had some unknown and powerful force overcome this mutually acknowledged domination and banished Belial from Earth? Horrified, Darian shook his head in disbelief: that could never have happened. Even archangels had no strength to control Belial. Yet where was the demon prince and why were there no signs of carnage and battle? Wouldn't his companion have resisted and fought back?

Against all common sense, Darian needed to break back into the house, seek clues to what happened and to see if anything remained safe. There were places inside like the Chamber of Summoning that only he could ever enter ... at least it had been sacrosanct in the past. He gave a curious, piercing whistle hoping to at least recover Misha but the dragoncat did not appear. His entire world had been stolen even down to his pet.

'I think perhaps we had better move on, put some distance between the house and ourselves,' Hardwick urged. 'Reggie said they were rounding up and imprisoning anyone with occult leanings. You must be on top of their list of most wanted.'

Darian pushed him away and ran up the steps to the obstructed door, trying to pull away the iron bars with his hands, but the barrier to his home would not yield and he fell back, bloodied and bruised, snarling with frustration.

'That bloody hellion Fate! The bitch has been toying with me all along. I thought it was too easy, the lucky breaks and fortunate escapes all along our expedition. Softening me up for this ...'

Exasperated and fearful, Hardwick grabbed his arm and tried to force him down the steps.

'Cyrus, in the name of all the gods, we must go. Now. Stroude will have spies everywhere, waiting for your return.'

The alchemist turned towards Hardwick, his voice bleak, 'And where shall I go, old chap? I have nothing left to fight back with. All I possess is a bargaining chip: I know the true location of the Bane of Souls.'

Hardwick shook his head, puzzled, 'Why would you do that? Betray an ally and friend. The Bane is with Count Bartrev.'

Sitting down on the top step in front of the house, Darian looked up with a grim ghost of a wry smile. 'Is it, Miles? I must beg to differ.

Though puzzled by the cryptic remark, Hardwick pushed it to one side, determined to drag the alchemist away from danger and force him out of this depressed state. Always highly-strung, Cyrus's quick wits and arrogance had kept him one step away from his enemies ... until now. His attention was distracted by a flurry of grey wings, a jackdaw – clearly deranged, flew down and flailed around Darian's head. Hardwick tried to drive it away with his bowler and cane.

'Cambion, remarked the alchemist in a weary tone, 'I wondered when you would reappear in my life.'

The air around the bird twisted and shimmered, became a dark mist from which the shapeshifter stepped forward, head down, hands raised in a gesture of surrender. 'You have every reason to kill me, Cyrus. And I will not stop you ending my miserable, treacherous and unnatural existence,'

When neither man made a move against him, a somewhat disappointed Cambion continued, 'But then you would not know where to find Belial and your possessions.'

Darian finally snapped out of his fugue, leapt to his feet and grabbed the little man by the throat, lifting him several feet from the ground. 'Why should I bother, you treacherous little sewer worm? I am a wealthy man, I can live anywhere in the world, leave this festering cess pit of a city and start again. You can take your secrets to hell for all I care.'

But his words were empty bravado, he could not get on with his life. Not with Belial missing. Another vile sensation tore through his body, one he recognised, a painful wound that did not heal or soften with time. One he'd experienced every day and night since losing his wife, barely controlled by his lifelong search to find a way back to her. Now to his utter astonishment and defying all attempts at disavowal, he felt that pain again … for Belial? This could not happen, would not happen! The Fallen Angel in human form was nothing more than a contrivance, a living weapon he'd summoned to aid and protect him in his nefarious adventures. But Darian knew he would not enjoy a single moment of peace or contentment. The search to travel back in time for his lovely Egyptian princess must wait. First, he had to find and rescue the Prince of Hell.

Sensing his hesitation, Cambion found the strength to fight back and escape from Darian's grip without transforming and stood his ground. 'I don't believe you. If you walk away now, you will have lost and the great Cyrus Darian never loses.'

'Magerian kept me alive to tell you where the major has taken your stuff and imprisoned Belial,' the shapeshifter continued. 'A trap of course but since when have you ever turned down a challenge?'

It all made some sort of warped sense now. Magerian was a cunning and gifted sorcerer, one whose powers he had seriously underestimated. So Stroude had employed the evil bastard to capture Belial as a trap for him, a compliment and admission of Darian's superiority in occult matters. It would be a pleasure to defeat them both. His thoughts were the distraction Cambion needed, transforming into a swift, the shapeshifter made an easy escape back to his new masters. It was only the benefit of their dubious protection that prevented him from becoming the beast and ripping both Darian and Hardwick to bloody shreds. That pleasure was still to come.

'I suspect we have made a grave mistake allowing that creature to slip from our grasp,' murmured Hardwick, 'I should have wrung his neck while he was still a jackdaw.'

Darian gave an indifferent shrug, 'The man is most slippery to contain, why else did I employ his skills for so long.'

The shapeshifter was the least of his worries, not with agents of Her Majesty's Government and a bounder of a sorcerer ranged against him. It seemed the past protection he had enjoyed from the ruling elite of this country was a thing of the past. With no sign of the Lady, he had never been so vulnerable to his many enemies.

52

The abbess heard footsteps approaching through the corridor of rough stone walls and flagstone flooring. Purposeful but feminine, she prepared herself to say some mollifying words to one of her sisters.

She welcomed in the tall young nun and beckoned her to sit down. Though head of the order, the abbess's cell and office were no more comfortable than any other in the convent. A plain pine wood table and two chairs, a statue of the Blessed Virgin and a single shelf of religious themed books were all the furnishings of her office. Yet none doubted her authority.

The abbess waited until the younger woman had composed herself, tucking a stray auburn lock of hair back into her tight, starchy wimple.

'I know why you are here this morning, my dear sister. And I am happy to be the bearer of good news.'

She smiled as her words triggered a spark of excitement in the young nun.

'Not long now and all our plans, patience and sacrifice will be rewarded. They are both coming sister, and nothing will stop them from reaching the abbey with their noisy demands.'

She took the young nun's hands in hers and gave them a warm, affectionate squeeze.

'And we will be waiting.'

Something was wrong; Major Stroude felt it on a deep, instinctive level. His sudden, unannounced arrival at Fursey Abbey with the trapped demon and Magerian in tow had not alarmed the Abbess or her novices. Everything was warning him this was a grave mistake but he could not deviate from his intended plan now. Where else could he go with his prisoners without alerting the unwelcome attention of the Prime Minister?

Stroude had everything he'd planned for in one place, a sanctified holy place of safety. Artefacts and devices gathered from the English occult community, all now in the service of Queen and Empire. He had everything in place to capture and disarm the notorious Cyrus Darian. The new world order was within his grasp. So why did his every nerve-ending tingle with a creeping sensation of dread?

Magerian's co-operative behaviour continued and using his dark powers, he manoeuvred the wraith with their hellish prisoner down into the secret chamber beneath the abbey. To the relief of all, Belial had not regained consciousness but even so tightly bound remained a potent force of chaos and destruction. Stroude would have preferred for the prince to be sent back to Hell while still in human form, but Darian's Chamber of Summoning remained barred even to Magerian. And what else could tempt Darian to this confrontation other than the desire to free his companion?

Stroude's young team carried down the confiscated goods from Darian's home. The bravest man in the squad carried a metal cage at arm's length containing the wraith-bound and unconscious form of the curious beast that had attacked them in Pleasance Square. Magerian had called it a dragoncat and described it as Darian's pet but the huge roaring, rampaging creature that had confronted them was far from the coiled bundle of red, black and gold fur in the cage. Stroude shuddered at the thought of it breaking free of its wraith-constraint in the claustrophobic chamber and only relaxed when the Abbess directed its placement within the sanctified circle.

'Thank you for entrusting us with such dangerous creatures and objects,' the Abbess bowed her head in a formal gesture towards the major. 'I trust now you have secured Darian's prized possessions, we will be seeing far less of you in the future. There can be little left in the country for your squad to seize.'

Her stern, cool gaze met his, her manner commanding, 'Unless you mean to go and purge the entire empire of its occult content. I really think you should make that your first priority on returning to London tonight.'

'That will be a matter for Her Majesty's Government to decide, ma'am.' Stroude kept his voice clipped, controlled, refusing to be intimidated by this cloistered female. 'Nor will you be seeing the back of me and my team so soon. We will not have completed this mission until Cyrus Darian is in custody, awaiting execution, and I have good reason to believe he will be making his way here at any time.'

There was a curious flare of animation in the nun's grey eyes before returning to their glacial stillness, 'Execution? None of the other captured practitioners of the occult have faced this?'

She glanced over to the clearly alarmed, heavily shackled Magerian, 'Or do they?'

Major Stroude realised he had spoken too hastily but continued unabashed, 'Don't worry, Magerian, if you continue to co-operate, your neck will be spared the hangman's noose. But in the interest of the security of the Realm and Empire, Darian is a rogue cur, a rabid pariah who needs to be destroyed. Hopefully by a well-aimed bullet resisting arrest, saving the Crown the cost of imprisonment and trial.'

53

'I cannot believe I am going along with this suicidal folly,' grumbled Hardwick and not for the first time on his train journey to East Anglia with Darian. As he sat in a second class department, disguised in clothing befitting a member of the lower orders, his words fell on deaf ears. Darian had not spoken since boarding the locomotive and not just from his long held distaste for public transportation. Instead he had stared out of the window with eyes that did not observe the passing countryside but looked to some other, inner landscape. One, Hardwick suspected, was not a good place to be.

With no supernatural back up or devices at his command, Darian was deliberately heading towards an obvious trap with nothing but his swordstick and the spent force that was the Ghostbinder for self-defence. No doubt gambling Stroude and Magerian would not know the device would not work again. He had spurned Hardwick's suggestion of rallying the magicians and mages still free in London and laughed openly at the suggestion of freeing those incarcerated in that remote prison on Dartmoor.

'Not one of those inept fools would lift a finger to help me, old chap,' he had told Hardwick. 'They loathe and fear me in equal measure no matter how amiable they may seem face to face.'

So, here they were, just two men against the determined Major Stroude and his squad of well-armed fanatics ... and the evident power of the evil Magerian. Madness. And for once, Hardwick's faith in his friend seriously wavered. Had Darian finally given into the bleakness in his heart and soul? The core of ice he tried to hide with nonchalance and bravado but which Hardwick could plainly see when the mask slipped. It seemed so. Yet loyal to what could be the bitter end, Hardwick had turned his back on his wife and a safe future and now sat opposite

CYRUS DARIAN AND THE GHASTLY HORDE

Darian in a scruffy train carriage rumbling through a flat, bleak and featureless landscape. A harsh, cold rainstorm slashed at the smoke and dust encrusted windows creating grimy streaks across the glass. It seemed only the elements were weeping for their imminent demise.

They alighted from the locomotive three stops before they needed to at March, a busy market town and sought out the nearest local livery stables. There Darian hired two good horses, paying generously, enough to buy the animals outright. Like their riders, there was a good chance the horses would not be returning home. The alchemist astonished the horses' owner with his deranged largesse – clearly all foreigners were mad. Meanwhile, an increasingly agitated Hardwick bought provisions for their journey, storing them in saddle bags for the long ride to Fursey Abbey.

As they left March, heading north, the rain clouds petered out and warm sunlight glared up from the wet road, the heat raising a thick white mist from the surrounding sodden fields. Their fit, strong horses were keen, skittering and shying at shadows and birds as they trotted out along the open road. Both Hardwick and Darian were experienced horsemen and allowed the animals to work off their excess energy without reproach but their mood was as depressed as their mounts were high spirited.

At first, as in the train journey, they rode in silence but once the horses had settled down, Hardwick halted. 'I've gone this far with you, Cyrus so you know my intentions are to back you up all the way. But I think I deserve some candour from you.'

Darian reined in his bay mare. The inventor gained no comfort from his bleak tone.

'If you want to know my plan, I do not have one. I will understand and think no less of you, Miles, should you turn back now.'

He reached down and patted the restive mare's neck, soothing her in his native Farsi, 'In fact, I should have insisted on coming here on my own. But once a wretched foreign cad and all that …'

Darian's voice trailed off, the lack of his familiar nonchalant bravado sent a chill of foreboding through his companion, one that no amount of warm sunlight could dispel.

Giving their mounts frequent stops for rest and grazing, the travellers made good progress, helped by a flat landscape with no tiring steep hills or rough terrain. They had not encountered any other travellers during their ride; it was as if they moved through an empty land devoid of human life. Only the distant barking of a dog and an angry human voice raised in admonishment brought back a touch of reality to their journey.

It was obvious that Darian had spent time studying the route for, as the shadows lengthened, he headed for a particular stand of indigenous trees and bushes with, at its centre, a glade blessed by a natural spring-fed pool ringed by willows. Though there was still enough daylight to carry on, Hardwick accepted the wisdom of stopping here to camp for the night. There was no guarantee of finding an inn on the road ahead in such remote countryside far away from busy thoroughfares or rail routes. Nor did they want Stroude and his minions to be forewarned by locals of their progress towards an unequal showdown. Surprise was in this case the slimmest and most brittle of advantages.

The horses accepted the restraint of tethers, more interested in cropping the fresh grass in the glade, well hidden from the road. Hardwick lit a small fire and the men ate their supper and rested their aching muscles. There was no sign of the morning's rainstorm, the earth was dry now, soft and warm, the air redolent of the drifting summer scents of wild flowers and grasses. Bees droned, the horses cropped the grass in content, Hardwick's eyes grew heavy and he settled back on a makeshift cushion – his jacket folded over a saddle. He watched as Darian crouched over the fire, poking it occasionally with a stick, his manner desultory, haunted by what was to come.

Hardwick awoke as cool air touched his face, darkness had fallen during his many hours of slumber. Rubbing an aching neck, he sought out Darian across the glade. The fire had burnt out and it took a few moments to adjust his eyes to the night but Hardwick made out some movement by the tethered horses. Darian had saddled them both and now led them towards him.

CYRUS DARIAN AND THE GHASTLY HORDE

'There will be clear skies and a good moon tonight, near enough full to be able to travel by,' Darian announced handing Hardwick the reins of his horse. As he prepared to journey on, the inventor noted a remarkable change in Darian's demeanour, his friend had recovered his usual animation and restless enthusiasm. But if something had happened while Hardwick slept, Darian had no intention of telling him. So the drastic change of mood remained a mystery.

They arrived at the outskirts of Fursey Abbey within an hour of daybreak, catching sight of the moonlit Norman chapel from a gap in its surrounding yew trees. Darian turned to his friend as they directed the horses' heads towards the meagre shelter of a spinney. 'You've helped me get this far, Miles and for that I thank you. You have supported me more than I could ever deserve. But there is no need to risk your life and freedom. Please, turn back while you can.'

'What are those hackneyed old sayings? In for a penny, better be hung for a sheep? I've got this far, Cyrus. Let us finish this unpleasant business now.'

Despite his noble-sounding words, Darian had never doubted the inventor's loyalty and valour, bred into Hardwick's aristocratic class for centuries and something he had shamelessly exploited in the past. This time was no different.

Once in the meagre shelter of the spinney, they removed the saddles and bridles, releasing the horses to fend for themselves. There was no point tethering the animals with little likelihood of their riders returning to care for them. Hardwick's spirits fell to deep depression as he watched the horses amble off in search of fresh grass, they represented an escape route, a glimmer of hope that he would survive this adventure. If Darian felt any of this sense of dread, it was not apparent in his relaxed manner.

Hardwick's low spirits turned to outright horror when instead of approaching the abbey by a furtive route, Darian strolled openly down the middle of the track, swinging his walking cane in a jaunty manner as if out for a morning stroll. He was carrying the canvas bag containing the Ghostbinder. The inventor ran to his side, attempted to pull him off the track. Despite the early hour, Hardwick had some idea religious types began their devotions at day break, the lightening sky warned this was not far away.

Darian prised away his companion's grip, his voice calm, resigned, 'There is no point attempting subterfuge, old chap. We have been observed and reported on for some time. They know we are here.'

'Cambion!'

'Indeed, in a variety of winged guises. I should have brought a rifle.'

With understandable reluctance, Hardwick continued along the track beside the alchemist, each step along the stony path resounding like thunder to his nerve-stretched senses. Insanity? Or part of a brilliant plan of Darian's? He would soon find out as they strode into the clearing surrounding the Abbey. Could a trap be more obvious? There was no sign of carriages or tethered dirigibles, just the silent, still dark Abbey. By now there should be candle light flickering through the narrow leaded windows and the plaintive sound of the nuns chanting matins.

'We could still try some attempt as surprise,' whispered Hardwick in an effort to prevent the alchemist striding straight up to the main entrance of the abbey.

'Far too late for that, Miles.'

The old oak door opened with a creak that sounded like the crack of doom to Hardwick's frayed nerves and the men stepped into an entrance hall empty but for some unlit tall sconces and a well-worn statue of a sainted monk and the blessed virgin.

'There is no point sneaking up on us, gentlemen, we are fully aware of you and your weapons.'

As Darian's voice echoed through the cloisters, a group of heavily armed young men stepped out of the shadows, aiming their pistols at the heads of the new arrivals. Once the prisoners were secured, Major Stroude stepped forward, small, pale eyes betraying his anxiety ... this was far too easy. What dastardly scheme had Darian hatched? The major barked an order for the perimeter of the abbey to be searched for henchmen, human or more likely supernatural. No one walked straight into a trap with such insouciant ease. Even Cyrus Darian.

'I am here for my things,' Darian stated with cold simplicity, triggering an outburst of nervous laughter from the major.

'Are you now? And just how do you expect to get them back in your current predicament? Search him … and Hardwick.'

One of the young men stepped forward, hands shaking … Darian was also a necromancer, a man who controlled an army of the dead and consorted with demons. The idea of touching him and triggering some hellish attack was foremost in his mind. Stroude's minion nervously checked the prisoner's arms and back and was about to pat down his chest when Darian spoke, causing the man to jump to one side in alarm.

'You know Stroude old chap, you really should choose your cohorts with more care. This fine fellow is becoming quite aroused, not so much searching my body than caressing it.'

Before the blushing and outraged young man could respond, the temperature in the abbey appeared to plummet. A stooping tall figure, gaunt features cadaverous in their pallor appeared, his ankles and wrists shackled.

'Cyrus Darian …' Magerian's top lip curled with hatred as he spat out the alchemist's name as a curse. The sorcerer did not want to be in this situation, he'd hoped Stroude's squad would have finished the man off by now with an assassin's bullet. Though he bragged about his superior magickal powers, inside he doubted his ascendance over Darian. Even surrounded by superior forces, Darian was clever, dangerous and unpredictable.

'Hello, old chap,' Darian returned with a humourless grin, 'I see time has been most unkind to you, you need to get out in the fresh air more, eat some fruit. Or better still, crawl back under the nearest damp stone.'

Stroude signalled to his men, 'Our business is concluded. We will take the prisoners back to London for trial.'

'Prisoners?' Magerian's eyes flashed with alarm, was this the treachery he'd been expecting all along?

'Darian and Hardwick …' the major snapped back a curt

reply, 'regrettably I will continue to require your expertise to eliminate the danger from Darian's demon and creature. Consider yourself employed in the service of Her Majesty's Government. Betray this trust and you will meet the same fate as Darian. Now take his bag, it is bound to contain something occult and dangerous.'

Stroude turned to the alchemist, 'You had your chance, Darian, something to dwell on during your last moments.'

'I am here to take back what belongs to me. My stolen possessions. Which includes my demon.'

Darian's stubborn and fearless stance was baffling, the man was clearly defeated and was powerless. Had he gone insane? The man's companion, Hardwick clearly thought so, the gasp and look of horror on his face spoke volumes. Stroude ordered the captives to be taken from the abbey and locked in a prison vehicle, no longer hidden from sight and waiting in the courtyard. But any move was blocked by the silent arrival of the abbess and her nuns who stood in front of the entrance, a serene but curiously eerie presence in the pre-dawn gloom.

'I see no reason why Mr Darian should not be reminded of all he has lost with his lifetime of unholy transgressions.' The abbess's voice had a core of steel hitherto unheard, 'Take him to the vault, maybe the true extent of his loss will engender some repentance. It is never too late to find salvation.'

Stroude could barely contain his fury. He knew a confrontation with the nun was on the horizon but not yet. Instinctively he realised that having Darian in close proximity with his demon, even Wraith bound, was highly dangerous.

'Ma'am, with all due respect, this is a matter of state that does not concern you or your gentle sisters.'

'You are within my abbey, Major Stroude, I have complete jurisdiction here. Now take him to the vault.'

To his horror, the highly religious men of his squad obeyed the abbess without question, his recruitment for the most zealous young recruits backfiring with a potentially disastrous result. There was nothing he could do without betraying his own agenda. Neither his men nor the sisters had any inkling all the occult devices would be soon turned over to the military under his command. Making sure his own pistol was ready for use, Stroude followed them down to the increasingly less secret chamber.

Nobody could see Darian's eyes flash with fury behind the dark lenses as he saw the prone form of the demon and Misha, his caged, comatose pet. Belial should never be helpless. It was an appalling insult to his status as a Fallen Prince of Hell. It even made Darian uneasy about releasing him. Belial's revenge would be bloody and spectacular and maybe not discriminate between enemies and allies.

He turned his attention to his surroundings. The vault was a treasure house of wondrous items, occult materials worth all ransom of every king that ever lived to one such as he. Darian spotted his own items among the haul, struggling to remain calm at the outrage. Time to bring this situation to a conclusion. One way or another.

'For that last time, Stroude, gentlemen, ladies, I am here to take back only what is mine. Release Belial and the creature and instruct your men to remove my items from the hoard and assemble them in the courtyard.'

Stroude stepped forward and waved his pistol close to the alchemist's face, 'Now I know you are insane. There is nothing you can do, you have lost everything, including your mind.'

Magerian opened the canvas bag and pulled out the Ghostbinder, pointing it at Hardwick's head, who feigned fear at the empty threat.

Ignoring the clicks of readying weapons, Darian reached into his coat pocket and pulled out a delicate silver-framed mirror, the innocuous, feminine item triggering a nervous laugh of relief among the men. Not so Magerian who recognised what it was and its power.

'Get that off him! Now!' He screamed, dropping the Ghostbinder and shielding his face from the reflective surface before scrambling away, seeking shelter behind a pillar. Darian raised the mirror high, 'Release Belial and the creature or I will smash the mirror.'

'What kind of idiotic threat is that?' Stroude shouted, confused once more by Darian's apparent lunacy. 'Take it off him.'

When none of his squad stepped forward, Stroude marched across the vault ready to seize the mirror but was beaten to it by a hysterical Magerian, shielding his eyes from the shiny surface and the threat of seeing his own reflection. He raised his manacled fists, determined to knock the Bane of Souls out of Darian's hands before he could use it.

'I really wouldn't do that,' Darian's voice was calm, mocking, turning the mirror to shine into Magerian's face. The sorcerer backed off, scurrying away again like a startled spider and gibbering in fear.

'Shoot him!' Stroude demanded but none of his men made a move, unnerved by Magerian's terror. Growling in frustration at their weakness and inaction, the major raised his own pistol, aiming for Darian's head but was thrown to the ground by a powerful vortex of cold air that whirled around the vault, screeching like a *bansidhe*. Confusion and fear escalated into chaos, as people sought shelter from the eerie wind, only for it to disappear as suddenly as it came. In its place, a golden light bathed the stone chamber in a beautiful yet disturbing miasma, there was no comfort or warmth in this luminosity, indeed it triggered ancient, primal sensations of serious foreboding within all in the chamber.

The wild, agitated air returned, this time, the vault echoed with the deafening sound of buzzing like a million bees trapped within the stone walls. Darian dropped to his knees and pulled Hardwick down with him. 'Lie down Miles, remain on the floor in a gesture of respectful submission ... don't argue and do not speak one word.'

Hardwick obeyed as the golden gleaming became more vivid and deeply disturbing, coalescing into tall, almost human forms. The vault now was filled with a group of male and female, pale, haughty beings from a different plane of existence. Their eyes were captured rainbows of glittering iridescence; their hair was long, straight in metallic hues of silver, gold and green. Darian recognised them as a gathering of Fae warriors dressed in intricate silver armour, all armed with an array of astonishing and eldritch weapons of unknown purpose.

'I made contact with the Fae at the willow grove pool while you slept,' the alchemist whispered to Hardwick, as what appeared to be their leader approached, holding his hand out for the Bane of Souls. Darian kept his head down as he addressed the Fae royalty in their curious, fluid language.

'I have kept my part of our bargain, your Majesty. The Bane is safe and once more in the hands of its rightful owners. In return, I asked for protection from those who would steal it and use it for harm. And the return of my possessions.'

'Greedy little human,' the Fae King's voice was emotionless. 'You say you brought our stolen treasure back to us from its hiding place but why should we believe you.'

'I could have kept it from you, used it for myself,' Darian replied somehow remaining calm, 'but it is here, as I promised.'

Terrified, Magerian shuffled forward, shouting 'Don't believe him! Cyrus Darian is a notorious liar. He will trick you.'

The Fae's eyes blazed with golden fire at the impudent interruption, sending Magerian flying across the vault, hitting a far wall with a sickening thud of breaking bones. He then turned back to the still prone Darian.

'We of the Fae are not fools nor are we ignorant of the ways of mankind. Your notorious and untrustworthy reputation precedes you, Cyrus Darian.'

'I make no secret of my character, Majesty,' Darian replied, 'but I have your artefact, The Bane of Souls … I travelled all the way to Russia, risked my life many times to return it to you.'

The Fae king returned across the room to his warriors and quietly spoke with them before facing Darian and holding out his hand, 'Give me the Bane and I will vanquish your enemies. Our agreement will be fulfilled in the honourable way of the Fae'

Already in considerable shock at the appearance of these unearthly beings and the explosive, unnatural violence against the sorcerer, Stroude's voice rose in a babble of panic, 'What is going on? What are these people? What do they want with us?'

The Abbess in a subtle move held onto his arm with a surprisingly tight grip. 'If you value your life, Major and that of your men, I suggest you remain quiet and still. Your fate is in the balance now and Darian has the upper hand.'

Darian paused for what seemed a long time to the terrified humans, deliberately, enjoying his moment of victory.

'Leave me Magerian and Stroude, the sisters and the major's men can leave. And of course, I want Belial and my pet freed from those accursed wraith.'

The Fae leader nodded with solemn grace as he accepted the Bane of Souls from Darian's hand. 'I must add a condition, human, The Prince of Hell's fury will be destructive to all, even my kind will not be immune. I will release the Wraith but he will remain like this until you are alone and can attempt to contain his vengeance. I wish you luck in that exploit.'

'*Thank you,*' sighed a deeply relieved Darian, dreading the moment the demon found himself free and in sight of humans to punish. Any humans.

'I suggest the good sisters and Stroude's squad leave now in some haste and keep going until you reach Wisbech. Otherwise things could get messy.' Darian announced, picking up the Ghostbinder and switching it on, 'I have unfinished business with these two gentlemen.'

He inclined his head and discovered all the nuns had vanished apart from the Abbess and one tall novice. Unwilling to desert their commander, Stroude's men lingered in a show of determination but as the Fae King turned to direct his deadly golden gaze in their direction, they ran for the door and fled the chamber. It was too much for the major, who dropped to the floor, head in hands and began to pray. Only the abbess remained standing, head high and fearless.

Raising the Bane of Souls, the Fae King concentrated its power on the tightly wound amalgam of Wraith, the mirror dazzled as before, releasing its halo of dancing stars before fusing them into a blinding silver light. The Wraith became contorted, twisting and screaming with soul-freezing agony as the light hit their spectral forms. Some fought back, detaching from the binding in a blur of dirty blackness and horrific, deformed faces spitting foul acid, the essence of their festering evil. It was no match for the Bane's old earth magicke radiance, as the light touched their writhing forms, they screeched in agony, recoiling back to the shadows with a hiss of hatred.

For good reason, the badly injured Magerian feared Belial's release more than the power of the mirror. Dragging a broken leg, the sorcerer edged towards the Wraith and raising his staff, tried to force them back into their binding spell. Tortured by the touch of the mirror's light and furious at being controlled by a mere living mage, all the Wraith split into their individual selves and attacked Magerian. His body jerked in uncontrollable spasms as shards of concentrated evil pierced his body, again and again until it could no longer maintain a cohesive form, exploding into a red mist that sprayed across the vault walls and floor and over the cowering Stroude.

Once again, the Fae King directed the Bane's light at the Wraith horde who finally accepting defeat, fled, disappeared into the fabric of the chapel then beyond to disperse into the world of the living.

The Fae King inclined his head in a slight gesture towards Darian, signalling their deal was completed and after a return of the dizzying vortex of shrieking air, the Fae were gone and the chamber returned to shocked silence. Darian still had the Ghostbinder in his hands but was forced to drop it to the flagstone floor as residual Bane energy coursed through it, a fortunate move for the metal bubbled and disintegrated into a molten puddle of melting copper and brass and liquefied glass.

Darian helped the inventor to his feet and then strode towards his possessions, touching them with a shudder of pleasure. He turned his attention to the still prone form of Belial, the beautiful youth appeared to be asleep, something the demon in human form never did.

'Sweet dreams, my dear, hellish friend,' he murmured. 'When you awake, you will be back home with me again. I cannot trust you to revive in the sanctified place ... too much temptation to wreak bloody havoc.'

Misha the dragoncat was wide awake, growling with agitation at being caged, Darian released her and laughed as she squirmed and wriggled around his body in a frenzy of fur and purring.

Stroude had risen to his feet and recovered his composure, once again pointing his pistol at the alchemist, 'Nothing has changed, Darian. Now you have given away your only bargaining chip, your situation is far worse.'

He strode over and snatched a bejeweled Egyptian reanimation sceptre from Darian's hand and placed it back on the stolen hoard. 'You are still under arrest by the command of Her Majesty's Government and your goods are still forfeit.'

'Actually, he is not.'

Everyone turned to witness a curious change in the Abbess. She appeared younger, more curvaceous, her eyes sparkling with wry amusement. 'But both he and Lord Hardwick are *my* prisoners now.'

The abbess gave a most unchaste and seductive smile, approaching Darian while unbuttoning her severe habit and pulling off her wimple, releasing a tumble of raven locks. She tore off the nun's garb and stood resplendent and brazen in a tight, red silk corset and petticoats.

'Do you not recognise me, *mi amore*?'

What was now a beautiful, dark-eyed woman traced the outline of Darian's face with her slim, elegant fingers and kissed him. Her taste and perfume was unmistakable, familiar from uncountable erotic trysts. The Lady! He now knew all this was an elaborate sham. If Fursey Abbey existed, this was not it but her itinerant Emporium of Magickal Curios in another clever guise. No wonder the other nuns had disappeared, they had never existed but were illusions created by the Lady's power of glamour. There was another revelation; the tall nun accompanying the phoney abbess also began to disrobe revealing the amazonian form of Lady Athena Hardwick. What manner of trickery was this?

'We think you have both been extremely naughty boys,' the Lady continued, putting her arm around Darian's waist and giving it a squeeze that was far from affectionate. 'Bad boys that needed teaching a lesson. You have betrayed me with your shameless thefts for many years, my darling but don't think I have indulged your kleptomania from my affection and desire for you.'

Athena strode over to her husband and grabbed him by the cravat, giving him a shake like a chastised cur, 'How dare you abandon me in Europe in the company of those dreadful people. And for what? More foolish escapades with that base born foreign rogue?'

Pinned in the corner by the snarling dragoncat, Major Stroude's indignation gave him courage to speak out, 'All of this ... the abbey ... the nuns ... everything was an elaborate deception? Nothing more than a convoluted supernatural hoax fuelled by lovers' quarrels?'

'It appears so, old chap,' remarked Darian, still reeling at the lengths the Lady and Athena Hardwick had gone to. 'It seems we have all become the victims of women scorned. Is there anything in this world more dangerous?'

'Back to business,' the Lady stepped away from Darian, her manner no longer seductive but cold and imperious. 'I will take all these stolen items as my own. No doubt their previous owners will come to me to get them back ... but only at a good price. Thank you Major Stroude, you have considerably improved my profits.'

Darian moved towards her, his voice low, switching on his charm as her lover, '*Mi querida, mi amor,* surely you will allow me to have my possessions, *mi preciosa,* you would not see me unhappy and bereft, would you?

The Lady gave a slight shrug of indifference, stepping away from his outstretched arms, 'Maybe ... but only after I have removed all the items you stole from me. And do not think I do not know each and every one you have so shamelessly taken.'

'*Mie scuse, tesora,*' Darian persisted, feigning a sincere apology, 'may I have my Amulet of Greel and the Asgard ring back first? I feel bereft without them.'

An embarrassed Hardwick focused his attention away from

the supercilious glare of his furious wife and onto the dumbfounded Major Stroude, still pinned down by the snarling dragon cat. Hardwick snatched the pistol away from his hands and aimed it at the major.

'Let him go,' commanded the Lady. 'His zealous lads have fled, and after trying to explain to his Prime Minister where all the confiscated items are gone, he will be a spent force.'

Humiliated but far from defeated, Stroude took his cue and stormed out of the vault and away from the abbey ... which was no longer an ecclesiastical building of Norman in an East Anglican forest but an elegant Georgian town house in Mayfair, beside Cyrus Darian's home. Stroude staggered away, dazed and disorientated, heading for his home and a bottle of his strongest whiskey. Darian's parting, arrogant smirk was fused into his memory. This was far from over.

If there were government agents watching his home, Darian ignored them, preferring to savour the sweet taste of victory. He had gambled his life and that of his companions on the innate honour of the Fae nobility and it had paid off. He could never call on them again, their co-operation was a one-off, but he was alive and Belial was free. Laying the demon down on his front step, he prepared to gently reawaken him, reaching into his slumbering soul with the power of his own. Now came serious peril.

Belial's eyes flickered and opened, ablaze with hellfire, his face contorted with fury, the same blinding anger from just before the Wraith spell bound him. Darian had no choice but to defuse the demon in the only way he knew how, by grabbing his face and kissing him. Instantly, his mind and body risked destruction, overcome by the assault of celestial power surging from Belial. As the demon regained his conscious thoughts, Darian struggled on, a mere human fighting searing demonical wrath with the one weapon he had, the emotional power he had over the cursed Fallen Angel.

It worked.

Shaken and exhausted, Darian stood up and held out his

hand to the still prone demon, 'Perfect timing, my beloved friend. I seem to be having a little difficulty getting back into my home.'

For the first time Belial looked vulnerable, almost human, an unsettling sight for the alchemist who relied on his strength.

'What happened? Why am I on your steps?'

Darian put a supporting arm around the demon's narrow shoulders, 'All will be revealed – over the finest vintage cognac in the house but first – my front door?'

The alchemist stood back as Belial, though still dazed, made light work of the iron bars denying entry into the townhouse. Hardwick and a still fuming Athena followed behind as Darian once again became master of his home. Inside, he discovered with a sigh of relief that the Lady had returned his things … well, nearly all his things. Darian was unbothered, he would enjoy stealing them back again.

With Athena seeking out her old room from the brief time she had lived in the townhouse, a refugee from tormenting Wraith, her chastened but unrepentant husband sought out a private word with Darian. Possibly his last private words if the determined Lady Hardwick got her way.

'So, Cyrus, at last you can get on with your life without the curse of an army of ghosts tagging along behind you,' Hardwick added with a relieved smile. The loss of the Ghostbinder meant little now its purpose had been fulfilled. Without the Bane of Souls, it was only a pile of melted metal and glass after all. Darian nodded, 'Absolutely, it was such a crashing bore, all those angry wafting nuisances getting in my way.'

His left hand opened his coat wide, revealing a glint of gleaming gold, the top of a cylinder – Michael Lewis's original small and intricate prototype.

'But I've selected a choice few from the ghastly hordes, having the nastiest ones under my control will come in handy, don't you think, old chap?'

Aftermath

Within a few days, Darian's home came under close scrutiny again and not just from Stroude and his remaining agents. Far from being in disgrace with his master, the Prime Minister, Stroude had turned defeat into victory. The mages and occultists were still imprisoned on Dartmoor, the most evil, Magerian was dead by his own hand and as far as the government knew, the appropriated supernatural items all destroyed. Stroude doubted a man with so little imagination as Bowring would believe they were stolen by a shapeshifter disguised as a nun. Stroude's campaign had lost a battle but would still win the war.

But other eyes gazed at the now restored townhouse in a Mayfair square, quietly returning to ghost free normality. A large carrion crow sat on an opposite roof, the beast rejoicing that his prize was still alive and that the sweet joy of ripping Darian apart and devouring him was still within his grasp. The crow preened his glossy black feathers in the wan summer light, miraculously filtering down through the layers of smoke and toxic filth that Londoners called fresh air. Life was good and soon it would get a whole lot better ...

Pain. Confusion. Fear. The loss of physical form was a crushing blow, a sudden and violent transition from life to death. The spirit thrashed about, spiralling out of control between celestial dimensions. Lost and frightened at first, the newly-departed spun in panic unable to focus on incomprehensible surroundings. Then anger. Anger overcame fear. In anger identity was recalled, the manner of its loss understood and the person responsible remembered. Any thought of moving on to the *Beyond* was abhorrent. Not when there was unfinished business back in the world of the living.

CYRUS DARIAN AND THE GHASTLY HORDE

The newly formed Wraith, more powerful in death than in life, focused its hate-filled essence on the face of its enemy and returned to London ...

About the Author

Raven Dane is an award-winning fantasy author based in the UK. Her published works include the highly acclaimed *Legacy of the Dark Kind* series of dark fantasy/sci-fi crossover novels (*Blood Tears*, *Blood Lament* and *Blood Alliance*).

However, Raven's skills in fiction don't end there. Her comedy fantasy *The Unwise Woman of Fuggis Mire* – a scurrilous spoof of high fantasy clichés – was met with great enthusiasm by the reading public. In more recent years Raven has met with critical acclaim for her steampunk/occult adventures *Cyrus Darian and the Technomicron* and *Cyrus Darian and the Ghastly Horde*.

Cyrus Darian and the Technomicron was the winner of the best novel award at the inaugural Victorian Steampunk Society awards 2012.

Raven also has many short stories published in anthologies including one in *Full Fathom Forty*, a celebration of 40 years of the British Fantasy Society, and the first annual of ghost stories from Spectral Press, called the *13 Ghosts of Christmas*.

Further works include poetry, published in an anthology of pagan verse.

Other Telos Titles By Raven Dane

THE MISADVENTURES OF CYRUS DARIAN
Steampunk Adventure Series
1: CYRUS DARIAN AND THE TECHNOMICRON
2: CYRUS DARIAN AND THE GHASTLY HORDE
3: CYRUS DARIAN AND THE DEMON (forthcoming)

DEATH'S DARK WINGS
Alternative History Novel

ABSINTHE AND ARSENIC
Horror and Fantasy Short Story Collection

Other Published Novels

LEGACY OF THE DARK KIND SERIES
Thrilling Vampire Series
1: BLOOD TEARS
2: BLOOD LAMENT
3: BLOOD ALLIANCE

THE UNWISE WOMAN OF FUGGIS MIRE
Comedy/Fantasy Novel

Other Telos Steampunk and Horror Titles

TANITH LEE
BLOOD 20
20 Vampire Stories through the ages

TANITH LEE A-Z (forthcoming)
An A-Z collection of Short Fiction by renowned writer Tanith Lee

GRAHAM MASTERTON
THE HELL CANDIDATE
THE DJINN
THE WELLS OF HELL
RULES OF DUEL (With William S Burroughs)

PAUL FINCH
CAPE WRATH AND THE HELLION (Horror Novella)
TERROR TALES OF CORNWALL (Ed. Paul Finch)

SIMON CLARK
HUMPTY'S BONES
THE FALL

FREDA WARRINGTON
NIGHTS OF BLOOD WINE
Vampire Horror Short Story Collection

DAVID J HOWE
TALESPINNING
Horror Collection of Stories, Novels and more

SAM STONE

KAT LIGHTFOOT MYSTERIES
Steampunk Adventure Series
1: ZOMBIES AT TIFFANY'S
2: KAT ON A HOT TIN AIRSHIP
3: WHAT'S DEAD PUSSYKAT
4: KAT OF GREEN TENTACLES
5: KAT AND THE PENDULUM
6: AND THEN THERE WAS KAT (forthcoming)

THE JINX CHRONICLES
Dark Science Fiction and Fantasy, dystopian future
1: JINX TOWN
2: JINX MAGIC
3: JINX BOUND (forthcoming)

THE VAMPIRE GENE SERIES
Vampire, Historical and Time Travel Series
1: KILLING KISS
2: FUTILE FLAME
3: DEMON DANCE
4: HATEFUL HEART
5: SILENT SAND
6: JADED JEWEL

ZOMBIES IN NEW YORK AND OTHER BLOODY JOTTINGS
Horror Story Collection

THE DARKNESS WITHIN: FINAL CUT
Science Fiction Horror Novel

CTHULHU AND OTHER MONSTERS
Lovecraftian Style Stories and more

KIT COX
DR TRIPPS: KAIJU COCKTAIL

PAUL LEWIS
SMALL GHOSTS
Horror Novella

STEPHEN LAWS
SPECTRE

RHYS HUGHES
CAPTAINS STUPENDOUS

HELEN MCCABE
THE PIPER TRILOGY
1: PIPER
2: THE PIERCING
3: THE CODEX

TELOS PUBLISHING
www.telos.co.uk